FARLANDS

THE ANTLANDS SERIES / BOOK 3

FARLANDS

GENEVIEVE MORRISSEY

ANTLANDS.COM

Published by Genevieve Morrissey.

ISBN: 978-1-7351096-6-4

Cover design and interior formatting: Mark Thomas / Coverness.com

For Sarah and Frank

CHAPTER ONE

I'd killed my Aunt Jane, so my dad was the only family I had left in the world. Dad was away at sea. Being a sailor, he usually was. My mom was… gone. Run off. The only other kin I'd ever had besides Mom and Dad was my aunt, who I'd just left laying on the floor with her face all gray and her mouth hanging open. I didn't kill her on purpose, although I admit I pretty much hit her as hard as I could, and I swear that deep inside me I was sorry she was dead. But Aunt Jane'd always said I was selfish, and I guess she was right, because all I could think about now was myself and the fix I was in.

The only way out of it I could see was to put on boy's clothes and run away to sea. I'd been wanting to do that for years anyway. But by the time I landed the jab that knocked Aunt Jane backwards into a door that gave way and took her down with it, we'd been trading punches for a while, and Aunt Jane always gave as good as she got. Both my eyes were blacked and I had too many bruises generally to look like a good candidate for a ship's boy now. I needed to lie low awhile and get my face right before I tried to get on a ship.

So I run away and spent the rest of the night in a stable. I'd slept there before. It was dirty, but warm from the horses. Men would come there early to get their animals, so I left before daybreak, and after that I wandered the streets, trying not to be seen. Early is a good time for stealing food, when the shopkeepers are getting ready to open. I was helping myself to bread when I remembered a place that might do for a temporary hideout. I'd found it by accident a few years ago on a school outing, if you can believe I ever went to school; a little room at the top of a secret staircase in the town library.

I didn't figure I could stay there long. The room didn't look like it was used much, but it was kept nice, so I guessed somebody must be coming by it from time to time. I didn't know—or care—whose room it was, but it had a bed in it. My head ached and one of my eyes was so swole up I couldn't see out of it. Any place with a bed seemed like a piece of paradise to me.

Also, it was getting light. I wouldn't say the town authorities was ever real enthusiastic about chasing murderers, but they'd get after me eventually—especially when they heard I was only a girl and not known to be armed. I needed to get off the street. I snuck up to the town library's back door and let myself in, and then crept up to the little hidden room. A fur blanket on the bed warmed me up the minute I crawled under it. I must have been hurt worse than I'd thought, because I slept most of the day.

I slept most of the next day, too, only getting up when the library was closed to go downstairs for water and to empty my slops. The next day was the same, except I brought a couple books back up with me. You wouldn't guess it if you knew me, but I liked to read. When I was awake, I laid plans for getting away—where I could steal the right clothes, mainly, and get a proper sea chest—and I thought about Aunt Jane. I was sorry for what I'd done to her, but not enough to wish her back again.

I'd lived with my aunt since I was nine. She beat me regular, but I probably deserved it. Now and then she let one of my "uncles" beat me though, and I didn't like that. Auntie made me call any long-time man she had "Uncle" (six months was a long time for Auntie), and said uncles had beating rights over me, same as aunts. I didn't agree. She took away most of what I got begging or stealing—mostly stealing now, since I wasn't young and pathetic enough to beg anymore—but she almost always left me enough to eat on, so that was all right. She sold my clothes off my back if she came up short on the rent, or to save the trouble of washing them, and she hired out my bed from under me if someone else wanted it for a night, or a week. I honestly didn't blame Aunt Jane for any of that, though. At least, I didn't blame her enough to kill her over it.

But when she took my mother's ring, she went too far. Not because it was my mother's. I ain't sentimental about my mother. Not at all. But the ring was the only thing I had that was all mine, and I loved it for that. Everything else I had I'd stole from somebody or was only mine to use, like the dirty couch in the upstairs hallway at Aunt Jane's that I was only allowed to sleep on if nobody else wanted it. By rights, the couch was Auntie's. The house I lived in was Auntie's. The food I ate was Auntie's. Everything was Auntie's. She never let me forget that. But the ring was mine.

Curled down tight in the bed at the library, I decided I wouldn't have killed Aunt Jane on purpose even for taking my ring. She hit me, and I hit her back. Fights was a normal thing with us. But I'd never wanted to hit her so hard she'd go down and not get back up. Ring or no, I would never have done a thing like that intentional. Even with a fur blanket over me, I shivered when I remembered how she'd lain still in a way nobody alive is ever still and wished— almost wished—it had been her that killed me, instead of the other way.

Since I had to hide—and murderers was hung in Fortress City, so I definitely had to hide—the little room in the library was the best hiding place I could have asked for. Aside from the bad dreams I had, I was comfortable there. I was too comfortable. I was so comfortable I stayed on for five days; reading and sleeping and eating what I could scavenge, as much at ease as a baby before it's born.

Until the day I heard a key slip into the lock. As I sat up, very fast, the door opened and a woman walked in.

She wasn't young. She wasn't bent over, I don't mean, but her piled-up hair was gray. She must have thought she could take care of herself, because instead of backing off when she saw me, she came the rest of the way in and shut the door behind her. She never took her eyes off my face. "Well, well. What have we here?"

I wasn't dressed, but I jumped for the door anyway.

She was quick for an old person. Before I got halfway there, she'd pulled a chair in front of herself to block me.

"That's far enough," she said, not turning a hair. "Get back in the bed. No, get under the blanket again. What are you doing here? Besides reading, I mean."

When I just stared at her, she moved the chair to behind her, and sat in it.

"All right," she said, "here's an easier question. What's your name?"

"Mary."

"Lies bore me. Tell the truth. What's your name?"

I sized her up. She was taller than me, but as I said before, she wasn't young. Even without a weapon, I could have taken her, easy. She didn't seem to understand that.

"Let's not play games," the woman said meantime. "I could have you arrested for trespassing. If you answer my questions, I might not. What's your name, and what are you doing here? I'm guessing you're a runaway."

"I'm not a kid." I stuck my jaw forward. "I can go where I want. No one owns me."

"Then you have no reason not to tell me your name."

She'd find out soon enough anyway. I said, "It's Claire. No—that's the truth! It's Claire!"

"Claire what? Who are your parents?"

"What do you care?"

Her voice got sharper. "Answer me. Where do you live?"

"Here."

"Don't be tedious. Who did you live with before you came here? Come on: You must have lived somewhere."

The only answer I could think of was the true one, which, as I said, she'd find out soon enough anyway. "With my Aunt Jane."

The woman thought this over for a minute. "Jane Joyce?"

This surprised me, kind of. My aunt wasn't the only Jane in town. "Yeah. Her. The dead lady. And I'm the one killed her." I crossed my arms, hoping I looked tough that way.

The woman's answer was different from the one I expected.

She raised her eyebrows but not her voice. "Really? When?"

"Huh?"

"When did you kill her? Today?"

I started to say something—I'm not sure what—but the woman interrupted me. "My name is Sarah, Claire. I saw Jane Joyce alive in the market a few hours ago, so either you've been very busy this morning, or you didn't kill her. I haven't heard of any other recent murders, and you don't look like you've been out, so I'm going to assume for now you didn't kill anyone."

"I did!"

The woman—Sarah—laughed. "How long have you been staying in this room? For that matter, how did you know it was here? Few people do."

I answered her with just noises, not being able to get out any actual words. I was sure I'd killed Auntie. After I knocked her down—not entirely meaning to, as I said before—I'd stared at her for five minutes at least. She never moved or breathed that I saw.

"I did," I mumbled.

Sarah sighed. "Look, I don't know what happened between you and your aunt, but whatever it was, it wasn't as bad as you imagined. In fact, when I saw her, she looked better than you do. If you want to go home and patch things up with her—"

"No!"

I didn't know I was going to say that, but once it was out, I knew I meant it.

"You don't want to go back?"

"I'll *never* go back! She took—" I didn't want to talk about my ring. "Everything."

I was glad—I mean it—that Auntie wasn't dead, but she still took my ring and give me a beating in its place. If nobody was hunting me, I could go where I wanted, and where I wanted to go was anywhere but Aunt Jane's.

For no reason I could see, Sarah's smile got bigger. "Well, you can't stay here." She got up from her chair. "My husband died in that bed. I'm sure you'll understand when I say that makes it a special place for me."

I can tell you, I never left anyplace quicker than I left that bed. Somebody had *died* there? Ten thousand gods! "You washed the sheets after, right?" I shuddered and looked around quick for any sign of a ghost.

Sarah said she had. "But now they'll have to be washed again. As will you. When did you last have a bath?"

"Don't remember."

"I'm not surprised. Besides your aunt, who else hits you?"

She was staring at my back. I put my clothes on faster. "Nobody. Fell down some stairs."

"Well, bundle your things to take with you, but leave *my* things on the table." Her eyes bored into me like a second Aunt Jane. "*All* of my things."

Damn her. I'd found a lot of nice stuff in the drawer of the table that stood on one side of the room, and I'd helped myself to most of it. I unloaded my pockets slowly, hoping she wouldn't notice if I kept a few things back, and tried to distract her. A stack of handwritten papers were on the desk; hundreds of sheets tied up in bundles. I pointed. "What's them?"

"A book."

"They don't look like a book."

"I should have said, they're the manuscript of what would someday have been a book. A dictionary."

"A dictionary? What language?" To be honest, I didn't actually care what language the papers was in. I just wanted the woman to understand that just because I was dirty and a thief didn't mean I didn't know what a dictionary was.

"Farlandish. Where's the knife?"

I'd sold it.

"There wasn't one," I lied.

"There certainly was. Where is it? Did you sell it?"

"By the gods, lady, there wasn't no—"

"Get it back. Do whatever you have to and get it back. How old are you?"

I named the age I wished I was. "Sixteen."

"What year were you born? No, don't bother to answer me. You hesitated. That's all the answer I need. If you're going to lie about your age, you need to figure out what your birth year should be and memorize it. You look…twelve."

"Fifteen!" I was fourteen.

"Fifteen still means you should go to school. We'll discuss that later. For now, bring your things and the sheets."

"Where we going?"

"To another room I have. One you *can* stay in. It's nicer than this one and warmer."

"Why?" I pulled the sheets off the bed careful enough (I hoped) for a ghost not to mind.

"Why am I letting you have the room?" Sarah looked at me like she was wondering that herself. "Well, why not? The room's empty anyway, and I don't want you on the streets. Also, I don't like your Aunt Jane any better than you do."

I couldn't keep from grinning when she said that. Since I wasn't Aunt Jane's murderer after all, I figured I had a right to grin at bad things people said about her.

After thinking it over, I decided I had a right to wait until winter was over and I had the sea chest I wanted before I went to sea, too. Winters at sea was brutal, my dad always said.

Sarah opened the door for me and locked it behind us when we were out.

Downstairs, there were people in the library. They stared at me.

I tried not to notice. "Where's 'Farlands?' I never heard of it before."

"It's a long way from here. All the way across an ocean."

"There's places across the ocean?"

"Whole worlds of places."

"And the people talk different in them?"

"Very differently, yes."

"I want to go there."

"So did I, once," Sarah sighed.

She looked like she might cry, so I dropped the subject.

CHAPTER TWO

Old people like Aunt Jane said that back when Fortress City was Fortresstown, it didn't used to be divided into nice parts and bad parts. It used to be all the same. All bad is what I think Auntie meant. But things change, as everybody says, and the part Sarah and me walked to was one of the nicest neighborhoods in Fortress. Since that meant it wasn't anywhere near Auntie's house, I was glad.

Mostly glad.

"Ten thousand gods!" I gasped when we finally stopped at a house. "Are you—are you one of the *Farmers*?"

From the face Sarah made, you'd have thought there was something wrong with being rich.

"Just put the sheets down next to the door," she said, letting us in. "We'll deal with them later. After we have something to eat, we'll see about running a bath for you."

The food she gave me was the best food I ever ate, and the bath I took afterwards was the best bath. The bath was hot. I hadn't had too many baths in my life total, and none of them was ever hot. I liked it a lot.

I loved it so much, in fact, I stayed in it, washing everything twice, including my hair, and opening the tap from time to time until I'd used up all the hot water there was. Then I got out and put on clean clothes Sarah had brought me that used to belong to her granddaughter. They were such nice clothes I'd have stolen them except Sarah said they were mine to keep anyhow.

She said, "Give me a call when you're dressed, and I'll show you your room."

As I was putting on the shoes that went with the clothes—nice leather ones, with no holes in them—I heard talking from downstairs. I tiptoed to the top of the stairs and lay down on my belly to listen.

Sarah said, "I'm sorry I didn't hear you come in, darling. I was upstairs making up a bed."

"What bed?"

I risked a quick peek. The "darling" person looked so much like Sarah—only younger—I guessed she was Sarah's daughter.

"I have a guest. I suppose I can call her a guest. Claire."

"What Claire?"

"*Claire*. She's a girl, not a 'what.' A stray. I think she's a runaway; and she's definitely a thief, so keep an eye on your things." Since this was only the truth, I wasn't insulted by it. "I found her squatting in your father's room at the library."

"You found her in *Father's* room? And you brought her *home*?"

"It's not as bad as it sounds. She's only fifteen—or says she is. Anyway, if I don't take her in, she has nowhere else to go but the streets or Jane Joyce's."

"Jane's? You mean...?"

"I mean Jane's her aunt. Claire's mother is 'gone'—I don't know what that implies, but it's all I've been able to get from her—and her father's at sea. Claire and her aunt had a fight—physical—and Claire imagined she had killed her. She hid in the library to evade the authorities."

"You brought home a— a *hoodlum* who struck an old woman?"

"Don't underestimate Jane. Claire's bruised from head to foot."

"No doubt she's been abused, but you said yourself she's a thief, Mother. Of course, now that I think of it, she naturally *would* be a thief, because all the Joyces are thieves. What on earth are you thinking?"

"Don't look at me like that. *You're* the one who keeps telling me I need something to take me out of myself."

"I meant you should get a cat!"

"Well, I didn't happen to find a cat." I couldn't see her, but from her voice I guessed Sarah was smiling. "I found Claire instead, and she needs a place to stay and a little kindness. She needs regular baths, too. Just indulge me in this, Laura, please."

Laura didn't answer for a minute.

Then she said, "You know she's only here for what she can get, don't you?"

"Well, so are we all here for 'what we can get,'" Sarah said. "What's the point of life but seeing 'what we can get' out of it? I promise I'll be careful."

There was a knock at the back door just then. I scuttled away to find someplace to hide.

Luckily, when Sarah called out to know who was there, a man—not Aunt Jane—answered her. I relaxed again and crawled back to have a look.

The man was a sailor—an officer, by his clothes—and just about the ugliest fellow I'd ever seen. Sarah called him Timmy. Timmy had a sea chest on his shoulder, a real beauty, that Sarah told him to put down anywhere. Then she asked him how Mary was.

"Ain't been home yet," Timmy said. "Thought I'd bring you your box first."

If it was Sarah's sea chest, she'd been at sea sometime, probably. That was interesting.

Laura asked the sailor, "What do you know about a Claire Joyce, Tim? Have you heard of her? She's Jane Joyce's daughter."

Which was all wrong, of course. Sarah corrected her. "She's Jane's niece, not her daughter. And her surname's Dunn. Her father's a sailor. Do you know any sailors named Dunn?"

I hoped Timmy would say yes. I hoped he'd say my dad was the finest sailor he'd ever known and was on his way home—no, already landed—right now.

Instead, Timmy said he didn't know the name. "How old's the girl?"

"Fifteen or so."

"Old enough to be trouble." Timmy grinned. "Which she will be, if she's a Joyce. What's she doing here?"

After hushing Laura before Laura had a chance to say what *she* thought I was doing here, Sarah said, "Will you ask around? See if anybody can tell you anything about Mr. Dunn."

Timmy said he would, and then the three of them talked for a few more minutes before Timmy left.

Laura said she had to go, too. "Are you sure you know what you're doing, Mother?"

"No, not at all. Your father was always in favor of second chances, though."

"For everybody but himself. Maybe you could put her out in the stable. Just to sleep, I mean."

"Laura!"

"It was only a suggestion. You're coming for dinner tonight, aren't you? Bring Claire, of course."

Without asking me first, Sarah said, "We'll be there."

*

The dinner went all right.

Laura's husband's name was Tom, and he was very nice, and Tom and Laura had kids named Wolf and Anne. Anne was my age and Wolf was older. The two quarreled a lot with each other but spoke kind to me. I behaved myself. I didn't swear much, and I didn't take anything, either—although only because Laura kept a sharp eye out. I didn't think Laura liked me. Couldn't blame her.

As I'd already figured out from the sea chest, a couple days before Sarah caught me in the library she'd come back from a voyage. She'd been to an island called Annasland, which I'd heard of but didn't know anything about, where she'd gone to plant a tree for her brother, Wolf's and Anne's Uncle Daniel. It took me a while to figure out the tree meant Uncle Daniel was dead. I already knew Sarah's husband River was dead, too, so I wasn't totally surprised when the evening turned out to be kind of a grim one, with a lot of eye-dabs and sniffling. The food was good, though. Nothing wrong with the food.

When Sarah and me were getting ready to leave, Tom told Sarah she seemed more like her old self.

"I think it's time for a new adventure for you," he said. "That's the final thing missing to completely restore your spirits."

But Sarah said she'd had enough of that. She said she didn't even like the word "adventure" anymore.

As we walked home, I asked her why.

"Because I'm old and alone."

"You got kids, though."

"My children have their own lives and their own adventures."

"Oh." Made sense. After a minute, I asked, "Why did your husband die at the library? Did he live there?"

"Oh, no. Well, only in his last few days. The room at the library is a replica of a room in a Forest home. River was born in a Forest, and at the end, just before he died, he wanted to go 'home.'"

"He was a Forester?"

"That's right."

"Are you one? Because I thought Foresters never marry anybody but other Foresters."

"Sometimes they marry outsiders," Sarah said. "It's not common, but it happens. Our son Robin is married to a Forest woman, and they're even allowed to live in a Forest, which is a change from the old days. He's only a 'Friend of the Forest,' though. Not a Forest citizen."

"Are you sad your husband didn't want to die at home?"

As soon as I asked it, I thought this might not be a nice question, but Sarah took it calm.

She even smiled. "Home was wherever River was."

The knife I'd sold had been River's, of course, and when Sarah said the thing about him and home, it made me embarrassed to have stole it from her. I was so embarrassed, in fact, I stayed away from her house for two days. I slept in the stable and lived on the street, and told myself I loved it because I was free.

Only I didn't love it, because I was dirty and hungry, and I didn't feel free because the little knife cut my conscience. On the third day, I snuck back into Sarah's house and stole a picture frame from her. The money I got from that, plus everything I'd saved, was enough to buy the knife back, which I did. Sarah pretended not to notice about the frame, and thanked me for the knife and even kissed me, so though I was sad about being broke again, I was happy to have made her happy. I'd never made Aunt Jane happy. If I'd brought Aunt Jane gold and diamonds, she'd have complained because I didn't bring pearls and emeralds, too.

I didn't want to steal from Sarah no more, but I still needed money, so I stole stuff from a shop instead. And got caught.

It wasn't the first time I'd ever been caught, but this time I was in more trouble than other times because of my nice clothes. The shopkeeper called a constable to arrest me, and the constable—who knew me—figured I'd stole 'em. It was a reasonable guess, but wrong. I'd never thought before about what clothes cost in a shop; shops wasn't usually where I got mine. But it turned out that with the shoes added in, I was wearing a good amount of money on my back.

"I didn't steal nothing," I told the constable, "and Sarah Farmer give me these clothes."

The first part of that was a lie, but the second part was true, only the constable didn't believe it.

Luckily, Sarah heard from somebody that I was in trouble and came to the jail, where she not only told the constable I was being honest about the clothes, but also that whatever else I'd taken was meant to go on her account. Everybody knew she was lying, but in Fortress City, if a Farmer says something, it's taken for truth. The shopkeeper apologized, and the constable turned suddenly polite. As he let me loose, he wished me a good day. It must have just about killed him.

"Why did you do that?" I asked Sarah as we walked back to her house. "I'm a thief and stupid for getting caught, too. Why didn't you just leave me to get what I have coming?" I growled because I was embarrassed.

"What you 'have coming,'" Sarah answered back, sharp, "is a decent life and people who care about you. I'd be happy to provide both. But you have to stop stealing, Claire. It's wrong."

"I guess it's right to starve, then."

"You aren't starving."

She was right. I wasn't starving, and didn't have no real reason to steal. But I didn't like to admit I was wrong. "I am in my heart!" I snapped back.

I didn't mean to say it out loud, and I didn't think Sarah'd understand it when I did, but Sarah looked funny when I mentioned my heart and stopped walking.

"What is it?" she asked, looking at me earnest. "Is something missing in your life that I could provide? I know you've lost your mother, but—"

"It ain't my mother." I looked away. "It's nothing to do with her. I just want— I want something back. Something that's mine, only Aunt Jane took it. It's nothing to do with you, though, and I swear I won't steal no more."

I was lying. I'd steal until I got what I needed to get my ring back. I just wouldn't steal from Sarah.

But Sarah asked me to tell her everything, sounding so kind that though I'd swore to myself I wouldn't say nothing about my ring to nobody *ever*, I ended up telling her...a lot. Not everything; but a lot.

When I was done talking, Sarah asked, reaching into her pocket, "How much do you need? How much does whoever's got the ring now want for it?"

I didn't know, exactly. "He told me one price first, but when I got that much, he told me a different one."

"Typical. All right, what's the new number?"

I didn't like to answer this, but by now I was in too deep to keep anything back. I admitted the "new number" wasn't a...number. "He wants something else."

Sarah slipped her arm around me. "Has he hurt you?" she asked me, quiet.

"No," I said quick. "He just...talks. You know."

"But he hasn't...?"

"No."

Sarah started walking again. "Good," she said, brisk. "Then I don't have to kill him after all. Is the ring valuable?"

I couldn't talk for a minute because I was laughing at the idea of Sarah killing someone—though on second thought I remembered the way her eyes'd bored into me at the library and thought maybe it wasn't a joke. "It's only valuable to me," I finally told her.

"Because it was your mother's?"

"No," I answered, short.

"Claire, it's all right for you to care about your mother. It's perfectly natural, in fact. It's natural for you to care about your Aunt Jane, too. Whatever their faults, they probably had some loveable qualities, too."

I ignored the part about my mother. "Aunt Jane don't."

I said it firm, but if I'd been honest, I'd have admitted I did miss my aunt now and then. She was my dad's younger sister and probably not as old as she looked, and when she had food in the house, a few coins in her pocket, and no men beating on her, she liked to sit and talk, mostly about herself. She'd always start by complaining about how she'd been stuck taking care of her grandmother, then her mother, and then me when my mom…left…and never had a single minute of pleasure in her whole life, but when she ran out of that kind of rubbish, she'd go on to tell funny stories about how she'd been a teamster winning prizes racing wagon teams in her young days, and how she'd dance all night at festivals, robbing her partners one by one as they whirled around the dance floor, and go home with her pockets full of their money.

I reckoned the stories were mostly lies, but they were interesting lies, and I loved hearing them.

Eventually, though, something'd set Auntie off again, and she'd start cursing and throwing things like usual.

"Whatever your mother did," Sarah said, "she probably had her reasons. Tell me what this ring of hers looks like."

I said it was gold, and had a little blue stone in it.

"We'll get it back," Sarah said, solid as bricks. "And here—take some money." She put coins in my hand. "A bulwark against temptation."

I didn't know what a "bulwark" was, but I took the money.

A couple nights later—real late—I heard someone at the door again. I got up, and when I snuck to the landing to listen, I recognized the ugly sailor's voice.

"Nobody can say where he is," Timmy told Sarah. "Bill Dunn comes and goes mysterious."

"What do you think?"

"Oh, I got no doubt he's a pirate. Or a smuggler."

"Do you think she knows?"

"He'd be a fool to tell her."

"And the ring?"

I couldn't make out Timmy's answer to this. He left, and when Sarah started coming up the stairs, I scurried back to bed.

At breakfast next day, Sarah was all smiles. "No worse for wear, I hope," she said, and put my ring straight into my hand.

I was so surprised for a minute, I just stared at it. When I could talk again, I asked, "Did it cost you a lot? I'll pay you back for it, I promise."

"Nothing to pay. It didn't cost me a penny."

I didn't believe this, but I was afraid I might cry if I tried for real to thank Sarah, so I made a joke instead. "Only just the price of a bullet, maybe. Or did he use a knife?"

"A knife? Who used a knife?"

"That ugly sailor. I'm betting he was the one got my ring back."

"Don't call Tim ugly. He has a beautiful soul."

"Too bad he can't wear his soul where his face is, then. What'd he use? A gun or a knife? Or maybe just knucks. Was it knucks? Mr. Beautiful Soul don't look the type for knucks, though, being so skinny like he is."

"Violence was unnecessary. He didn't go alone, of course."

"Ten thousand gods, you've got a gang!" I laughed. "Can I join up?"

Sarah liked the joke. "Maybe when you're older, dear."

*

D&R was the biggest, most powerful company in the Valley, and Sarah owned two thirds of it. One third of that was her own from money she'd put in when the company was started, and the other third had been her dead brother Daniel's. Sarah said Daniel's daughter Helen should have got his part, but she was a Forester so she couldn't own anything. The other third of the company belonged to Laura, who'd inherited it from River, her dad. Sarah's family relationships were too complicated for me to keep track of. She had other sisters—two, I think—who didn't have anything to do with D&R, and about ten thousand nieces and nephews and cousins, but it was perfectly clear that her owning two thirds of D&R meant Sarah was very, very rich. I'd promised myself I wouldn't rob Sarah *personally*, but I figured if there was any place in the world where I could get myself a little money that nobody would even miss, it was from D&R. With that in mind—but with no intention, like I said, of stealing Sarah's personal stuff—I asked her one time what she did with all her company's cash.

"You must have piles of the stuff," I said. "You know it isn't safe to just leave it around, right?" Naturally, what I was hoping was that she *did* just leave it around, and that she'd tell me where.

But Sarah said first she was grateful for my concern, and then that she invested her money in pies to keep her fingers warm in, which wasn't any kind of answer or even funny. I wanted to know what the real answer was—just out of curiosity, as I said before—so I kept my ears open.

It turned out nobody in the family hardly ever talked about money. Maybe they just had so much of it they were bored of the subject. When the Farmers talked about D&R it was only about the people who worked there or what new things the company might make. It was never about how much money the place was raking in or where they kept it.

They talked about problems at the company sometimes too—but only private, when they thought I wasn't around. To help them be private, I usually excused myself to go up to my room during visits from D&R folks, where I could listen at the top of the stairs without anybody knowing. I still didn't hear anything about where their money was, but I did find out other stuff, such as that the Flying Machine project wasn't going too well, and that another company had stole one of D&R's ideas. Laura was furious about that one. I found out other things, too—like that D&R had bought some "hot steel."

Steel isn't usually something I'm interested in, if you want the truth. A lot of the things D&R makes are steel, and I guessed without anybody telling me that the company must buy tons of it. But when Tom didn't wait for me to make my own excuse to go upstairs, but sent me himself the minute he walked in Sarah's door, supposedly to look for a jacket Wolf'd left, I got curious. Before I was all the way gone—I didn't hurry—Tom was already talking about the steel to Sarah and showing her his hands, which were red and blistered.

"We're having to check everything in the warehouse," he said very quiet.

He also said he'd reported the steel to the Forests like he truly expected the Foresters to care what happened to his hands. "The Forest masters are keeping an eye out."

Since I was sure Foresters already knew that steel could get hot, and that hot things can burn hands, I didn't see the point of "reporting" about it to them unless there was more to the story than I was getting.

Sarah said, "Someone's taken this war as an opportunity to loot. Did any active radios leave D&R?"

I think "active radios" was what she said.

I'd never heard any radios called "active" before. I didn't know what Sarah meant by that. I also didn't know there was a war—though on second thought, it didn't surprise me to hear there was. It seems like there's always a war somewheres.

I waited to hear more, hoping for something really interesting, but all Tom said was, "We're checking that. I've informed the town authorities."

As far as town authorities were concerned, I figured Tom could have saved his breath. Things like governments and laws and "authorities" got wiped out on the continent by the Ant Cataclysm, and for a thousand years after that Men had to be their own authorities. Governments are back now—sort of—along with lots and lots of laws, but as far as "authorities" go, Men's own selves are still mostly the only ones they ever pay attention to.

After that, Tom and Sarah talked about other stuff until I came down to say I hadn't found Wolf's jacket, and Tom went home, leaving me no wiser.

The only thing I'd learned from the conversation was that steel might be able to be hot in a different way from the one I already knew about, and that radios could be active. I stashed this information in the back of my brain in case I ever needed it.

That day, like most of my days now, was good. My ring was back on my finger, I had plenty to eat, no beatings, and a clean bed to sleep in. I had nice clothes and hot baths. I liked Sarah, and I could almost even let myself believe Sarah liked me. The only thing I needed to feel perfectly peaceful inside was to have my dad back again, and Sarah had people looking for him. Life was almost perfect.

And then Rose and Robin came to visit, and ruined it.

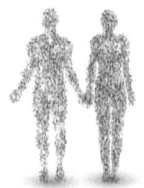

CHAPTER THREE

A t first, I was excited to hear Rose and Robin were coming. Rose was a real Forester, and Sarah's son Robin had been living in a Forest—Evergreen—for years, so he was almost a Forester, too. I'd never met a real Forester. I'd heard they were snooty, but Sarah said Robin and Rose weren't. She also said they were looking forward to meeting me, too, which I doubted.

On the day the two were supposed to arrive, Laura and her family came to Sarah's house, and everybody but me took turns running to the window every five minutes to look. I stayed sitting where I was because I wasn't really family, so it didn't seem right for me to act too curious, but inside I was as excited as anybody else. When a vehicle finally pulled up outside, I rushed out with the rest of them.

Robin was the one of the pair who looked like I thought Foresters are supposed to look; tall and dark, with dark eyes. I guessed he took after his father. Rose was smaller and light-haired. Everybody but me hugged and cried and kissed, all asking each other at the same time how everybody was, like they only had five minutes left to talk before the world ended. I stayed off to one side until Wolf dragged me forward and shoved me at Robin, who pretended not to mind that he had to hug me. I liked him for that. Then I got pushed in Rose's direction.

Rose was…different. Not just different from her husband. She was different from everybody. I can't say how. I don't know what words to use. She was just—different. She wasn't beautiful, exactly, though I liked looking at her. But I felt like if I looked too close, into her eyes, maybe, I'd see something scary there. I couldn't avoid her. As soon as I got near her, she put her hand out to me. Naturally, I put mine out to her, too.

Then, without meaning to, I said, "No!" real loud, and took a step backward. I didn't do it to be rude. I couldn't stop myself.

Everyone stared at me. All the talking and laughing stopped for a minute, and somebody—Laura, I think—gasped out loud.

Rose was the only one who didn't seem to notice or mind. She stuck out her hand farther, and when she reached mine, she shook it like normal. Also like normal, she said, "How do you do, Claire? I'm Rose."

My face was on fire, but I managed to say, "How do you do?" back, and everybody started breathing again.

The rest of the day went fine. I didn't have much to talk about, but nobody else could shut up. Rose and Robin went on and on about Evergreen, especially the fancy, big school they had there where Robin was a teacher. When Wolf said he wanted to go to the school himself, I noticed both Sarah and Laura snuck looks at me like they wanted me to say the same—which I didn't. There was some talk about D&R, but only the usual. At dinner there was enough food for forty, and the party didn't break up until midnight, when Laura and Tom went home and everybody else went to bed.

A few hours later, I was wide awake again. With a nightmare.

It was the one I always had, where I was laying in bed with a woman next to me. I was awake, but the woman was asleep. Then a noise from the next room woke her up, too, and she got up. The bed creaked—a sound I knew as well as I knew my own voice.

I asked, "What?"

"Nothing," the woman whispered to me. "Go back to sleep."

She got up and went out, and when she closed the door behind her, my dream ended, and I woke up sweating and shaking, like I always did, with my heart pounding. For some reason, no matter how many times I had the dream, it still scared me.

I didn't want to fall back to sleep and maybe have the dream start over, like it did sometimes, so I got out of bed and walked to the window. The sky was getting light. Pretty soon it would be morning.

Somebody knocked at my door.

Rose asked through it, "Are you all right?"

"Yeah." My heart was like a hammer against my ribs. "Yeah, I'm fine."

"May I come in?"

"You don't need to. I'm fine."

"You had a bad dream."

"Yeah. Something I ate, probably."

"May I help?"

I said no, and lied that I was going to sleep again.

Rose said, "I'm just down the hall, if you need me."

"Thanks. I'm fine, though."

As soon as I was sure Rose had gone back to her own room, I got dressed and went out.

Two hours later, I was at the river landing, sitting on a piling, when Tom came.

"Rose thought you might be here," he said, kind and smiling like he always was. "What's up?"

My skin crawled. How did Rose know where I was?

"Nothing," I answered. "Just needed some air."

Tom said I probably needed breakfast, too. "I'm on my way to work. Want to come with me? I'll show you around D&R, and we can have breakfast together."

I was hungry, so I said yes to this. I ended up spending all day with Tom at D&R and I had a good time. Then we went home to Sarah's for dinner, where Rose made me nervous all over again.

The whole week was like that—days full of picnics and games and fun things; scary nights full of bad dreams and Rose prying. The funny thing was, I *liked* Rose. She was nice. But I was also scared of her, and I didn't know why. My dream got worse and worse, until one night when Rose came to my bedroom door, she pretty much told me straight out she was coming in to "help" me whether I liked it or not.

I opened my door, though not wide. "I'm fine," I muttered, unfriendly. "What do you want? I don't need help."

Rose ignored me. Pushing past me, she said, "Let's talk about that dream of yours. Hop back into bed."

She was Sarah's guest, so I couldn't throw her out. I did what she said. Rose tucked the blankets around me nice, asking me if I knew where she was from.

I said, "Yeah. Evergreen Forest."

"That's where I live now," Rose answered. "I'm not from there originally. I'm from the Island Forest."

I guessed she was trying to distract me from my bad dream, so I played along. "Yeah? That's interesting. Is it nice there?"

"Very nice. Do you know anything about the Island Forest? Who its people are?"

"Foresters."

"Foresters—but also Hybrids. Most of us are Hybrids."

"Oh."

"Do you know what a Hybrid is?"

"No."

The strange feelings Rose always gave me came back—strong. I shivered. "You should go," I said, sitting forward. "You should go back to bed."

"I make you uncomfortable."

She did, but it didn't seem like it would be polite for me to say so. "No, I like you. I just— I mean, they'll worry. Your husband'n them."

"Nobody will worry. Let's talk about your dream first. Then I'll go."

I know I said Rose was nice. Did I mention she was pushy? I looked away. "It's just a dream. I've had it lots of times before."

"It frightens you."

"No. Well—not much, anyway."

Rose said, "Let me ask you a few questions about it. Sometimes it's easier to answer questions than to tell a story. At the beginning of the dream, you're in bed, aren't you?"

She was right. "Yeah."

"And someone else is there, too."

"Yeah."

"It's a woman, isn't it? Who is she?"

I shrugged. "I don't know."

"Maybe we can figure that out. Shall we try? She may be someone you know."

I wiped my hands on the sheet. "I don't care who she is. What difference does it make who she is?"

"Sometimes when people think a dream all the way through, they don't dream it anymore. That would be nice, wouldn't it? Your dream doesn't have an ending. Let's give it one and see if that helps."

"Maybe I don't want it to have an ending."

"Because it might not be a good one?"

I didn't answer this.

Rose went back to her questions. "There's a noise outside the room where you and the woman are sleeping, isn't there? And it wakes you both up."

I started to correct her. I started to say it woke the woman up, but I was already awake. But then—and this is the weird part—I realized Rose was actually right. The woman and me had both been asleep and dreaming. "How do you know that?" I asked, suspicious.

"Is that what happens?"

"Yeah. We wake up."

"What happens next?"

"She gets up."

"The woman gets up. And you don't know who she is?"

"I already said I don't!"

"Yes, of course. What happens next?"

"She gets up. And the bed squeaks."

"Had you ever heard that squeak before?"

I laughed. "Only about a million times. That bed always squeaked."

"You know this bed?"

I pulled the blankets up to my chin. "It was ours."

"Yours and—?"

"It was mine! Just mine! Who else's would it be, dammit?"

But it wasn't just mine, and I knew it. Rose knew it.

Since it was looking like Rose wouldn't go away until she'd heard the whole story, I decided to just tell it and get it over with. "It's *hers* and mine," I admitted, impatient. "And she turns and looks at me, and—"

"The woman turns?"

"Yes. She turns and looks at me and she tells me to stay in bed. She says, 'Stay here. I'll be right back.'" I wiped my forehead with the sleeve of my nightshirt. "It's hot in here."

"What happens next?"

"Next—I stay, like she says to. Only she don't come back. She never comes back." Before, I couldn't look at Rose. Now I looked and couldn't look away. "I didn't want her to go!"

Rose took my hand and squeezed it. "And then?"

"That's all."

"No, there's more. Isn't there?"

"No! Yes. I don't know. I never got this far before."

"Let's go farther. What's next?"

I said a bad word—two—but gave in. "Noises," I said. "There's noises."

"Voices?"

"Yeah, voices."

"Loud voices?"

"He's yelling."

"There's a man there?"

"No!" My voice came out scareder than I'd meant it to. There was a man there.

Rose closed her eyes. "I see him," she said. "He's angry."

"No! There's just her! Just my mom!"

"The woman is your mother?"

25

Rose asked that—and then my dream went crazy. Everything went crazy. Crazy things started happening right in front of my face. I could see them.

"What's he doing, Claire? What's the man doing?"

"No!" I yelled. "No, no, no!"

The crazy stuff stopped. All of a sudden, I was back in my room at the Farmer house, only now I was standing in front of the window. Rose was beside me. "Back to bed," Rose was saying. "Back to bed and get warm."

I let her lead me back and tuck me in again, and then I started to cry.

I hate crying.

Rose wanted to comfort me, but I shoved her away. I hated her, too. I told her I did.

"Who do you hate, Claire?" Rose asked. "Not me, I think. I think you hate that man. What was he doing when you ran to the window?"

"I don't know." I knew what *I* was doing when I ran to the window. I was—dying. But not exactly. I mean, it was kind of *like* dying—like how I thought dying would feel—but also like a dream. A kind of dream where I saw things, and felt things, and even smelled things like when I was awake, but where I couldn't *do* anything, like in a dream. In this dream, the man was hurting me. Only somehow, it also *wasn't* me he was hurting, it was my mother. It was both of us. That didn't make any sense, but that's how it seemed. She—we—wanted to yell for help, but we couldn't. We—me and my mother—squirmed and struggled, but at the same time, it was like we couldn't move.

Then we stopped struggling. All we wanted now was just to breathe. We wanted one good, deep breath. The man held us tight, and wouldn't let us have it.

Then—about the time I got to the window I guess—everything went quiet in my dream, and I could breathe again, as much as I wanted. But my mother was gone.

"There, there," Rose murmured. "It's over. The dream is over."

I rolled away from her, all the way to the other side of the bed. "Why did you do that? That wasn't nice."

Rose patted me. "I know it was hard, but you needed to talk about what happened. You had to get it out and not keep it locked up inside you."

"It was lies."

"It was a memory—part of a memory. One day I think you'll remember it all."

"No."

"Who was the man who hurt your mother, Claire? I saw his face, but I don't know who he was."

If I hadn't been too tired to move, I'd have hit her. "You never saw *nothing*," I hissed. "It was *my* dream."

"I can see your dreams. You can see mine, too, if you want."

"More lies. You're a liar!"

"I can see them because I'm a telepath. And so are you."

I closed my eyes. "They're all dead."

"The Ants are dead, you mean. But I didn't say you and I were Ants. Remember when I said I was a Hybrid? Hybrids are also telepathic. You're a Hybrid, Claire. You're a different kind of Hybrid from me. Your thoughts are hard for me to read. But I understand you enough to know that you could learn to read my thoughts, too, and the thoughts of other Hybrids. I could help you to learn, if you wanted me to. I could teach you."

"I said you're a liar!"

"Your mother must also have been a Hybrid."

"My mother was a—" All I could think of to call her was a navy word. "She was a *deserter!*" I cried. "She deserted my dad and me! She didn't like us."

"Please believe me that I sensed something very different! I believe your mother loved you very much."

"You don't know. You weren't there. I hate you. Everything you say is lies."

I hated Rose—but when she put her arms around me, I let her. I let her hug me, and I let her rock me, and when she talked to me on and on, soothing, about how my mom loved me and stuff, I let her talk. I fell asleep to her talking, and when I woke up, it was afternoon.

*

I got up and dressed, and then I went downstairs and acted like nothing had happened. Nobody was fooled. I tried all day to be normal, except for not looking at Rose—because I couldn't—and not eating much—same reason—and as soon as I could, I snuck away to the docks again. Tom came and got me like he had before, pretending he just happened to be passing by on his way home from work. I knew different. I knew Rose had sent him. Tom took me to his own house instead of Sarah's, and I had dinner with him and Wolf and Anne while Laura went to her mom's.

I guessed Wolf and Anne didn't know anything about what had happened, because they were the same as always to me, but Tom was extra-nice, which I hated. After dinner we played games. I was in a bad mood so I taught Wolf and Anne to play a gambling game I knew how to cheat good at. I didn't like the game very much. I only taught it to Wolf and Anne because Laura and Tom didn't want their kids to know gambling games. Tom staked us all anyway, and when I won everybody's money—cheating—he just laughed. I didn't enjoy myself, and at the end, I gave everybody their money back. I slept over at their house.

After that, I got up early every morning to leave Sarah's before anybody could see me or stop me, and stayed out as long as I could. Since Rose knew about me liking the docks, I didn't go there anymore. I went other places. But if I didn't come back to Sarah's by nightfall, Tom always found me and brought me to his house. The whole family must have been spying on me for him to always know where I was. Rose told somebody—I couldn't remember afterwards exactly when or who—that she felt bad for upsetting me when I "wasn't ready." As if anybody could ever be "ready" for a pack of lies piled on top of bad dreams. Rose had promised—almost promised—that if I talked about it, I wouldn't have my nightmare anymore, but that was just another lie. I had it most nights now. Something inside me felt rotten and hurt.

Time to run away.

I'd been "good" for months—wasted time, I can tell you—but now I stole again. I snuck into Tom and Laura's house and stole a suit of Wolf's clothes. Probably nobody minded. The clothes were old, and everybody was always offering me clothes anyway, if I wanted any, which I didn't. But I didn't ask first, so it was stealing, and I would have stole Sarah's nice sea chest, too, except that would have been too low even for me to go. Sarah loved that chest. Her husband River had give it to her.

I changed into the clothes in Anne's room and left my girl-clothes there, and then I tied my hair back like boys tie theirs and dirtied my face and my fingernails because boys is always dirty. Then I went down to the docks on the river again and did another bad thing, because why not? What was one more bad thing on top of the others I'd already done? I bribed the captain of a lighter headed downriver to Coast-town to take me aboard.

Somewhere near Coast-town, my "strange" feelings went away, and I was me again. Being me wasn't exactly something to be proud of, but it was something I was used to, at least. I hung around the harbor for a day, getting the lay of things, and slept rough that night. I admit I missed my bed at Sarah's and breakfast, too, when breakfast time came and went with me still empty as a drum. But later I picked up a few coins helping people with their trunks and things, and once I'd had a meal, I felt good again. Pretty good, anyway. I was free and beholden to nobody and old enough to take care of myself.

I was still only fourteen, and ship's boys have to be sixteen, but I figured if you reckoned age by savvy instead of by years, I was old enough to go to sea, so I started looking for a berth. I only had a small bundle and not a sea chest like a regular sailor, due to my not stealing Sarah's, and I wasn't exactly what captains was usually looking for in a ship's boy, in that I was strong for my size but not big, or a boy. But I figured if I kept trying, sooner or later somebody would give me a job. Then, once I'd got my first place, everybody'd see how hard I could work, and one place would lead to another, and I'd rank as a seaman in no time. Simple as that.

CHAPTER FOUR

I t was simple, all right—only not easy.

For a long time I didn't have no luck at all. I talked to a lot of officers—even a captain or two—asking for a trial, but all of them told me the same thing: Go home. It was easy for me to ignore this advice on account of not having a home to go to.

Finally, I got an offer. It was a bad one—a cut of two sailors' pay in return for doing part of their work. Not a big cut, either. But it was the chance I'd been looking for to show what I could do, so I took it. The two sailors wasn't young—I guessed about my dad's age—and they were both only ranked "seaman" themselves, which was a bad sign, but at least they were nice to me. When I told one I wanted to find my dad, he said, "Got a dad myself." That seemed friendly.

"I'll work hard," I told them both. "I'm a very hard worker."

"You sure will!" one said, slapping me on the back so hard I almost fell over. Their ship—my ship—the *Antelope*, was headed straight to Johns Island, where I'd heard from Aunt Jane my dad sometimes went.

The *Antelope* turned out to be an old wooden sailing ship. Like a lot of other old boats, she was so leaky and slow she couldn't turn a profit trading unless she sailed overloaded and undermanned. Even the ship's longboat, perched up on the deck, was packed full of cargo. Exactly how the sailors was supposed to get off if the *Antelope* foundered—which she looked like she might—wasn't clear. The deck was so crowded with chicken-coops and pens of sheep that the dinghy had to be towed behind.

I'd planned for days what I was going to say when I saw my ship for the first time, and like a fool, I went ahead and said it: "She's a handsome lady."

Antelope was so opposite of handsome the sailors slapped their thighs and just about laughed themselves sick.

One of 'em slapped my thighs, too. I thought of my dad and how much I wanted to see him and didn't do more than just shove the sailor's hand away.

The sailors had told me it wouldn't be any problem to have me aboard. They said sailors like them hired "assistants" all the time. They were lying. When the first officer saw the three of us, he yelled, "Dammit, send that female ashore! We sail in an hour!" How he knew I was a female, I don't know.

I was scared by the yelling, but the sailors said it was just bluff, and wouldn't let me leave. One pushed me behind a sheep-pen and told me not to make noise, and as soon as the first officer got busy somewhere else, the two sailors put me to work cleaning up after the animals. It was hard work, and dirty, but they kept me at it until the ship sailed and a couple more hours after that. Then one of them took me below.

With the ship as overloaded as she was, I wasn't surprised to see that the crew-quarters was small. Bunks was hung above bunks, three high.

"Get in there," the sailor ordered me, pointing to a middle one. "It's mine, but we ain't got a spare for you. It's big. We can share."

"I can't share with you!"

The sailor said sure I could, but added after a look at my face that we'd never be in it two at once anyway. "We'll have different watches, see?"

This made sense, so I climbed in the bunk. The blanket was stinking, and there wasn't no pillow, but I put my bundle under me and lay so I could peek out and watch what was going on.

The watch was changing, with sailors coming in and out, claiming bunks and stowing their gear. The sailor said this watch was his and went away—to eat, I figured out from listening to the talk around me. I was hungry, but I was even more tired. I put my head down, and in five minutes, the rocking of the ship sent me straight to sleep.

I woke when the sailor whose bunk I was in climbed in beside me. It was dark. The sailor clapped his hand over my mouth as he stretched out, so I couldn't ask what I wanted to ask, which was if it was my watch now. He'd said we'd never be in the bunk two at once, and now here he was, so I figured it was time for me to get out, but when I tried to, the sailor put his leg over me so I couldn't. I was too surprised to say anything.

After a minute, he took his hand off my mouth. "Now, missy," he whispered. "Let's see what you got in there."

He fumbled at my shirt buttons.

"Stop it," I whispered back. "Let me get out."

He muttered something. I didn't catch exactly what.

I could've screamed, I guess, but screaming—even talking at all—might make my situation worse. There were men sleeping all around me, and it dawned on me the job the sailors had brought me aboard to do included parts I hadn't bargained on.

"I gotta, um… I gotta go to the toilet," I ventured.

"Later."

He had half my buttons undone. His breath stank.

"No, really." I tried to squirm away. "I *need* to. It won't take long."

"Dammit, lady, that can wait!" The sailor pushed himself against me, and if I hadn't already figured out what he had in mind, I'd have guessed it then.

I fell to begging. "Please! I'm bursting!"

A sleepy voice from a nearby bunk muttered, "Shut up, can't you?"

The sailor—he had started on his own buttons by now—hesitated just enough to give me time to roll away from him and out of the bunk. I landed half on the sailor sleeping below, but luckily the fellow was too tired to do more than curse.

I ran for the nearest ladder.

To be honest, I didn't expect to make it. I thought the sailor'd come after me. But he must've believed me that I'd come back, because I not only made it to the ladder, but onto the deck, where I headed for the chicken coops I'd cleaned around earlier.

The spot I picked turned out to be the exact place on the lee-side rail the sailors generally pissed over, but I hid there anyways. It was safer than trying to move.

Toward morning, I found a better hiding place behind the sheep pens and watched from there as the sun came up. The sailors who'd brought me aboard hunted for me now—both of them. After they'd looked in a place near me, I snuck out from the sheep pens and moved to the place they'd looked, figuring they wouldn't be back there soon.

When they didn't find me, the sailors got mad, and told the first officer they thought there was a stowaway aboard.

The first officer had other things on his mind.

"Get back to your work!" he yelled at them. "Stowaway? Like hell! As long as she don't set no fires, I don't care to know about it."

The sailors started looking for me again.

I hid behind the galley stove until the cook spotted me and pulled me out by the arm. "Who the hell are you?" he asked, harsh. "Damn me, you're a girl! How old are you, girl? Twelve?"

"Sixteen."

"In a pig's eye you are. What are you doing on this ship?"

I explained about my "job." He said "pig's eye" to that, too. "You are in a whole heap of trouble, girlie," he told me, very serious. "You got family?"

"Got a dad. I think he might be on Johns Island. That's why I want to go there."

The cook shook his head. "A whole *heap* of trouble. Can you reach your dad by radio? Do you know where he's staying?"

When I told him I didn't, the cook said a word I'd never heard before but I guessed was bad. "Got a mom? Grandma? Friends? Anybody in reach of a radio?"

I thought of Sarah. She had a radio right in her house. But I'd run off on her, so I said no.

"Booger." The cook thought for a couple minutes, then cocked his head. "In here," he said, dragging me to a cupboard. "Don't make a sound."

The cupboard was where the food was stored, and it was filthy. Honestly, Aunt Jane would have kept it better. The first thing I saw when my eyes adjusted to the dark was a big cheese, and the second thing I saw was three rats eating the cheese and using it for a piss-pot at the same time. Me and the rats stared at each other while just the other side of the door, sailors argued with the cook.

When the sailors went away, the cook pulled me out again. He repeated, "Who are you?" but before I could answer, said, "Never mind. I don't want to know." Then he gave me a chunk of bread. Rats might have chewed it—peed on it, too—but it was the first food I'd got in more than a day so I took a big bite.

The cook dragged me by the arm to a place where he could see the deck. "I'll pass the word the captain's got you with him in his cabin," he whispered to me. "He's drunk enough he'll stay in his bunk until tonight or so, but after that…!" He shook his head. "I don't know what to do with you. We've got to get you off this ship. You're in a heap of trouble, like I said."

"I want to go to Johns," I told him.

"Johns Island is a week away. You could never hide that long." He stared at me a minute. "You're a girl. Use what you got."

Without letting the cook see me do it, I turned my mother's ring on my finger so the pretty stone was hid against my palm. "I've got money," I said then.

"That ain't what I meant, but it might do. Where is it?"

"My— the bunk I was in."

"You left it?"

"In my bundle."

"It's gone, then. Your bundle, too. If you can't radio anyone, you'd better find yourself somebody shipboard to look after you. You ain't real pretty"—I knew this—"but you're young enough you might get an officer. An officer's your best bet."

I set my jaw. "I'd rather die."

"Without protection, you might." He thought for a minute. "Look there: You see the scuppers?" He pointed out a place on the deck. "Nobody goes near them. They stink. You get there and you hide, all right? Give me time to come up with something."

I got to the place without being seen, and it was just big enough to give me cover while I ate my bread. The place did stink. I hoped the cook was a fast thinker.

I'd said I was willing to die, and sitting there in the scuppers, I worried death might be the only way out for me. Thing was, I'd have to stay uncaught and undead until nighttime, or else when I threw myself overboard, I'd likely be seen and "rescued." The thought of dying didn't bother me as much as I expected it to. I was more curious about it than sad. I wondered if death was the end of everything, like some people said, or if it was just the beginning of something new. Whatever it was, I hoped it would have my mother in it. Sarah'd said my mom must've had reasons for running off. I wanted to ask her what her reasons'd been.

As the cook said he would, the captain stumbled out of his cabin around nightfall, bloated and cross, and when I wasn't with him, the sailors started hunting for me again. By then the scuppers where I was hiding were filthier than ever, which was partly my fault, since I couldn't leave where I was even to answer nature's calls. I was so dirty there was no chance I'd get "protected" by an officer now.

I felt so bad that when I heard somebody coming, I almost stood up to save whoever it was the trouble of finding me.

It was the cook.

Standing near me—but looking in another direction—he asked, quiet, "Can you handle a boat?"

I eyed the longboat nearby.

"Not that one, ninny. The dinghy. Can you row?"

"Yes."

"Can you go down a rope to it?"

We were two decks above the water, and I'd never gone down a rope to anything before, but of course I said, "Sure."

"Which way's north?"

I pointed.

The cook smiled a little. "All right, then. When I say, get to the dinghy. There's a rope and a bag on the deck aft. Use the rope, and take the bag."

He walked away.

"Wait!" I shout-whispered after him.

The cook stopped and pretended to look at the chickens in their coops.

"Why're you helping me?"

The cook risked a quick look in my direction, I guess so's to be sure I saw the sneer on his face. "Because you *need* help, stupid. Why do you think?"

"I can't help you back, though," I reminded him. "I got nothing."

He answered this like he was talking to an unbright child—which was about right, now I thought of it. "You're a fool, like lots of us are at your age. But if you stay on this ship, things are likely to happen that'll turn you vicious." He looked straight at me. "The fewer vicious dogs I got to share the world with, the better I'm suited. Good enough?"

This made sense. "All right."

The cook was already moving off again.

A long, long time later—maybe fifteen minutes—I heard him say, "Go."

At my first step, I slipped in muck and almost fell. I'd been crouching so long my legs was cramped. I forced myself to keep going, first stumbling, then walking, and when my pounding heart forced blood to my feet, I ran. I ran the length of the deck and lunged for the coiled rope waiting for me. A bag made of rough sacking with a strip of cloth for a handle was next to the rope, and when I put the bag over my arm, two bottles inside clinked together. Something to drink, thank the gods!

Going down a rope was a lot harder than it'd looked when I saw real sailors do it. I didn't get the hang of stopping myself with my feet right away so went down faster than I wanted to and scorched my palms. I landed in the water instead of the dinghy, but didn't mind the dunking. The sea was cold, but compared to me it was clean. I grabbed onto the dinghy's side and let the *Antelope* drag me along for a minute or two. It was like washing away the ugliness of the day. Then I climbed in, and I managed not to capsize, either.

As I settled myself, the dinghy's painter dropped into the water in front of me—one last nice thing the cook did for me. I waved to thank him, but it was dark, and I don't know if he saw. Despite her bagging sails, the *Antelope* moved away from me quick, and in a few minutes, I was alone on the water.

CHAPTER FIVE

I checked out the bag first—especially the bottles. I hadn't had anything to drink since the day before. I told myself I wouldn't be greedy, but when the bottle got to my mouth I couldn't stop myself from taking a good long hit from it. I promised myself I'd make up for it later.

Then I had a look at what else the cook had packed.

There was a piece of cheese, maybe from the wheel I'd seen in the ship's pantry. Having seen what the rats was doing to it I wanted to throw it overboard, but food was food, so I washed it off overside instead. The salt water made my hands sting. Besides the cheese, there was a chunk of something I wasn't sure about, though it was possibly pickled meat. I washed that, too.

The last thing in the bag was a small tin of ship's biscuit.

This was a prize, and not just for the biscuit in it, but because the box had a map scratched onto its lid. A rough shape at one side of the map had "continent" written on it, and a dotted line from "continent" to an oval labelled *Antelope* showed the course the ship had sailed since putting to sea. Johns was northeast from Coast-town, but according to the map, we'd traveled almost due east instead. I didn't know why. It probably had something to do with the currents. Straightest course is shortest course, sailors say, so the cook had done me a big favor to show me how we'd sailed so I didn't waste any time going south. There was also a line of arrows drawn on the map's "sky," with a ball for the sun in the middle of it to show me that the arrows were the sun's path. To finish the picture, there was even a little compass rose drawn on the bottom right corner.

"All I need to do to get home," I heard myself say out loud, "is row west."

But—row for how long?

I tried not to think about that. Instead, I unshipped the oars and with one eye on the stars, I pulled—I hoped—for land.

*

I hadn't rowed long before I knew my rope-singed hands would never take me all the way home, even if the continent was nearer than I thought it was. By moonlight I could make out that my palms were starting to blister. I stopped to think about what to do. Gloves were what I needed, only I didn't have any.

I did have the food bag, though. I pulled off its cloth handle and wound it around my right hand, which was sorer than the left one. Then I tried one careful pull. The trick seemed to work, so I tore the whole bag into strips and wrapped up both my palms. I could row again.

By moonset, my thumbs hurt. I hadn't covered them, and I was pretty sure they had blisters now, too. I stopped rowing again and thought more about my situation.

I had to sleep. My whole body—brain, too—was screaming for it. And it would be better for my hands if I rested them a while, too. On the other hand, the dinghy didn't have an anchor, nor the sea where I was a bottom to anchor on, probably. If I wasn't rowing, I'd drift, and who knew where I'd drift to?

But there was nothing I could do about that. I'd dozed off twice already just while I was thinking. I stretched out on the dinghy's damp bottom and was asleep before I knew it.

My old dream woke me up. My mother—the woman was definitely my mother; I admitted that to myself now—got up from beside me, and the old bedstead creaked. She said she'd be back. She never came.

The creaking woke me up, only it wasn't the old bed creaking, it was the dinghy. The wind had picked up, and she was rocking. It was morning, and though I didn't know exactly where I was, I knew which way to go. Time to be on my way.

But first, breakfast—hard biscuit and water. Not as much water as I wanted, but some. My thumbs was blistered, just like I'd thought; only they were worse than I'd thought, with raw spots not only on the pads but down the sides of them. I rearranged the strips of cloth on my hands to cover these new bad spots, and once that was done, I started rowing again. No rest, and no more water, I told myself, until noon.

The sun took days, it seemed like, to get overhead. I knew the dinghy's bow was pointed toward the continent, but I didn't know if I was really moving in that direction, or even moving at all. If I was rowing straight against a current, I might be working hard to sit still in the water. I just had to keep rowing and trust that the cook would have found a way to warn me about a current.

Just when it felt like the muscles in my shoulders had caught fire, the sun made it up the last few degrees to noon, and I could finally let myself have a drink. I took two swallows, and I made them big ones. I'd liked to have had a dozen more.

Food, on the other hand, didn't look very good to me—especially the pickled meat, which was slimy. In fact, I threw the meat overside without a second thought. But was cheese—even biscuit—actually worth whatever extra strength they gave me if they made me more thirsty? I wasn't sure. I made myself eat two bits of cheese and a biscuit, and I let myself have just one more small gulp of water to digest them with. Then I recommenced rowing. I reckoned I still had a long way to go.

By mid-afternoon, my face was so hot I knew it was sunburned. I didn't have a hat, of course, nor any means of making one, so I rowed with my chin on my chest to avoid the worst from above. I couldn't do nothing about the reflection off the water. In late afternoon, I had another drink—less water than I wanted, but probably more than I could afford.

In the evening, I unwound the strips of cloth from my hands. I wanted to rearrange them and maybe make them more comfortable. The inside strips stuck on, and the only way I could get them off was by soaking my hands in seawater. Soaking them hurt a lot. A whole lot. I said all the bad words I knew and added the one the cook'd used that I didn't know the meaning of. This time when I tied my hands up again, I made sure every inch of skin was covered.

I figured that under the big moon that was rising, I could row a couple more hours at least, but that's not what I did. What I did was drop like a stone into the bottom of the boat and sleep. I didn't do it on purpose. One minute I was awake, and the next I was awake again, only the moon was down, and I was lying on the boat's bottom.

It was close to morning, but still dark, and I was crazy, crazy thirsty. The second water-bottle was almost empty. I wondered how long a person could live without water. I'd heard once about a man who went for months without a single bite of food—that's what he said, anyway—but what about something to drink? He must've been drinking right along. Was it a good sign that I wasn't hungry, or a bad one? I went back to rowing, but I almost didn't care anymore if I got anywhere. That's the truth. I almost didn't care.

When the day was finally over—I don't remember too much about it—I forced myself to eat part of a biscuit and a bite of cheese, then let myself have all the rest of the water in the second bottle. It wasn't much. Tomorrow, I'd already decided, was my do-or-die day. Tomorrow would see me ashore—or dead. The pus from my blisters had soaked through the wrappings on my hands by now, and my shoulders hurt so bad sometimes I cried. I cried with no tears. I remembered stories about people who got lost in the Antlands and drank their own pee to survive, but I didn't feel sorry for them the way I used to. Anybody who wasn't too dry to pee at all was better off than me and had no reason to complain. I didn't have tears anymore, and I didn't have piss. I just had a long way to row. The sky clouded over like it might rain, and I thought rain might save me. But the clouds, thin and high, blew over.

The salty ocean water was beginning to look good to me. Of course, it'll kill you to drink salt water. Everybody knows that, including most of the fools who go ahead and drink it anyway and die. But was it better to die from drinking salt water or from drinking no water at all? A couple times I held one of the bottles over the side to fill it, but the pain of salt water on my blisters always stopped me and made me pull the bottle back empty. All my dad's people for generations back—some of my mom's, too—were sailors, and I told myself that the burning in my hands was a warning from them to die from no water at all. Anyway, I pretended it was their warning. It made me feel better to pretend somebody somewhere cared enough about me to give me warnings.

By nightfall, I'd got to pretending my seafaring ancestors were sitting in the boat with me and I could talk to them—which I did. Later, there were sea monsters with them and sometimes my Aunt Jane. I wasn't out of my head enough to entirely believe they were real, but it was a comfort to have them there and not be alone. The best thing about death, I decided, was that I didn't have to row to it. I could take my ease now. Death would come and get me right where I was.

That being the case, I lay down and tried to get comfortable. Another time I'd have thought the wet bottom of a dinghy made a bad bed, but now it was fine. I closed my eyes. I didn't mind anything except that I didn't have a paper or anything to write with. I wanted to write to Sarah and tell her I was sorry for running off. I wanted to thank her for being nice to me, and ask her to thank everybody else who'd been nice to me, too. When I'd written, I'd fold the note and put her name on the outside so whoever found the dinghy would know who to give it to. Everybody knew the Farmers and D&R. Sarah'd get the note and read it and know I hadn't run off from being ungrateful to her but only from being stupid. On second thought, I'd write a line to the cook on the *Antelope*, too. Couldn't hurt.

I slept, and woke, and slept some more, and each time I slept, I didn't expect to wake up again.

CHAPTER SIX

I'd just gotten to a comfortable place in my dying, where I was peaceful and nothing hurt, when the dinghy, for some reason, slued sideways and bumped. I didn't care to be disturbed, and the bump, especially, annoyed me. The dinghy went back to bobbing, so I turned my face away from the sun that was burning me and closed my eyes again.

Another bump. Then another, and then a change in the way the boat bobbed. One of the oars squeaked in the oarlock. The sound reminded me of my mother's old bed that we'd shared and ruined my peacefulness. I sat up.

The bumping was a gentle surf nudging the dinghy against a sandy beach. Somehow, I'd made it to land.

By crawling, I managed to get up into the dinghy's bow, and in one pull I didn't think I had strength enough left to make, I got my belly over the rail. From there I rolled over the side and into the water, which was like fire on my blisters and sunburn, but woke me up all the way, which was good. I swam a few strokes toward the beach, then got my feet under me and walked. There was no way I could bring in my boat, which I felt bad for. She'd done me good service, and I would have liked to have kept her. But I did manage to get ashore and a dozen steps toward some bushes ahead. When my legs gave out, I moved on by crawling, and eventually by wiggling like a snake through the sand. I got to the bushes at last, rolled under their shade, and tried to decide whether to get back to dying or get up and try to find clean water.

I couldn't get up, so I guessed I'd have to die. That's what I was doing a little later—dying under the bushes—when I heard talking.

I opened my eyes a crack. Two men, backs to me, were pulling in my dinghy.

I was so far out of my head that their talking sounded like gibberish, but it was plain they didn't see me. I opened my mouth to shout to them, but only a whisper came out.

On second thought, I wasn't sure I wanted to get their attention after all. They were men, both bigger and stronger than I was, and probably no better than the rest of their kind. I let my eyes go back closed and considered my situation.

When I looked again, the dinghy was ashore, and one of the men had a canteen to his lips and was drinking.

I didn't necessarily want to live, and I for sure didn't want anything more to do with men, but I did want a drink. I wanted to drink buckets full of water, and I wanted to feel water—cool, if possible, but at least not salt, poured over my face. My eyes on the canteen, I opened my mouth again.

What came out this time wasn't the yell I meant it to be, but it was loud enough to be heard. The men turned toward me and stared.

The shout took the last of my strength, I guess. After shouting, I went back to sleep—or whatever what I was doing was called—and didn't know anything more until I was rolled onto a blanket and lifted. My face was wet, and when I licked my lips, the salt-crust was off them. I'd got half my wish—to have my face washed—but didn't get to enjoy it happening.

"Water," I croaked, in a bullfrog voice. "Bucketful."

Instead of a bucketful, the men gave me about enough water to fill a thimble. Then they lifted the blanket again and carried me off to—? Somewhere. I had no idea where they were taking me and didn't care.

I don't remember much more about what happened that day. Someone gave me a tiny drink from time to time. Someone tried to unbandage my hands. I think I screamed when they did that. Somebody screamed, anyway. It was probably me. Somebody tried to undress me, too. I probably screamed more about that, but I don't remember. Whether I yelled or not, somebody undressed me anyway, because the next time I woke up I was wearing a clean shirt and drawers instead of the salty ones I'd had on before. I guessed by now everybody—whoever everybody was—knew I wasn't a boy.

People talked around me in soft voices. Sometimes they talked to me. Someone asked me who my people were. I shook my head. "Nobody," I whispered. "Got no family." I wouldn't say where I'd come from, either.

In Valley, but with a strong accent I didn't recognize, someone finally said, "Here. Drink this," and gave me a big drink of something that wasn't water, and wasn't tasty, but was wet, so I swallowed it all. That was the last thing I did, or knew about, for quite a while.

*

When I woke again, I was cool and in my right mind. The sun was just coming up, and there was a tent over me instead of bushes. I was too weak to move much, so I looked at the only thing I could see without turning my head—a young man sitting on the ground beside me reading a book. He was dark, with dark eyes, and looked to be a few years older than me.

The young man glanced up, saw my eyes were open, and immediately put his book aside. "How are you?" he asked.

His voice was different from the one that had offered me the sleeping drink but had the same accent.

"Good," I whispered—sounding anything but. "Drink."

The young man held up my head, very gentle, and gave me water.

While I was drinking, he called to someone else, and another man came and knelt down on the other side of me. This man was older, and he smiled.

"Awake at last, eh?" the man said. "How do you feel?"

I answered, but didn't recognize the voice that came out of my mouth.

"That's all right," the man said quick. "You'll sound like yourself again soon. Do you think you could tell me your name?"

A lie's usually safer than the truth, but harder to come up with. The only name that came to me right away—besides my own—was my mother's. I croaked, "Catherine."

"Hello, Catherine. My name is 'Doctor.'"

The hell it was, I thought. Nobody's name is "Doctor."

Pointing to the young man, Doctor said, "And this is Dan."

I tried to offer my hand, polite, but remembered when I raised it up and got a look at it that my hands was hurt. The rags I'd put on had been cut off and they were bandaged instead, the bandages so thick my hand didn't look like a hand at all.

"Are you in pain, Catherine?" Doctor asked. "Aside from your hands, I mean."

"Not—a lot."

"Do you think you could eat something? You need to."

"I could drink, maybe."

"Some soup?" He looked at the young man—Dan—and Dan got up quick and ran off.

Dan came back with soup, and after the two men together had propped me up on soft bundles, Dan fed me like a baby, since I couldn't use my hands.

Seeing that I was embarrassed, Doctor said, "It's only for a day or two. Tell me about yourself, Catherine."

There was nothing I wanted him to know. "*Are* you a doctor?" I asked.

Smiling his nice smile again, the man said, "I am," then repeated, "Tell me about yourself."

"Nothing to tell." I flexed my bandaged fingers, which made them hurt. "I'm just—normal."

"I'm normal too." Doctor nodded. "We're all normal around here. Well, maybe not Dan." Dan seemed to like the insult, because he laughed. "What normal place are you from, Catherine?"

I tried to avoid this one, too. "Is this the continent?" I asked.

"Yes."

"I'm from the continent. Whereabouts are *you* from?"

"I'm from the Islands. You know the Islands?"

Some teacher or other had mentioned them, but the only island I knew for sure about was Annasland, where Rose was from. In my mind I heard her say, "I'm a telepath and so are you."

Without thinking, I blurted, "Gods, you can read my mind!"

Doctor laughed. "Do you think I'm a telepath? No, sorry. I'm not."

I wasn't sure whether to believe him. "Some people from islands are, though, right?"

Doctor said some were, but he and Dan weren't, and I felt better.

Doctor had given up on getting me to say where I was from, I guess. Instead, he asked, "Where were you going in that rowboat, Catherine?"

I wished I hadn't given my mother's name. I jumped when he said it.

"Johns," I blurted.

"Johns Island?"

"Yeah."

"Why did you want to go to Johns?"

"Because my dad might be there."

"So you do have some family?"

Damn me, I'd said earlier that I didn't. "No. Or—yeah, maybe. I don't know. Dad might be dead. That's why I was going to look for him on Johns. To find out."

"And you thought you could row there?"

I decided the next time I met with strangers, I'd pretend I was a deaf-mute. That way, I couldn't talk myself into places where my choice was to either tell the truth—some of the truth—or have people think I was stupid.

Stupid seemed worst of the two, so I admitted, "I was on a ship first. I was a sailor."

"Was the ship the *Antelope*? That's the name on the dinghy."

"Yeah, the *Antelope*."

I was hoping he'd just let it go, but instead Doctor pushed, "And?"

It was too late to lie now. "And some sailors bothered me. They wouldn't stop bothering me, so I had to get off. You know."

"I see," Doctor said, lips tight. "And the *Antelope* was heading for Johns Island?"

I nodded.

"Well, Johns is a fit place for that kind. It's a stinking hole. Which is too bad, because it used to be very nice."

I looked Doctor over very careful—his face, I mean. Something about him reminded me of the cook who'd helped me and made me think maybe I could trust him.

But I wanted to be sure, so I asked him the same question I'd asked the cook. "Why're you helping me? I got nothing to pay you for your trouble. All my money was took on the *Antelope*."

Instead of giving me an answer about vicious dogs or something I could understand, Doctor said, "You're too young to be so cynical," and got up. "I'll be back in a few minutes to work on those hands again, Catherine." He added a sentence or two to Dan in the language I'd heard them using earlier and walked away.

I'd just have to keep watching and see if I could figure out their angle for myself.

For a few minutes, Dan and I just looked at each other. Then Dan said, "You never got around to telling us where you were from. Is it someplace near here?" Laughing, he added, "Although if you don't say either 'Coast-town' or 'Port,' I won't know where you're talking about anyway. This is my first visit to the continent, and Coast-town and Port are the only two places I've seen."

"You from the Islands, too?"

Dan frowned a little. "Well, one of the islands, I guess you'd say. Anyway, where're you from?"

"I was aiming for Port," I said—letting Dan guess, if he wanted to, that Port was where I lived.

"We're nearer Coast-town," Dan told me. "We were thinking of taking you there, in fact. There are doctors in Coast-town."

There were doctors, and also about a thousand people who knew the Farmer family. D&R had warehouses in Coast-town. Dan and the other men wanted to be rid of me, and I could understand that—but I couldn't let them take me to Coast-town.

So I said no, not Coast-town, and made up a story about how all my family had died there and going back would make me too sad.

I was proud to see I hadn't lost my knack for lying. Dan was totally fooled.

Unfortunately, he was also totally sad for me, which was embarrassing.

"Oh, it's a long time ago now," I said quick. "I'm over it."

Only then I realized that if I was over it, I could go to Coast-town, so I changed this to, "I mean, I'm mostly over it," and turned the subject. "What made you come to the continent? Are you traders?"

The question seemed to make Dan uncomfortable. It was plain he wasn't used to making up stories like I was. "Sort of," he said. "Well, not me. I'm here to visit family. But my uncle and the rest are traders. Of a kind."

"What's that mean? Are they traders or not? What do they trade?"

"They don't trade anything—yet. What I mean is they're looking for something."

"Something to trade?"

"Something somebody else is trading."

Then it was Dan's turn to change the subject quick, which he did by saying his uncle was called "Captain," which was another name I didn't for a minute believe was real. He also said the fourth man in the group was named "Wise." I didn't know whether to believe that one or not.

"Wise is on guard-duty right now," Dan said.

Just as he was saying this, Wise himself walked up to the tent, carrying a long gun.

At sight of the gun, my stomach turned, and I looked around quick for Doctor, hoping I wasn't wrong that Doctor wasn't the type to let other men hurt me.

But Wise left the long gun outside the tent when he came in, and when he spoke, he spoke gentle. I breathed again.

"How are you feeling?" Wise asked me.

Close up, I recognized Wise as one of the men who'd found me on the beach. He looked a little older than Doctor. "I'm good," I said, trying to sit up a little better to show him how strong I was. "I'll be out of your hair real soon."

"No hurry," Wise said. "Get well first."

"Going to sleep?" Dan asked, speaking to Wise. To me he added, "Wise was up most of the night."

Wise said yes, and then he said something more—just a few words—to Dan, in the language I'd heard the men speaking among themselves earlier.

Dan answered back in the same foreign-talk, and Wise walked away.

I asked, sly, "Is that Island? What you were speaking?"

Dan said it was.

Only—it wasn't.

I knew it wasn't because I spoke pretty good Island myself. Island is a lot like my native language of Coastal-speak, whereas the language the men with the false names was speaking among themselves wasn't like Coastal-speak at all.

The men were as big liars as I was. Which was interesting. I wondered how many other things they were lying about. And why.

*

My hands, when Doctor came back and unwrapped them, were tore to pieces and oozing. Honestly, I took one look and thought I'd ruined them permanent.

My ring was gone. That didn't surprise me. I figured the men had took it. In one way, losing my mother's ring was like a stab in my heart; but in another way, it was almost a relief to see it gone. I knew the men's angle now, and didn't have to feel beholden to them for feeding and looking after me. Nobody does anything for free, and most people would've said a jeweled ring was a fair exchange for a life. Not my life, maybe. But some lives.

But just as I finished thinking all this, Doctor fished around in one of his pockets and pulled out a poor, bent up thing that wasn't hardly a ring anymore but was still beautiful to me.

"I'm sorry," he said, laying it on one of my palms. "Your hands were so swollen I had to cut it off your finger. It looks bad, I know, but I believe any competent jeweler could repair it."

I was so happy to have my treasure back, I almost forgot to thank Doctor for it. Bent as it was, I still loved the look of the little blue stone against the gold.

After helping me tuck the ring away in my pocket, Doctor washed my hands in a basin of clean water, soaking the parts where the bandages stuck. After they were clean and he'd looked them over careful, he smeared salve on them, bandaged them again, and said they'd heal up fine.

"They will be scarred, though," he warned.

Like I cared about scars. I patted the pocket that had my mother's ring in it and couldn't keep back a smile.

Doctor smiled too, for a minute. Then he turned serious. He said, "I noticed... I couldn't help but notice—" and then stopped.

"Yeah?"

He looked me straight in the eyes. "Someone has hurt you."

I thought I knew what he meant, and shook my head. "No, I'm only hurt from rowing, and the sun and stuff. I got away from the *Antelope* so quick nobody had time to touch me."

"I mean before the ship." Doctor reached and ran his finger over a scar on my cheek I got when Aunt Jane flung the pieces of a broken plate at me and I didn't duck quick enough. "Here, for instance, and your back."

He must have been the one who undressed me.

To be fair to Aunt Jane, she'd chucked the plate at my head because I was the one who'd broke it. The marks on my back weren't as easy to explain. Mostly I'd got them times Auntie'd been mad in general and the thing I did wrong was to get in range of her belt.

I didn't know what to say about the beltings, so I looked away and stared at a tree. And lied. "I fell," I said. "It's nothing."

"Was it your parents?"

The question made me mad, kind of. My mom hadn't cared for me enough to stick around and raise me, but she'd never beat me. And my dad didn't usually hit hard.

Not as hard as he could've, anyway.

I snapped, "No!"

Doctor stared at me for a minute. I didn't look, but I could feel it. "Do you want to talk about it? I've been told I'm a good listener."

I sneaked a peek, and he looked kind, but I didn't want to talk. I shook my head and stared at the tree some more.

"Whatever happened, you didn't deserve it," Doctor said. "I hope you know that. All children deserve nothing but kind treatment."

"I ain't a child."

"You were when you got some of those scars."

I guessed, being a doctor and all, he could tell how old scars were by looking. I said, "You can't say what I deserved. You weren't there to see. Truth is, I was mostly nothing but trouble all the time."

"No amount of 'trouble' on your part could justify what was done to you," Doctor said, firm. Then he asked again if I wanted to talk about it.

I didn't. "It's nothing," I repeated.

To my relief, he gave up pushing.

We talked about other things for a while. Doctor didn't say anything important, but I listened close to see if I could pick out more lies in his conversation. Tell the truth in pieces, and when you put the pieces together all you ever get is whole truth; but tell a lie in pieces, and the pieces don't generally go back together same way twice. I figured if I kept the men talking, and kept checking their stories against each other, they'd eventually tell me everything I wanted to know.

With this in mind, I asked Doctor, "Whereabouts you all heading?"

He said they were following the Inland Valley Road, and then turned the tables on me. "What about you, Catherine? Where are you planning to go?"

I shrugged and said I didn't have no place particular in mind. "I want to be a sailor, but with my hands like they are, I can't do that right now. I guess I'll just walk until I get someplace." The name of a town came to me—Tenoaks. I'd never been there, but I'd heard it was on the Inland Road. "I might go to Tenoaks."

"And do what when you get there?"

"Dunno. Work."

"With those hands?"

Stealing was the work I had in mind. Depending on what you take, stealing don't need to be a job that's hard on your hands. But if you don't know for sure what kind of company you're keeping, it's always best not to be the first one to mention thieving, so I said, "With whatever hands I got. My money was took by those rats on the *Antelope*, and I ain't the kind can beg."

"No, of course not," Doctor said. From his expression I guessed he thought I meant I was too proud to beg. I really meant I wasn't pretty enough to be good at it.

Doctor patted my arm then and told me to sleep, and went off to take his shift of standing guard.

For two days, I mostly slept, sometimes ate, and when I wasn't doing either one of those things, talked with Dan.

Dan loved to talk. Along with a whole bunch of other things—such as his entire life story except where he really came from—he told me the other members of the Liars were Doctor and Wise, who I knew about already, and a third man that was Dan's uncle. The Liars all called Dan's uncle "Captain," which I didn't believe for a minute was his real name. I'd seen Captain once or twice right after the Liars rescued me, but after that he'd gone off somewheres alone and he didn't show up again until I was back on my feet. Then he rolled into camp driving a one-horse wagon with his saddle horse tied on behind.

As Captain jumped down from the wagon-seat, he threw the reins to Dan. Looking very doubtful, Dan turned to me. "Do you know how to do this?"

"Do what? Unharness a horse, you mean? Sure. Don't you?"

Dan admitted he didn't. "Will it bite?" he asked me, eyeing the wagon horse. "The one I ride tries to bite me."

I started unbuckling the harness—clumsy, from all the bandages on my hands. "What for? Are you rough with him?"

Dan took the buckle I was working on and unbuckled it himself. "Uncle says I'm the opposite. He says I'm too tentative."

Dan got the rest of the harness off by unbuckling where I pointed, and even took the bit out of the horse's mouth when the time came, though anybody could've seen he didn't want to. "Before we got here, I never saw a horse except in pictures. They're bigger than I expected."

"Don't they have horses in the islands?"

"No."

This was another lie to add to the stash the Liars had already told. The Islands had horses. And wagons.

Dan said that though he didn't care much for horses, he'd love a chance to ride in a vehicle.

"If you know about vehicles, I guess you must've been in a town," I said.

"Coast-town. Have you ridden in any?"

"I've stole a few rides, if that counts." I grinned. "If they go by slow, sometimes you can jump up behind." Jump up—and take a swat or two from the driver's stick, if they was smart enough to carry one. I didn't mention that part to Dan. "Vehicles are nice. They're ugly and they stink, kind of, and they break down a lot, but horses break down, too."

The horse, which Dan'd tied to a tree by now, chose that exact second to take a long piss. "Vehicles aren't the only things that stink," Dan muttered, while I laughed and laughed.

At mealtime that day, I finally got to meet Captain proper.

I could see why the others called him "Captain." He was youngish—about Doctor's age—but the kind of person who, young or old, always gets chose for a leader. He was tall and good-looking, which look leaderish to other men, and though he spoke quiet, he spoke like he meant you to obey him. His first glance my way was so sharp it went through me like an awl.

Earlier, I'd heard Captain and Wise and Doctor talking to each other in "Island-speak." Now they told Dan and me what they'd been talking about. Captain had gotten word by telegraph that they needed to change their plans slightly and leave the Inland Valley Road for a couple days to meet someone on a trail.

Dan liked the idea of taking a detour. He said he wanted to see the whole continent. "Who are we meeting? Anybody I know?"

Captain said yes, that one of the people was a friend of Dan's. He gave her name as "Shy," which I put down for another lie, because nobody is named "Shy." He said, "Shy will have a little girl with her. We don't know the little girl's name yet. I hope she'll be able to tell us soon."

I perked up a little.

Most people don't know this about me, but I really like kids. Mind you, I don't *say* I like them, because if you're female and say you like kids, you'll be expected to take care of everybody's. I asked how old the little girl was.

"We think about seven or eight."

"Months?"

Captain smiled. "Ah…no. Years."

"Seven or eight years, but she don't know her *name*?"

Turned out there was a reason the little girl didn't know her name. She had a real sad story, which Captain proceeded to tell me.

He said the little girl and her mother, along with some other women, had been kidnapped from an island by pirates. On the pirates' way back to the continent with them, a big trader spotted the pirates' ship—the pirates' ship was named the *Bee*, Captain said—and chased it.

There aren't any sea-police to stop pirates. The way pirates're dealt with on the continent is that any trading ship that captures a pirate ship and brings her and her crew to a town to be punished gets to keep the pirate ship's cargo as a reward. Naturally, that makes all traders want to catch any pirates they see. Some traders' whole trade is catching pirates, in fact—which in my opinion just makes them another kind of pirate, but let's not get into that now. The town the trader brings the pirates to gets to keep whatever it gets from selling the pirates' ship, which generally gets bought by—more pirates. And that's the way it goes, round and round.

As I said, let's not get into it.

Anyway, the trader chased the *Bee*, trying to capture her, and the captain of the *Bee*, not wanting to get captured, threw the women he'd kidnapped—they were all women—overboard.

Fortunately for the women, the captain of the trader stopped to pick up the ones who weren't already drowned, so the *Bee* got away. The little girl was one of the females the trader'd rescued, and she hadn't spoken a word since, which was why nobody knew her name.

It was the saddest story I'd ever heard, and made me cry a little.

"Did her mother drown?" I asked, wiping my nose on my sleeve before I remembered I was wearing Dan's jacket.

"We assume so," Captain said.

"You going to take her home?"

"We hope to eventually. Right now, we're going to help Shy take the child to Beechlands Forest, where there are people who might be able to help her. At this point, we don't know where the little girl's home island is."

"I know *she* don't talk, but was any of the grown-up women rescued? They'd know which island they came from, wouldn't they?"

Captain and Doctor explained together that the adult women were actually no help at all. They just called their island "Home" and didn't know how to say where it was beyond pointing generally in the direction of the sea.

They sounded like a pretty stupid bunch, if you want the truth.

"The adults have already been resettled on another island, among… culturally similar people," Captain said. "But the traders passed the little girl to another ship that had a doctor, and the ship's doctor gave her to Shy. Shy believes she's still too traumatized for resettlement. She doesn't eat, she can't talk, she has trouble sleeping… Shy is working with her."

"Shy's good," Dan said, confident. "She'll be able to help."

Captain said he hoped Dan was right.

After dinner, while Doctor was rubbing my hands with salve again and rebandaging them, I could hear Dan talking with his uncle Captain over by the corral. I could only understand one word of what they said, but I could understand that word *perfect*, because it was my name. Or rather, my mother's name. Between them, Dan and Captain must have said "Catherine" twenty or thirty times.

"Your hands are coming along nicely," Doctor told me while he bandaged, talking loud to cover up the conversation at the corral, I guessed. "Your face is better, too. Are you keeping out of the sun? You should wear a hat until that sunburn is better."

"…Catherine…" I heard from behind me again.

"Have a rest in the afternoons. Lots of rest will help you get well more quickly, and a nap will keep you out of the sun, too."

Luckily, I didn't have to wait too long to find out what was up with Captain and Dan. As soon as Doctor was finished, Captain came over to me and said, "You're heading to Tenoaks, I believe, Catherine? Is that right?"

To be honest, I'd forgot I ever mentioned the place. But I couldn't say that, so instead I nodded. "I guess I am. I mean, it's not too far to walk from here."

Captain and Doctor smiled at each other. "You're not easily put off by difficulties, are you?" Captain said—which I guessed meant Tenoaks was farther away than I'd thought. "As Dan has just reminded me, Tenoaks is near where we're going to meet our friend and the little girl, and you see that we have a wagon now." He gestured at it. "We'd be pleased to give you a lift to Tenoaks, if you'd like."

I thought my situation over. To go with them would mean days on the road with a bunch of men, but with my hands the way they were, I didn't have a lot of better options. The men seemed nice so far. Decent. More like the *Antelope's* cook than the *Antelope's* sailors.

Dan caught my eye and smiled, pleading.

"I'd be pleased if you'd have me along," I said.

*

I knew how to drive a wagon but couldn't, because of my hands. Dan didn't know how to drive a wagon, but somebody had to, so he got the job. As it happened, Dan turned out to like driving a lot better than he liked riding. He said the length of the shafts was just about the exact distance he wanted between him and a horse's mouth. We were on the Inland Valley Road barely long enough for him to get the hang of driving straight before we turned off on a rough side-lane, where the wagon needed some real managing, but luckily the horse was smarter and better-trained than Dan was, so we mostly stayed out of the ditches.

Everything Dan saw was new and exciting to him, which made me guess that wherever he was from—which was *not* the Islands—must be a pretty dull place. Even the busted-up remains of an ancient building, like you see everywhere, was interesting to Dan.

"Don't the Islands have any broke-down junk?" I asked. I knew perfectly well the Islands did.

Dan said they didn't.

I explored the ancient sites with him. I'd already seen too much wrecked concrete in my life to think it was "fascinating" the way Dan did, but I didn't mind the chance to look around ruins for pieces of steel or shards of good glass. Lashed to a handle, a piece of glass or steel makes a fine weapon, and a weapon in my pocket would have made me feel better. But the sites we passed were close to the trail, and had probably been scavenged a million times already. They didn't have anything left in them to make a knife from. All I found was a smooth, hand-size rock—better than nothing—that I kept convenient in my pocket days, and under my blanket at night. None of the men ever threatened or tried to take advantage of me. In fact, they were polite as they could be. It just seemed like, threats or no, I couldn't go back to being trusting like I had been before I'd climbed aboard the *Antelope*. That was probably a good thing, but it made me feel bad.

Anyway, me and Dan got on very friendly, as I said, which was almost funny, since we didn't have hardly anything in common. Dan loved school; I hated it. Dan was educated; I was ignorant as a summer day is long. Dan knew everything about building and fixing radios; I knew how to steal and fence radios. Dan's family were educated, important people. His father, name of Peregrine, was some kind of high elected official somewhere, and his mother Helen was a medical doctor. My family was—Aunt Jane.

But somehow Dan and me still found enough to talk about to make time in the wagon pass by quick.

One day after Doctor'd washed my hands with boiled water like usual and rubbed the last few raw spots with salve, he said I didn't need to wear bandages anymore.

"Your hands will finish healing better now if they get a little air and sunshine," he told me. "Keep them dry, though. Don't even wash them more than two or three times a day."

Except when I'd been at Sarah's, I'd mostly never washed my hands more than *one* time a day—if that. But I'd already noticed the Liars cared a lot about being clean, so I took this as a hint, and when camp was made that evening and everybody else walked down to a creek to clean up, I went too. I washed my hands good, and also my face, and though nobody said anything about it, I could tell they were pleased.

Afterwards, I sat by the campfire while it kindled and watched Doctor skin and gut a couple of rabbits for our dinner. Almost the best thing about traveling with the Liars was that one or another of the group hunted every day, riding out ahead of the wagon where the game hadn't heard us coming yet, and using a bow and arrows, like in olden days. I'd never got to eat meat regular before, and I liked it.

"Those are honestly cleaned better than ones at the butchers' in town," I told Doctor admiringly. "I guess you must have done a lot of skinning before."

"No, but I do a little surgery from time to time," Doctor answered me, smiling. "Surgery doesn't usually involve skinning, exactly—but it's similar."

"I keep forgetting you're a doctor. Did you have to be one because of your name, or did you get named after?"

I asked the question hoping it might trick Doctor into saying something he otherwise wouldn't, but before he could answer it, Captain spoke up and changed the subject.

"Do you like game, Catherine?" he asked.

Maybe the sight of the fat, juicy rabbits distracted me, I don't know. Whatever the reason was, I didn't think first, but—like an idiot—answered him honest.

"I like most kinds," I said. "I'm happy to eat any meat I can get, really, excepting rat. I mean, I'll eat rat if rat's all I can get, but I don't like it. No matter how it's cooked, rat always tastes dirty to me."

Well, shit.

One look at the Liars faces told me they didn't eat rat, and didn't think much of anybody else who did. Dan seemed almost sick at the idea of it.

I was trying to take back what I'd said, pretending I only meant I *guessed* rat wouldn't taste good, when Captain spoke up. "I agree with you, Catherine," he said. "Rats make terrible eating." He sounded so serene anybody might have believed he ate a rat or two himself every day.

Then he started talking about something totally different, and though I don't remember anymore what he said, I do recall that everybody pretended to be very interested in it until I could look at them again.

The rest of the evening, thank the gods, went all right.

*

Next day, we found Shy and the little nameless girl trailside, all by themselves in the middle of nowhere. Nobody seemed surprised by this but me. I looked all around—even stood up in the wagon for a better look—but there wasn't so much as a tiny village anywhere in sight.

Shy was tall and brown-eyed and probably what you'd call "attractive"—not that I'm any judge—so of course Dan made a fool of himself over her. Yelling "Shy!" like a lunatic, he didn't even wait for the wagon to stop rolling before he jumped out of it to greet her. The other men also said hello to Shy very friendly, but managed to keep their dignities.

Shy greeted them all back, using the same foreign-speak the men spoke among themselves until Wise explained that I didn't know "Islander." Then she switched to Valley to greet me, but didn't offer her hand. The little girl, meanwhile, didn't so much as raise up. She just lay against Shy's shoulder, her face turned away from us.

I took an instant dislike to Shy; I can't say why. Though she smiled and said all the right things, I just found something about her…mislikeable, if that's the right word. We talked for a minute, both of us sounding friendly, but before we'd exchanged ten words, Shy got a look on her face that made me think the mislike might be mutual.

"I hope we'll be friends," she said, with just enough extra stress on the word "hope" to make it clear she doubted we would be.

I made my lips smile again; turned; and started talking to the little girl.

Aside from the look on her face, which was blank, the kid looked like all she needed to be adorable was to put on some weight. She was a blue-eyed blonde with every feature that ever made anybody coo over a child, including a little dimple in her chin. She might've had dimples in her cheeks, too, if she'd ever smiled, but she didn't. Instead, her pale lips was curved down, and while everybody else talked and laughed, she stared off at nothing.

It was clear she was suffering.

I thought a cuddle might help, but with Shy holding her, I couldn't give her one. All I could do was put out my hand to her, and when she didn't take it (I'd already guessed she probably wouldn't), I took hers anyway, very firm, and shook it like a grown-up's. If there's one thing I've learned about kids, it's that they love being treated like grown-ups.

"How do you do?" I asked the girl, super polite. "My name is Cl— Catherine. What's yours?"

Shy stopped talking to Dan to answer for her. "We don't know yet."

"Huh," I said, still looking at the little girl, and holding her hand. "Well, I'm gonna call you Isabelle. Isabelle's a pretty name. I'll call you Isabelle, and if you don't like it, you can tell me your real name, and then I'll call you that instead. Deal?"

The kid pulled away a little, but just gentle; and when I didn't let her hand go, she looked straight into my face—although only for a real short time.

I smiled at her, and though "Isabelle" didn't smile back, I thought she kind of liked that I'd touched her.

Shy didn't. Shy hated me for it. She didn't say so, but I could tell.

While I'd been meeting and naming Isabelle, everybody else had talked it over and agreed that since Isabelle would have to ride in the wagon, Shy would have to drive it. Dan didn't like riding a horse, and I didn't like riding with Shy, but Isabelle was just too skinny and sickly to sit a horse, even in somebody's lap. After a quick meal—that Isabelle didn't eat two bites of—we started off again with Shy on the wagon-seat beside me and Isabelle lying between us with her head on Shy's lap.

Shy was a better driver than Dan, but she wasn't nearly as good a talker—at least, not to me. She'd talk with the Liars sometimes, in "Island-speak" even in front of me, which was rude, and the Liars didn't do it. But she didn't talk spontaneous to me and she usually didn't bother to answer when I talked, either, even if I asked her a question. Like, I asked her—twice—whereabouts in the Islands she was from, mainly to see what lie she'd tell, and Shy just looked at me.

Another time I asked her, "So, are you a trader, like your friends?" gesturing so she'd know that by her friends, I meant the men.

I wasn't being funny, but Shy laughed liked I'd made a little joke.

"A trader," she repeated, and added a snorty chuckle. "Well, as you know, I'm here to look after the child."

I did kind of know this, but I didn't like being answered snotty about it, and after a few more strange looks and not-answers from Shy, I talked to Isabelle instead.

Aside from being thin and sad, Isabelle seemed like other kids, so I figured she'd like what other kids like. I wrapped up my rock in my handkerchief—I mean Dan's handkerchief, that I'd borrowed—and showed Isabelle how she could cuddle it like a doll, which she did. I caught a bug and showed it to her. She wasn't much interested in the bug, but she wasn't totally *un*interested, either. I sang her a song. When we stopped once and Shy was busy and not looking, I even lifted Isabelle up to touch the carthorse's ear.

Shy saw and came running over. "Why did you do that?" she asked, snatching Isabelle away from me.

"Because she looked like she wanted to," I answered. "She's been staring at those ears all morning." I grinned at Isabelle. "You didn't expect that ear to twitch like that, did you? I reckon the horse is going to like you. You're very gentle."

I don't think it made Shy like me any better when, as I walked off, Isabelle reached out her hand for the horse's ear again. It was the first time I'd seen the kid be interested in anything, and Shy aside, I was kind of proud of myself about it.

It probably also didn't help that later at mealtime, Isabelle crawled into my lap instead of Shy's, and once she was there, even ate a little. Poor Shy had spent every meal before trying to get Isabelle to take even one bite, but the kid ate a dozen bites I gave her without being nudged. Next meal she did the same, and after that, Doctor suggested maybe I should have the job of feeding Isabelle all the time.

If Shy'd been friendlier, I'd have felt sorry for her.

Eating made Isabelle stronger, so she could walk a little and not be carried all the time. I saw Shy watching her do it—walk—and said, "Nah, she won't die. Pretty soon she'll be fine, in fact."

Shy laughed a little, kind of shaky. "I did think she might die. I was afraid she would." Then she asked me, "What does she think about? Does she think about her mother?"

Like I'd know.

On second thought, I decided maybe I did know. *I* thought about *my* mother. Isabelle was probably the same as me.

So I said, "Yeah, probably. She's not one hundred percent sure what happened to her, so she still hopes sometime she'll come back."

I felt guilty when Shy thanked me. I was really just making stuff up.

On the morning of what was going to be my last day with the Liars, Dan asked me, sudden, "You have a ring, right? Doctor said you do. But you can't wear it."

"Yeah, it's all messed up," I agreed, taking out my ring and showing it to him. "Doctor says it can be fixed, though."

"Is it ancient? It looks ancient."

I said I didn't know.

Reaching in his pocket, Dan pulled out a cord he'd braided from hairs brushed out of the horse's tails. "I had an idea that since you can't wear your ring on your finger, maybe you'd like to put it on this and wear it around your neck instead," he told me.

I said I would like it—a lot—so Dan bent my ring back into a circle, strung it on the cord, and tied the cord around my neck for me. He used a fancy knot that felt smooth against my skin. "There!" he said, looking proud of himself.

I'd never had a friend before who liked me enough to make things for me. I'd never had any friends, really. In a few hours we'd get to Tenoaks and Dan and I would have to say goodbye to each other. I was happy I'd have something to remember him by.

The closer we got to Tenoaks, the more traffic there was, and the wider and more trampled the trail got. Eventually it stopped even being a trail, and turned into an actual road. The way was all downhill because of course Mantowns're always built near water, and water's downhill from everything. Riding his horse up next to me in the wagon, Captain mentioned that the Tenoaks river was nice, but not big enough to carry ocean-going boats.

"But it joins a bigger river about ten miles from town," he told me. "When your hands have fully healed, you can probably get a ship from there to take you back to the coast."

I saw from Shy's look she was wondering why I wanted to go to the coast, so I explained, "I'm going to be a sailor."

To my surprise, Shy answered back, very serious, "It's a good life."

"You're a sailor?"

Shy was surprised. "You didn't know that? I guess I've just been so concerned about the child"—Shy had never yet called Isabelle by the name I'd give her—"that I've hardly thought about my *real* job. And I'm between ships, too. All sailors are lost souls when they're between ships." The smile she gave me was the first *real* smile I'd seen on her face.

Shy got serious again. "The child is sad that you're going away."

"Did you tell her? I didn't tell her yet."

"I don't need to tell the child anything," Shy answered me. "She senses it."

I looked down at Isabelle then and, dammit, Shy was right. Isabelle did look sad. She looked like she might even cry. This was bad, though better than her looking blank-faced like she had at first.

"Do what I do, Isabelle," I said to her, trying to make a little joke. "Tell yourself you never liked me anyway. Then you won't miss me."

Shy's back and voice both went stiff as an iron bar. "Does that work?" she asked, cold.

"Lying to yourself? Oh, yeah. I mean, it takes practice to get good at, like anything else. But if you keep it up, you can get so you don't know what's a lie and what ain't."

Just as Shy took a breath to say something more—probably something very anti-lie—Isabelle perked up. She'd just noticed the cord around my neck. Curious, she reached out her finger like she was going to touch it, then looked me in the face and quick pulled back her hand.

The gesture was shy and cute and made me smile. "It's all right," I told her. "It won't hurt you. See?" I pulled the cord from under my shirt and let Isabelle see the ring hanging on it. "It's just a pretty, not a weapon."

After staring for a minute, Isabelle put out her finger again and gently touched the ring's blue stone.

A picture of my mother come into my mind. "It was my mother's," I told Isabelle.

One time, years ago, I'd stuck my hand in the back of Aunt Jane's radio. Don't ask why. The instant I said "mother" to Isabelle, the same thing—the same pain—ripped through me like when I'd touched the radio wires. Everything went white, and all the air went out of my lungs. There might even have been a loud noise. I'm not sure.

Isabelle didn't know the word "mother." She didn't know any words in my language. But all the same, the instant I thought about my mother, she thought of her mother, too. I knew it. I *saw* it. Her mind was full of her mother, and at the same time, my mind was also full of her mother. I'd never even met her, but all of a sudden I could see Isabelle's mother and hear her and even smell her. I could feel her arms around Isabelle almost the same as if they'd been around me. I could see everything Isabelle was seeing, which was not just her mother, but her whole island and its people. In some way I didn't understand, Isabelle and me were looking together at how it had been on the day the Men came to it.

I saw Men with guns all around, and people who looked like Isabelle, only older, who were throwing rocks and sticks at the Men, trying to drive them off. Then I heard gunshots and smelled gunpowder, and a bunch of the rock-throwers fell down all at once. Isabelle didn't understand what had happened to them, but I knew they were dead. While this was going on, other Men were grabbing every female they saw and dragging them away. The Men didn't want children. They left the children alone. But they had Isabelle's mother, and Isabelle ran after them, fighting the Men and trying to pull her mother back.

"Isabelle, don't!" I called to her—maybe out loud. She was just a little girl. She wasn't strong enough to stop the Men from doing whatever they wanted. She'd only get hurt herself if she didn't let go of her mother. But Isabelle wouldn't let go. She wouldn't let go until another Man, coming up from behind her, shot her mother dead. He shot her mother dead, and made Isabelle run with the other women, who were being driven like animals toward the Men's ship.

To make things even weirder and scarier, at the same time I was seeing what happened to Isabelle's mother, I was seeing my own mother, too. It was like my dream back, but more shadowy. The bed was a shadow that creaked. My mother was a shadow who stood up, looked at me, and said she'd be back. This time, when my shadow-mother turned to go, I knew something I'd never known before. I'd never known what was going to happen to my mother when she left our room, but this time I knew there was a man waiting outside. I wanted to warn my shadow-mother, and I wanted to warn Isabelle. I flung myself after my mom and tried to tell her about what was outside. At the exact same time, I also flung myself after Isabelle, who was running with the other women from her island toward a ship.

But my mom dissolved away, and I couldn't catch Isabelle.

Only—I must have caught her after all, because now Isabelle was holding onto me, very tight. We hung onto each other as our mothers' minds faded away, and our own minds were left all alone.

Meantime somewhere far, far off, Dan was calling to his uncle to stop while Wise asked me several times, "Are you all right, Catherine?" When I couldn't answer, he jumped into the wagon beside me and took the reins from Shy's hands while Shy, as soon as her hands was empty, pulled Isabelle into her lap and hugged both her and me.

Once he got the wagon stopped, Wise reached the reins up to Dan to hold, while he got out and helped Shy out of the wagon from one side at the same time Captain was lifting me and Isabelle, still hanging onto each other, down from the other. Doctor was there, too, and all of us followed Dan as he walked the wagon off the road and into the bushes.

By the time we'd gotten to a quiet, private place, I was coming back, but Isabelle was still far off somewhere in her mind, and as blank-faced as she'd been the first time I'd seen her. Doctor put blankets around us. As soon as Wise would let her, Shy grabbed onto me and Isabelle again and held us harder than ever. Somehow I didn't mind it. I still didn't like Shy, but— No. Now I kind of did. Now I felt like Shy understood what had happened to me and Isabelle and could help us. I cuddled Isabelle close and lay my head on Shy's shoulder while the world slowly turned back right-side up.

Then I asked, my voice hoarse, "What?"

Before Shy could answer, in my mind I heard Rose again, saying, "I'm a telepath, and so are you."

"Oh, gods," I whispered. "I'm a telepath, aren't I? I'm a telepath."

Shy rocked us. "I had no idea you didn't know. I just thought— I thought you didn't like me."

"You're one too?" I answered my own question. "Of course you are. And so is Isabelle."

"Yes."

I knew another thing now besides that I was a telepath. "My mother's dead."

Shy rocked harder. "Gods, gods," she moaned. "I'm so sorry, Catherine. I am so sorry."

I rested against Shy for a long time, and Isabelle rested against me, while around us, the men made camp very quiet and built a fire.

CHAPTER SEVEN

I don't remember most of the rest of that day. I was cold and stayed by the
fire, but I don't know if I ever ate dinner. Later, Isabelle wanted to sleep
with me in the wagon bed instead of with Shy, and Shy let her. I worried I
might have nightmares, but I didn't. I don't think I dreamed at all.

In the morning, I woke up at first light. Isabelle was still sleeping.

Everybody else was already up, moving around and talking soft to each
other. I stayed like I was, eyes closed, and pretended to be asleep. I couldn't
face them. I was ashamed about the day before—all the fuss I'd made and the
crying and such. I was embarrassed that everybody'd known all along there
was something wrong with me, except…me. The Liars must have known I was
a telepath as soon as Shy did. She'd have told them. Shy must've known how
much I always lied, too. She must've known about all the bad things I thought.
She'd read them in my mind like in a book. Shy'd known everything, and I
hadn't known anything.

I was a fool, and to make things worse, I was also an Ant. I had to be,
because only Ants were telepathic. My brain'd been leaking all my secrets, and
I was the only one who didn't know it.

"Fool" was too nice a name for me. I was a clown.

I decided the only thing I could do to help myself now was to wait for everybody to get far enough away from the wagon for me to slip out without them seeing and run away. Cross-country, I could get to Tenoaks faster than they could, and once there, I could hide. I lay very still and waited for my chance.

But then Isabelle woke up and needed to pee. Little kids can't wait, so there was nothing I could do about it but help her out of the wagon and get her into the bushes.

It should have been private in the bushes, but it wasn't. Shy followed us. She helped Isabelle while I helped myself, and as soon as we were done, she hugged us both.

"Do you want to wash?" she asked. "I was just going down to wash. Come with me. We all want to talk to you, but there's no hurry. What we need to say can wait until you're ready."

I didn't think I'd probably ever be ready, but didn't tell Shy so.

The Liars—who didn't deserve to be called that as much as I did—were good campers and never stopped except in cover near clean water. There was a nice creek nearby, and I washed slow and careful in it, watching for Shy to turn her back and give me my chance to bolt. I combed my hair, too. I hadn't combed it for a while, so this took time, but Shy stayed with me anyway, combing Isabelle's hair and braiding the parts that were long enough.

Out of nowhere, she asked me, "Do you understand what I'm talking about?"

I jumped. "What?" As far as I remembered, Shy hadn't said a word since we'd got to the creek. Evidently she'd been "talking" to me silent, but I hadn't heard.

"Not yet? You will, though. Pretty soon." Shy must have been enjoying her morning, because she laughed. "I don't understand you very well, either. But I know I can learn to, and you can learn to read me too. We'll all learn together; you, me, and—Isabelle."

Before, Shy'd avoided calling Isabelle by her name—that is, the name I'd given her—but now she said it over and over. She said, "That's what I'm hoping—that you and I and Isabelle can all learn to understand each other.

Isabelle's the important one, of course. And I'm sure she can do it. Isabelle, I mean. Isabelle's very intelligent." Shy put "Isabelle" into a few more sentences, and then asked both of us, me and Isabelle, Isabelle, Isabelle, if we were ready for breakfast. "We have so much to talk about!" she said, sounding so happy it made me want to puke.

We went back to the camp, but I didn't feel like talking. I didn't feel like having breakfast, either—though I got Isabelle to eat a little. The men seemed to understand better than Shy did about this and reminded her gentle a couple times that talking could wait.

"Let Catherine rest for now," the doctor said. Since he'd spoke in his most medical voice, Shy did what he said.

I rested, all right. I was too tired to do anything else. I rested while the dream—I guessed it was a dream—about Isabelle's mother played over and over in my mind, and then I fell asleep. Isabelle slept in my arms, and when we woke up, it was afternoon and mealtime again. This time, me and Isabelle both ate, and afterwards we were almost our normal selves again.

That night by the campfire, Captain let Shy talk like she'd wanted to do earlier, and the first talking she did was to ask me if I'd consider not going to Tenoaks after all.

"We'd be happy to take you anywhere you want," she said, "but we'd love to have your company all the way Beechlands Forest, and you could help me so much!"

When I said I didn't see what help I could be, Shy launched into a little speech.

"You see, Catherine"—nobody says "you see" except in a speech they've rehearsed in their mind—"what I'd like to find out, through you, is what—and by *what*, I really mean *how*—"

She made a face and stopped. After thinking for a minute, Shy started over.

"See, it's my job… That is, I was given the job of finding out—if I could, I mean—because others of my people have already tried, with rather poor success—to learn how Isabelle's people communicate. And by 'how they communicate,' I don't really mean *how* they communicate, because of course we *know* how they communicate. What I mean is, I want to discover how to *read* their communication. If I can. Do you understand?"

"Not…exactly." I thought of something. "Wait—if I'm a telepath, how come I can't read what you want to say out of your mind?"

"Precisely! Precisely!" Shy made a little excited gesture with both hands. "That's *precisely* what I'm talking about! That's the difficulty the Reintegration Project is having!"

"Huh?"

Shy then talked for a while—quite a while—about something called the Reintegration Project.

The Project had been started almost as soon as the existence of Hybrids was discovered—though Shy didn't say when that was—and the idea of it was to make humans, Hybrids, and Ants be friends with each other. Something like that. The way the Project was supposed to make them be friends was that somebody—Shy didn't say who, but I guessed Foresters—planned to get a lot of Hybrids together with a lot of Ants and humans. Once they were all together, the Hybrids would talk telepathic with the Ants and out loud with regular humans until everybody understood each other.

"Wait," I interrupted. "Wouldn't the Ants kill the humans? And maybe the Hybrids, too?"

Turned out, the first time the three groups saw each other, that was pretty much exactly what happened.

"But just at first," Shy explained, looking embarrassed. "The three groups can co-exist now—within certain…parameters."

I guessed a "parameter" was a good, high wall between the Ants and the other two groups—possibly with guns ranged along the top.

The Project hadn't worked the way it was supposed to, Shy continued, because while the Hybrids could talk fine to the humans—Shy did it all the time—they couldn't talk to Ants at all.

I asked, "Is Isabelle a Hybrid?"

"No. She's a full Ant."

"So you can't talk to her with your mind?"

"It seems no," Shy said, sad. "I speak to her, but she doesn't understand me."

"Am I an Ant?" I guessed I probably was. That was why I didn't act right and tried to kill my Aunt Jane.

But Shy told me, "No. You're a Hybrid, like me."

I thought this over. "If I'm a Hybrid, then I can't talk to Isabelle, either. Which means I can't help you."

"But you *can* talk to Isabelle!" Shy got excited again. "You understand when she's hungry or thirsty or—or—when she wants to touch a horse's ear! And Isabelle understands you, too. You shared something with her, didn't you? You shared something about your mothers. I believe that means the way you communicate with each other must be close to the way full Ants communicate!" She seemed to sort of think about this for a minute before she added, "Maybe it's because you learned so late that you were a telepath. Most of us know it before we're born."

After this, Shy went on to say another ten thousand words or so comparing how I talked mental to how other Hybrids talked mental, winding up with, "Catherine, *you* could be the bridge we've been looking for all these years! *You* could be our link to the true Ant-mind!"

I said, "I hate to disappoint you," (I honestly did) "but being a link to an Ant-mind, especially a 'true' one, don't sound like a job I want."

"Don't pressure her, Shy," Captain spoke up.

Shy stopped talking, but her eyes went right on begging.

"Look," I said, when I realized I couldn't bring myself to just *ignore* her. "Even if I could understand Isabelle—which I can't—you don't want me for this job. You don't want me around at all, in fact. It's probably the Ant in me, but no matter how hard I try not to, I do terrible things that make people hate me."

This was nothing but the honest truth, but everybody took it as a joke. Wise and Dan laughed, and Captain answered me with a joke of his own, asking, "What do you mean by 'terrible'? Thorns in our bedrolls or actual violence?"

The rest of them made jokes then too (except for Shy, who never joked), saying stuff like thorns was all right, but for me please not to put sand in the soup. And so on. The whole bunch, except for Shy, as I said, kept up being funny—and they really were funny, too; I laughed myself—until Dan finally turned them more serious again by saying they truly did want my company and could take care of themselves.

Captain told me to sleep on the idea of staying with them. "It's late. We'll talk more in the morning."

I laid awake a long time that night.

I could think of reasons to go to Beechlands, like that I didn't have any place better to go, and I could also think of reasons not to, like that Beechlands was full of Foresters. My other experience of Foresters—which was to say, Rose—hadn't exactly left me wanting more. Rose'd been nosy and pushy and—this was the bad part—absolutely right in what she'd told me about myself. I could stand nosy and pushy. I was nosy and pushy myself. But *right about me* was going too far. If Rose was a typical Forester—and nobody'd said she wasn't—I needed to stay far away from Foresters.

But in the end, what I told everybody at breakfast was that, yes, I'd travel with them to Beechlands. Forgetting that Shy knew when I was lying, I even said I was looking forward to the trip.

What I stayed for was Isabelle. I stayed because Isabelle wanted me to stay. What had happened to Isabelle's mother—to both our mothers—made a tie between me and her that Isabelle wasn't ready to have broken. Even when she was asleep, if I said to myself, "Maybe I'd be better off on my own," Isabelle got restless, and her dreams turned bad. But when I thought, "Well, I might as well as stay with this bunch a while longer," she smiled and snuggled up to me, her dreams turning happy and peaceful.

"You win," I whispered to Isabelle now, and she smiled again. So did I.

CHAPTER EIGHT

O nce we'd passed Tenoaks and the road got quieter again, Dan went back to driving the wagon so Shy could ride, which she liked to do and he didn't. Since I was the one who could "talk" to Isabelle, Shy didn't need to be right beside her anymore. Like we had before, Dan and me talked all day long, and now Shy talked with us too, wherever the trail was wide enough for her to ride alongside us. Turned out, Shy really had as much to say as anybody. She'd only not said much to me before because she thought I already knew what she was thinking. Sometimes I thought I might be starting to "hear" her mentally a little bit—but I wasn't sure, so I didn't mention it.

At the same time Shy started talking, so did Isabelle. Sort of. What I mean is, being surrounded by our chatter all day long got Isabelle thinking there must be something good or fun in making mouth noises, so she made them. She didn't say any actual words. She jabbered mindless, like a baby. But her jabbers were mostly happy, where at first we'd only heard moaning and crying come out of her, and we all liked the change.

The morning after we rejoined the Inland Valley Road, I woke up to the sound of thunder far off. Then I sat up quick, wide awake, when I realized the sound wasn't thunder at all. It was cannon. The smell in the air wasn't rain, either. It was gun powder.

Captain was standing near the wagon looking straight west, toward the center of the continent.

"I was about to wake you," he said when he saw me. "Dress and eat, and see to Isabelle. Wise, Shy and I will be back in an hour or so."

"That's a battle, ain't it?" I looked where smoke hung like storm clouds, but lower.

He said it was.

As soon as me and Isabelle were out of the wagon, Captain and Dan took up a part of the wagon bed. The damn thing had a false bottom, which I'd never suspected before. A couple of long guns had always been kept around the camp, one for whoever was on guard duty, and another resting handy somewhere, but under the floor of the wagon was a regular arsenal—more long guns, plus pistols, and lots of ammunition. They all looked top quality, too. Captain strapped on a pistol and sent Dan with three more to Wise, Doctor, and Shy, and when he came back, Dan took one for himself. Captain looked for a minute like he might stop him, but didn't. Long guns was handed around, but nobody offered me anything.

Isabelle dressed herself willing but wouldn't eat a bite. She knew the smell of gunpowder from when the Men had come to her island and was scared out of her head. I "hid" her under a blanket, telling her it was a good, safe place, where no one would ever find her. She seemed to believe me but was still very frightened, so I also gave her my rock for "protection."

It seemed like forever before Wise, Shy and Captain came back. Dan took his job of lookout serious and wouldn't talk. Isabelle didn't talk either, of course, but I was getting to know her thoughts a little, and believe me, what she was planning to do with my rock to anybody who stuck his head under her blanket was ugly.

Luckily, nothing bad happened, and when the others came back they told Dan and me the battle was the first shooting to come out of a quarrel that'd been going on for months between a big country and some smaller ones. The two sides were about evenly matched, Captain said, so it was likely there wouldn't be a quick victory for either side, but more battles to come. He predicted we'd soon be meeting refugees on the roads. I noticed the guns didn't get put back under the wagon bed when we packed up the camp.

Just like Captain'd said, two days after that first battle the roads crowded up with stragglers. Most were wounded men going home to heal. Field hospitals were always full and dirty, and a wounded soldier's best chance was at home. Some had comrades along to help them, and some had their wives or other men's wives who were now widows. A few of the women had fought beside their men, but mostly they'd just helped to keep the camp. The soldiers were generally friendly, and sometimes funny, if you didn't mind rough language, and a lot of them said when they were well again, they'd go straight back and fight some more. The women mostly felt different. Wife or widow, most said they'd had enough and called war a fool's business.

They might've thought war was for fools, but that didn't mean they weren't as willing as their men to make some business out of it. I didn't see even one who didn't have things in their bundles they'd looted from houses along the way. Almost all the men had the army guns they'd been issued, which they weren't supposed to take from their army camp. I didn't blame them much for stealing those. The roads was dangerous. But I did blame them if they'd stole farm tools, and I especially blamed a man who'd helped himself to a cow and calf he was herding along home with him. I spoke sharp to him. I asked him how a farmer like himself could rob another farmer.

"That's just wrong and wicked," I scolded—sounding like my Aunt Jane, if you want the truth. "The man you took that from likely has family to feed, same as you."

I'd always had a temper. It had got me in trouble before. But it'd never got no one else in trouble, so I'd told myself whether I kept or lost my temper was my own business and nobody else's. But while I was yelling at the cow thief, I happened to see Captain, who was standing a little aside, slide his hand unobtrusive toward the pistol on his belt, and it came to me sudden that the man I was scolding like a naughty child was full grown, full armed, and—judging by his red face—full of offense at my tone. If I made him mad enough that he pulled out his gun and started shooting, I might not be the only one hit.

I shut up, but I didn't apologize. I didn't exactly know how to apologize. Luckily for me, when Doctor made a point of letting the man see him check that his long gun was loaded and ready, Cow-stealer took the hint and moved on.

For two nights after that, though, Captain ordered two-person night watches.

In other words, because of me, for two nights my friends—I wanted them to be my friends—got half as much sleep as they usually did. Nobody complained. Nobody scolded me for what I'd done. But I was ashamed and watched my mouth better after that.

A few days later three other men stopped by our camp, all cheerful fellows and not well-armed enough to scare us. They weren't loaded down with booty, either, but one had his bundle slung from a piece of metal that Captain took a definite interest in.

Though nice, the metal seemed ordinary to me. A squared-off bar rather than a rod, it had a greenish color to it, and when I looked close (which I only did because I noticed Captain looking close), I saw it had a square groove running the length of it. That was it. Nothing special. At least, I didn't think so.

But Captain, as I said, seemed to feel different. He looked close at the bar, like I mentioned, and then asked the man where he'd got it.

"Found it," the soldier explained, showing it off. "Laying right in the road. It's heavy to carry, but I thought it was too nice to leave."

A look I didn't understand passed between Captain, Wise, and Doctor, and the next thing I knew, Captain had the metal bar, and the wounded soldier had the four squirrels Wise'd shot earlier. The squirrels were supposed to be our dinner, and when the men took them instead, it only left us biscuit and water to eat that day.

"Under the green paint, that thing better be solid gold," I muttered to Shy. "I was looking forward to roast squirrel."

Shy laughed like she thought I was joking, but I wasn't. I was really planning to find a sharpish rock to rub some of the green paint off with so's I could see what the bar was made of. Before I could do it, though, Captain stuck it under the wagon bed on the opposite side from the weapons, at the same time saying to Dan and Shy and me, "Don't touch it. Absolutely do not touch it."

If it was gold, Captain intended to keep the gold all for himself.

Next day we turned from the road we'd been following, which led generally northwest toward Beechlands Forest, onto a smaller road. From what I could reckon—and I'd say I'm a pretty fair reckoner in matters of distance and direction—we were now heading back toward the coast rather than to any forest. I didn't say anything. Beechlands or coast was pretty much the same to me, and anyway I thought the change of route probably had something to do with Captain wanting to avoid meeting more refugees. One of the sides was now winning the war, we'd heard, which meant the other was losing, and depending on what they've lost, losers can be desperate. It was safer to avoid them, even if it meant going a little out of our way. I reckoned in a day or two we'd turn back west again.

We didn't. We kept going east.

Captain came back from scouting one morning and said he'd found a new route for us to follow. "The road's a little rough, but it's the fastest way to where we want to go."

Shy and me looked west across the valley toward Beechlands. I thought I felt Shy think something like, "At last!"

But when I looked, Captain was looking more east than ever. Due east, in fact. Sure enough, when we got to the road he wanted us to take, it led due east.

It also wasn't smooth enough to be called "rough." Or even a road.

"We can't take the wagon up this," Wise said when he saw it. "This is nothing but a cow-path!"

I disagreed. A cow would have been too smart to use it.

Captain's chin went out a little. "It's fine."

Doctor suggested leaving the wagon and packing the gear over. "Dan's turning out to be a fine driver, of course," he said—which wasn't a lie, but was an exaggeration—"but this way is too challenging for a relative beginner."

Captain didn't like the idea of packing, either. "We're in a hurry," he answered, stubborn.

Wise and Doctor looked at each other, and then Wise looked at Dan. "What do you think?"

Dan was always up for anything. Wrapping the reins tighter around his hands, he said, "Sure! Let's go."

At first, I expected the carthorse to stumble any minute and send us over the road's edge. The drop wasn't sheer, but it wasn't exactly a gentle slope, either, and in my mind I could picture the wagon tumbling end-over-end all the way back down to the bottom. I held Izzy—Dan's new name for Isabelle—in my lap and planned how the two of us would jump out at the first wobble. If Dan wanted to die that was his business, but I had other plans for myself.

But Dan drove careful, and though the road was just as narrow and steep all the way up as it'd looked from the bottom, nothing bad happened.

"Looks like we might live to get where we're going," I said to Dan as the road began to level out near the top of the hill. "Now that I think of it, where *are* we going? Do you know?"

"Beechlands," Dan said.

"Does that mean you don't know? Because you don't seem like the type to lie deliberate."

"Beechlands," Dan repeated. With a quick look at me—and a smile—he added, "Eventually."

"Eventually sounds about right," I agreed. "Why, though? Why don't we just go straight to Beechlands?"

"Well—business, like I said before. Uncle's got business."

The road bent ahead of us. Captain pulled up his horse. "It looks like there's a tree down," he called back to us, standing in his stirrups to look. "Stay here a minute. I'll check."

He came back to say there was a tree across the road, just like he'd thought, and called to Wise to help him clear it. Dan offered to come, too, but Captain said for him to stay.

"Wise and I can handle it," he said.

In the few seconds it took for Captain and Wise to ride to where the road turned, a lot of men—I didn't count how many—swarmed out of the bushes ahead and ran toward us. Some of them had guns.

Some of the men got between Captain and Wise and the wagon, and some got between us in the wagon and Shy and Doctor, who'd been riding behind. I hugged Isabelle tight to my chest.

Saying, "Down, down!" Dan pushed her and me behind the dash with one hand and drew his long gun from under the wagon seat with the other. I went down like he wanted us to, Izzy under me, but kept my head raised just enough to see some of what was happening.

Wise, Captain, Doctor, and Shy—all mounted, of course—had their pistols in their hands by now but didn't fire. The trail was narrow, and we were all so crowded onto it that if they'd shot, they might've shot each other. It was clear from the first minute that stealing the horses, not killing us, was the men's main goal, so the riders put all their attention on keeping their mounts constantly moving, turning, and rearing so as to make it hard for anybody to get hold of their bridles. The men wanted the horses so much their greed was a hindrance to them. Even the ones with guns didn't want to use them for fear they'd hit an animal instead of the man on it.

Just as I was thinking this, someone did shoot after all—it wasn't clear to me who—and a bandit went down. He screamed so horrible as he fell my blood curdled, and all the wrangling and commotion stopped for a minute. I threw Izzy over the side of the wagon and jumped after her—and a good thing I did because we wouldn't have got a second chance. Just as I landed, the carthorse, calm until then, panicked and begun to plunge and kick.

Captain shouted orders but in "Island," so at first, I couldn't understand him. Then, in the least handy bit of telepathy I'd experienced so far, I suddenly knew what language he was really speaking. It was Forester. The Liars was all Foresters, sneaking around Men's lands pretending to be Men. I was embarrassed not to have figured it out sooner. Holding onto Isabelle, I crawled into the bushes and hid with her there.

One thing about Foresters is they know how to fight. From where I was, I could see that if the men had worked together systematic, like the Foresters did, they could have unhorsed all the riders in five minutes. But instead, the men fought Man-style, everyone for himself. They were brave, sure; but the Foresters were brave, too, and had planning and method besides. Seeing them, men who'd had sense would've either changed their tactics or give up.

But the men didn't have sense—or rather, fear had made them reckless, I guess. They were probably going home from a battle they'd lost, and were afraid when they got there, they'd find their farms and towns plundered. There wouldn't be no harvest for a year or more, and most of them didn't have guns to hunt with. Our group had horses, a wagon, food, clothes, and the best weapons made. Since we didn't have enough for all the men, I reckoned when we were dead, they'd turn to fighting each other until eventually a few men went home with everything and the rest never went home at all. But that was only if they won. If the men lost or gave up, none of 'em'd get anything.

I was almost feeling sorry for them when a hand reached from behind me and grabbed Isabelle. A second later, another hand closed on my arm. More surprised than anything else, I jerked away.

I pulled free, but Izzy was still caught. With a look at me that said he wanted me to chase him, the man who'd grabbed us started pulling Izzy down the road. "Come and get her," he mocked—not in words, but with the way he dragged her behind him by one arm. He was dangling Isabelle in front of me like sweets before a child. "Come and get her."

Naturally, I went after him, just like he wanted. There was no way I was going to let anybody have Izzy.

Turned out it wasn't really Izzy he wanted. As soon as I got close enough, the man shoved Izzy aside and lunged for me instead, wrapping both his arms around me tight, pinning mine to my sides. I ain't a tall girl. When I butted with my head, I only hit him in his neck, instead of his nose like I wanted. The man jerked aside in time to make me almost miss him altogether and laughed at me.

"Ain't you the feisty one!" he said, like he liked it.

I didn't wait for him to say more. I butted him again, coming up from below this time, so his teeth snapped sharp together. The man's laugh turned ugly. He was angry now—an Aunt Jane grade of angry that made him want to hurt me.

He was stronger than Aunt Jane, and his hands was hard as iron. I saw quick that if I was going to beat him, I'd have to beat him by tricks. Sometimes with Aunt Jane, if I pretended to give up and stopped fighting, she loosened her hold a little. I tried that now.

Didn't work.

His arms still around me tight as ever, the man walked me, step by step, off the side of the road. He talked all the while, saying a lot of the same things the sailor on the *Antelope* had said to me while he pawed my buttons. Hearing them again made my blood first go cold and then boil.

Izzy was still standing where she'd ended up when the man'd flung her aside, and now, over my own thoughts, I heard hers. She was figuring things out. She reckoned the man was a pirate; she knew I was someone she loved. A pirate had killed someone else she loved (her mother); now a pirate was going to kill me. Faster than I can tell it and with a growl like an animal, Isabelle threw herself at the man, wrapped both her arms around one of his legs, and sank her teeth into his thigh. Izzy had a nice set of teeth, and whether by good luck or good aim—I don't know which—she got him up high, near his manhood, and hung on.

The pig-squeal of pain the man let out put new strength in me. I wiggled like an eel, kicked like a donkey, and butted like a goat all at once. I was every kind of animal and every kind of crazy, and Isabelle was just the same only crazier. She bit the bandit again, a little higher, and at the same time I got one hand free, pulled my rock from my pocket, and hit him square in the ear with it.

"Bite him again!" I ordered Izzy, and she did. She kicked him, too.

Between us, I think we gave that man the worst five minutes he'd ever had in his life. It was him trying to break free from *us* now, not the other way around. And when he finally did break free, he ran straight back toward the battle, happier to fight five well-armed and trained Foresters than two girls.

My blood was so high I had half a mind to go after him and give him more of what he had coming, but Izzy was crying by now. The scene in her head was the one where her mother fell down dead. I grabbed her in my arms and ran back into the bushes, deeper this time, while I thought what to do.

Shots came from behind us. The battle was evidently hotting up. Was it still between the Foresters and the men, I wondered, or was it man against man now? I wanted to go see, but didn't dare risk the road. I wanted to ask Shy, but couldn't hear her.

One more look at Izzy, her face white where it wasn't filthy, eyes big and frightened, and I decided to get her away. If the men won the fight, who knew what they'd do to her? Or rather, I did know. And if the Foresters was dead, I would be the only one between her and them.

"Come on, Isabelle." I took her hand firm. "We're getting out of here."

I didn't have to ask her twice.

*

The way was rough and rocky, and it got dark quicker than I expected, but I took Izzy all the way down to the bottom of the valley before I dared to stop. By then it was too dark to see our way, and we only found water by listening for it. Once at the creek, we drank and drank, but it wasn't a safe place for us to stay long. Animals would come to drink in the night, and in the morning maybe men. Not far away, standing out against the stars, were some biggish boulders. They looked like they'd keep off the wind, at least, so I led Izzy to them and found a place among them where we could sit. It was cold, and Isabelle didn't have a jacket. I wrapped her in mine and stretched out my legs to make her a lap. Izzy put her head down, and after shaking for a while, she fell asleep.

I dozed off and on, but mostly I kept watch all night. Sometimes I thought I caught the glint of animals' eyes turned toward us, and once I thought I heard men's voices. All I had was a rock—and surprise—to fight with, but the animals left us alone, and the men—if they were men—went by without stopping. Dawn looked like never coming, but then I blinked and suddenly it was light. I listened, but there was no sound of fighting, and when I sniffed no smell of gun powder in the air. Izzy and me were cold, stiff, and hungry, but I reckoned we were safe.

My idea was that we'd follow our own footprints back up to the place where we'd left the road, but I'd never tracked anything before, and tracking turned out not to be as easy as I'd thought it would be. I couldn't see the road from where we were, but I knew it was above us, so eventually I gave up "tracking" and just climbed. We had to go slow. Izzy wasn't strong, and now she was hungry, too. She'd never had dinner the day before, and all the breakfast I could give her was only bitter greens growing on the hillside. We didn't have a canteen. The best I could do for water was to soak my handkerchief in the creek before we started, and when Isabelle got thirsty, give it to her to suck along the way. I listened for Shy's mind, but either she was too far away for me to hear, or she was dead.

I hoped she wasn't dead.

We got to the road at last, a stretch I didn't recognize. There was no sign of any Foresters, but at least there wasn't any signs of Men, neither. My legs were shaking from the climb up. I found a level place, sat down, and pulled Izzy into my lap.

"We're on our own, Izzy," I told her. "Damn all Men, and damn all Foresters, too. Damn, damn, damn."

Izzy picked that moment to say her first-ever real word. "Damn," she repeated—speaking pretty clear, considering. "Damn."

I would have laughed, but I was just too tired to do it.

We'd sat for five minutes when Izzy all of a sudden went stiff and stared straight ahead.

There's no way to describe the sound of a thought. It's something you just have to hear. But I will say that every thought-voice is a little different from every other one. Izzy'd heard Shy's voice, and a minute later, I heard it, too. The two of us let out silent shouts of our own, and Shy answered.

Pretty soon, we heard another voice, very excited. This one wasn't telepathic, it was Wise's. "Where? Where?" he was calling.

"This way!" Shy called back to him, while her mental voice said to us, "Hang on! We're coming!" Then aloud she cried, "This way; this way!" again. After that I heard something I couldn't make out from Wise, and then Shy added, "No, I think they're all right!"

Foresters don't talk about the gods much. Some people say Foresters don't even believe in the gods. But as Shy and Wise came running up the road toward us, calling and waving, they were thanking the gods like a couple of priests. As they got near, me and Isabelle managed to stand up, and the four of us fell into each other's arms.

*

Once Izzy and me'd drained Wise's canteen, we felt better.

Something coming out of Shy's mind made me uneasy. "Where's Dan?" I asked, sharp. "Where's Doctor?"

They were both all right, Wise said quick. Or would be. Dan had took a blade to the upper chest and shoulder but wasn't hurt bad beyond that he'd lost a good bit of blood. Doctor had been knocked off his horse which then kicked him a few times. Just as I'd guessed they would, once Doctor was down, the men had gone instantly to fighting each other for his animal, who settled the matter of who'd have him by running away.

Shy went on from there to tell me the whole story.

After Izzy and me'd been dragged off, which only Shy knew at the time had happened, the fighting between the men and the Foresters went on for a while, with the men trying to take the Foresters' horses and the Foresters trying to keep them without having to kill any men. Dan had just got the carthorse calmed back down and was standing by its head when one of the men jumped onto the wagon-seat, thinking he'd take the reins and drive the wagon away. Two other men, wanting the wagon for themselves, jumped on Dan. None of the men had a gun, thank the gods, but the ones who jumped Dan both had knives.

Shy said that when Captain saw his nephew go down under the men, he turned cold and deliberate as a machine. He outright shot dead a man who was between him and the two who were attacking Dan, and then shot one of the attackers, too. Dan, on the ground, had got back his long gun by that time, which the men had knocked out of his hands, and he shot his other attacker himself, though only in the arm. I'd have preferred to hear he was dead. Shy "read" this out of my mind, and was shocked, but Izzy, who'd also understood me, grinned.

When Doctor was knocked off his horse and the horse ran away, three men ran after it. This gave Captain the idea of cutting the carthorse free, too. Sure enough, three more men followed the carthorse, which didn't leave a lot of Men behind to carry on the fight. Those decided pretty quick they didn't like the odds anymore and took off in several directions, helping their wounded and leaving their dead.

We'd all been walking while Shy was telling this, me leaning on Shy while Wise carried Izzy. By now we were in sight of the wagon, where Captain was looking after Dan and Doctor. Captain was watching for us, his face anxious, and when he caught sight of us he ran to hug me and Isabelle same as Wise and Shy had, though he didn't mention any gods.

When I first met Isabelle, she didn't understand that regular humans felt anything, since she couldn't feel things with them. Now she showed us she'd learned that we did by being worried and wanting to see for herself that Dan and Doctor were alive. She wanted to pet them, too—petting being an Ant's way of saying "I love you," I guess. I wouldn't let her touch Dan and Doctor, who were sleeping, but I said she could pet them later and she understood.

Nobody'd hunted, so there was nothing in the camp to eat but water and biscuit. Shy'd begun searching for us as soon as the bandits was driven off, and the others as soon as the wounded was tended to. But we were all hungry enough to make water and biscuit seem delicious, and after we'd ate hearty, we took turns napping the day away. No men, bandits or otherwise, bothered us.

CHAPTER NINE

I was all right that day and the night after. Happy, even. I was alive; Izzy was alive; and Dan and Doctor looked like they were going to be all right, too. What else mattered besides that we were alive? Doctor had got a kick to the head from his horse that made his face swell all up on one side, and though he said he was fine, Captain's opinion—stated very forceful—was that you could never know about these things. He made Doctor stay lying down for the rest of that day and the whole next one, which Doctor didn't like at all. Dan was weak and couldn't move much without his shoulder coming to bleed again. But those were little hurts compared to being dead like the three men whose bodies we left lying at the side of the road for a whole day before Wise and Captain together buried them. The three men wouldn't be going home ever, whereas we only had to wait a day or two for Dan and Doctor to get stronger and then be on our way again.

The morning of the second day after the attack, though, I woke up not happy at all. I woke up angry. In my dreams the night before, the men'd been stronger than us, and better organized, and had better guns. They'd been willing to shoot, and had. Who they shot switched around as the dream went on. Sometimes it was Wise or Doctor or Captain, and sometimes it was Shy or Dan. Sometimes it was all of them. But it was bad no matter who it was, because they were all my friends.

Asleep, I'd been worried about Captain, but once I was awake, I was mad at him instead. It seemed to me that if anybody was to blame for us getting into a battle, it was him. He was the one who'd been in such a big hurry to get— wherever it was we were going, that he'd lead us up a damn cow-path. The fact that he'd come out of the fight without a scratch on him only made me madder.

I was thinking about this after breakfast when Shy got me aside private from everybody else.

She had a knife for me.

"One of those men dropped it," she said. "It's not a very good knife, but it's better than nothing. I'll see you get a good one as soon as I can."

I'd been thinking I was reading Shy better and better. Now I knew it for sure. As soon Shy said, "dropped it," I knew she meant it'd fell from the man's dead hand. Shy saw that I knew and went red.

"Wait," she said, not looking at me. "I'll give you this one instead."

She offered me her own knife.

In my mind I saw someone give it to Shy. I guessed from his looks he was her dad.

"No, thanks. I'm fine with this one," I said, taking the first one she'd offered. "I kind of like the handle, in fact. It fits my hand."

Shy smiled, and I smiled back. All the important parts of the conversation had been silent, and I knew from Shy's look I'd understood it perfect.

"All right, Claire," she said, still smiling. "Keep that one until we find a better. The important thing is that you have some kind of weapon to defend yourself with."

It wasn't until Shy was walking away that we both realized what she'd called me. Luckily, nobody else had heard what she said but Izzy, who wouldn't—and couldn't—tell, but Shy promised she'd be more careful.

"Catherine was your mother's name, wasn't it?" she added as she walked away. "I can see why you picked it. It's lovely."

Because she could read my mind, Shy was coming to know everything about me. I didn't like it, but I didn't know any way to stop it happening.

A little later, when Shy was on guard duty and Captain had finally let Doctor get up, everybody except Dan, who was asleep in the wagon, was lounging around the fire. Maybe having a knife in my pocket made me braver, I don't know. All I know is I suddenly found myself crossing my arms over my chest, and saying, very severe, "Look: I want to know what's going on."

That didn't seem strong enough for how I felt, so I corrected it to, "I *demand* to know what's going on."

Judging by their faces, nobody'd expected I'd ever demand anything of the kind. They looked at each other, and then at me, blank.

Doctor asked, tentative, "You want to know—what? Specifically, I mean."

He said it so pleasant he…kind of took the wind out of my sails, if you want the truth.

I wasn't giving in, though. I repeated, "I want to know what's going on." I didn't use the word "demand" this time, but I kept my tone firm. "We're not going to Beechlands Forest. The direction we're going is the exact *wrong* way to get to Beechlands Forest. Which I don't care about, by the way. We can go to Beechlands or not, as far as I'm concerned—except I'm sorry for Isabelle and Shy if we don't, because they do care. The thing *I* care about is that Izzy and me almost got killed the other day. I think that gives me a right to know what's happening." Before anybody could answer me, I added, "Also Dan and Doctor almost got killed," because I didn't want anybody to get the idea I only thought about myself.

Nobody said anything, except Shy. From where she was standing guard, Shy told me (mental), "Go on."

She was on my side. That was nice.

I said again, "I want to know where I'm going. Also, I want to know who I'm going with. You ain't Islanders, and you don't talk Island-speak. My guess is you're Foresters."

Doctor glanced at Captain, who looked away. "You are correct," Doctor said, looking back at me. "We are Foresters."

"And Foresters are truthful," Shy's brain said. "Tell him to live up to that."

Having somebody as smart as Shy to help me argue was going to be great.

"Tell the truth like a Forester, then," I said, taking Shy's advice. "*Why* aren't we going to Beechlands? It's a Forest. Seems like you'd want to go there."

Captain stopped pretending he wasn't interested in the conversation. "We *are* going to Beechlands," he spoke up. "*Immediately*. Or rather, as soon as Dan can travel. It was my decision to leave the Beechlands trail, and I promise you I'm very sorry for it now."

He might've been sorry. He probably honestly was.

But he wasn't sorry enough for me.

My face went hot. "Do you even know what you're sorry *for*?" I cried—no, *demanded*. "Do you know what those men might've done to me and Isabelle? *And* Shy. Once they killed the rest of you, they wouldn't've left Shy alone just because she's a Forester!"

For a minute, I felt the bandit's arms around me, tight as a vise, and I heard him saying filth in my ear. I felt the sailor on the *Antelope* on me, too, fumbling at my chest. Of course, what'd happened with the sailor was my fault, not Captain's, but at that moment, it was all just the same to me. It was all just females being at a disadvantage to males, where size and strength mattered. "If I'm going to get killed, I don't want to die not knowing why. Tell me everything. It's only fair."

Both Wise and Doctor were looking at Captain now. Captain looked sheepish, but didn't answer.

Wise said, kind of pleading, "Loyal, Catherine's right. We owe her an explanation." Throwing a stick he was holding into the fire, he added, irritable, "I said from the first you'd be bored without a ship under you, and when you're bored, Loyal, you're dangerous. You should have kept the *Muriel* until the *River* was ready."

"What's he talking about?" I asked Shy. "*What's* loyal?"

Before Shy could answer me, Wise repeated again, more quiet: "Loyal…"

"Loyal is Captain's name," Shy explained. "Captain Loyal."

He was a *captain*? For some reason, him being a captain made me madder than ever.

"Look," I said to Captain—or, the captain. Whichever. "I want to know what's going on, and since it seems like you're the one got us in trouble, I think it should be you who tells me. The *Muriel's* a ship, ain't she? Where does she come into this?" Then I repeated, "You damn near got me killed," just in case he'd forgot.

Captain sighed first, but then said, "All right, fine;" and sat up straighter. "My name is Loyal Annason, Catherine," he began, "and until a few months ago, I was captain of the Forest ship *Muriel.*"

The whole story—leaving out some boring parts—was that Captain Loyal'd spent the last year of his time as captain of the *Muriel* chasing another ship around and never catching it. The ship he'd chased was called the *Bee.* I remembered when he said it that he'd mentioned the *Bee* earlier as the pirate ship that'd kidnapped Izzy and some of her people and then shoved them overboard when they were chased. The captain said now that *Bee* wasn't just a regular pirate ship, she was the master boss of a whole fleet of pirate ships. He said the *Bee* was the stinger of the group, so to speak, and sailed in where she was needed to fight off traders trying to stop other pirate ships. As far as anybody could tell, the *Bee* herself didn't usually carry any pirated goods. The women from Izzy's island had been an exception.

"And you couldn't catch her?" I asked. I was surprised to hear this because the *Muriel* was generally reckoned a fine ship.

"I could not." Captain Loyal made a face. "*Bee's* the fastest thing on the water and far better armed than *Muriel.*"

Not to worry, though, Captain Loyal went on. The Forest was meanwhile building a better ship themselves. *River*, which was due to be launched any day, would be as fast as *Bee*, or maybe faster, and at least as well-armed

"You're going to be captain of the *River*?" I won't deny I was impressed.

The captain said he was. He'd come back to the continent on purpose to step down as captain of the *Muriel* and sign on to the *River*. Wise and Doctor were supposed to move along to the *River*, too.

Only things had happened to delay the *River's* launch, and Captain Loyal—against Wise's advice, as Wise mentioned eight or ten times—decided that instead of staying with the *Muriel* until the *River* was ready, he and Wise and Doctor should all have a nice little holiday on the continent. They'd already picked up Captain Loyal's nephew, Dan, in Annasland and were supposed to take him to visit family in Evergreen Forest. Captain Loyal suggested they should *all* go to Evergreen Forest instead.

"Dan's from Annasland?" I asked.

"Yes."

"You all are?"

"Yes."

I asked, "You can't read my mind though, right? Only Shy can." I was already pretty sure about this, but wanted to be certain.

Captain Loyal agreed with this, then started back on his story at the place where, on their way to Evergreen, they'd found me.

While I was still sick, the captain had rode to Coast-town—I remembered him doing it—where he got word that the *Bee* had finally been caught carrying a cargo.

"Eleven Ant women and an Ant child," Doctor said, looking at Isabelle.

"What kind of cargo is *that*?" I asked, hugging Izzy closer. "What did they want people for?"

Captain Loyal said he didn't know. No one knew. "Shy was given the job of taking Isabelle to Beechlands to be helped, and since we were nearby, we were asked to escort her."

Shy and Izzy'd seemed to be all alone when we met them. I knew now from Shy's thoughts that there'd been other Foresters around, keeping watch to see they were safe. Shy was proud I hadn't seen them.

"You've done wonders with Isabelle," Doctor put in then, very sincere. "Shy initially doubted we could save her."

I knew this already. Shy'd told me.

"And—that's it," Captain Loyal added, like the story was done. "You know what happened after that."

"I know *what* happened," I agreed. "But I don't know *why*. Why did we stop going to Beechlands? I keep asking and asking that, but you never tell me."

Captain Loyal's look turned shifty, and instead of answering the question, tried to put me off with more compliments like Doctor's, about what a good job I'd done with Isabelle.

"That's not what I asked," I interrupted. I like praise as much as anybody, but not when it's only meant as a distraction. "I asked why we stopped going towards Beechlands. Also—why're we in such a hurry?"

"Who said we were in a hurry?"

"You did!" I snapped at him. "When Wise complained about that damn cow-path, you said, '*We're in a hurry.*'"

"You did, Loyal," Wise agreed, and winked at me.

Captain sighed again. After a minute, he said, "You remember those three Men who stopped at our camp one evening? Pleasant, but very dirty, and all slightly wounded?"

I did. "You gave them a bunch of our food."

"I *traded* some food, yes."

"Yeah. All the good stuff. For a metal bar you said we couldn't touch." I suddenly figured something out. "When you got that metal bar is when we changed course, ain't it?"

The captain nodded. "It's steel. We're following the trail of the men who dropped it. I believe they're headed to Harbor Town."

"You want to give it back to them?" I asked.

If the captain and the rest had been anybody but Foresters, this would have been a ridiculous question. One of the few things men can agree on is that found stuff belongs to the finder. The poor little bent ring I had hanging around my neck was proof that Foresters believed different.

But Captain Loyal said, no, he didn't plan to return it. "The steel is stolen," he said. "Looted from a..." He thought it over for about half a minute then apparently decided to just spill it. "...from a Forbidden Site. If I find the looters, I'm going to have them arrested."

Good luck with that, I thought. Out loud, I asked, "And the looters are in Harbor Town?"

"I believe so. That is, if they haven't already taken ship. I know I took a chance with your life, Catherine, and I apologize wholeheartedly for it. I allowed myself to get so focused on not letting that steel get into the hands of people who don't understand how dangerous it is that I forgot to be cautious."

"Dangerous?"

"Dangerous," the captain repeated. "It's not ordinary steel. It's *radioactive*."

I thought of the "hot" steel Sarah's son-in-law Tom had told her D&R might've accidentally put into radios. I'd got the name a little wrong, but I remembered it had burned Tom's hands.

"The man you got the steel from had his hands bandaged," I said. "They weren't regular burned, were they? They were radioactive burned."

"How do you know about radioactivity?" Doctor asked, sitting up straight.

"Somebody told me."

Doctor and the captain looked at each other and Doctor said I was amazingly well-informed. I liked that. Doctor went on to explain that looters not only took steel, but also other radioactive stuff from Forbidden Sites, and sold it off to people who didn't understand what they were buying. Then people got sick from it, Doctor said. Sometimes they died.

This was interesting. And terrible.

"I guess we're going after them, then," I said. "The looters, I mean. As soon as Dan can travel."

But Captain Loyal shook his head. "No. Chasing looters isn't my job. That's probably why I made a mess of it."

I heard Shy thinking that it was his job, really; that looters were just land-pirates; which sounded so clever I repeated it to the captain. "Anyway, you didn't make a mess of it," I added. "If you're right, we've all but caught those bastards already. As soon as Dan's ready, let's go get them before they hurt more people."

Shy's mind, sounding pleased with me, said, "Oh, Claire!" and looks went between the other Foresters that seemed to say they were pleased with me, too. I think I might've blushed.

Still looking pleased, Doctor got up and walked around the fire to where I was sitting. Squatting down and sticking out both his hands to me, he said, "My name is Masterson, Catherine. How do you do?"

When he told me his right name and called me by my wrong one, I got suddenly sick of my lie.

"My name's really Claire," I admitted, meanwhile taking his hands like Shy's mind was telling me to. "I told you it was Catherine because I didn't entirely trust you, but I do now. You're good people."

Masterson—Dr. Masterson—managed to thank me for my trust without sneering at the lie I'd told earlier about my name, which is more than I could have done in his position. Putting his cheek against mine, which was apparently something Foresters normally did that seemed…weird…to me—he repeated "How do you do, *Claire*;" and then added something in Forester that Shy told me meant "Friend of the Forest."

By now, Wise had come over to where I was, too. "Wise's name really *is* Wise," Dr. Masterson told me, standing up. "Although in fact he isn't always wise. You probably already noticed that."

Wise, grinning, took my hands the same way the doctor had done.

"Is Dan's name Dan?" I asked him, as we touched our cheeks together.

"No," Wise said, "we just call him that for charity's sake. His real name's—" He said a Forest word that Shy's brain translated for me as "Chamberpot."

I smirked and pretended to believe it. "Suits him."

Even Shy laughed at this, though she wasn't normally a laughy kind of person.

Wise and Dr. Masterson turned to Captain Loyal.

The captain said first, "You must be joking," and then, "All right, all right," and came and took my hands like the doctor and Wise had done. As we touched cheeks, he said, "I promise to have you safe in Beechlands in a week."

I pulled back and stared at him. "The hell you say!" I burst out.

"*Language*, Claire!" Shy protested, as the captain's eyebrows went up.

I knew I was getting good at telepathy when I understood right away that by "language," Shy meant mine was too raw for her. I tried to fix my mistake. "What I meant to say was, we're going to Harbor Town, ain't—*aren't*—we?" Besides my raw language, Shy apparently meant to fix up my grammar, too. "We're going to get the looters."

Before the captain could answer this, Dr. Masterson spoke up. "Claire's right, Loyal. We can't leave it now. Let's find someplace in Harbor Town where Dan can rest and Claire can look after Isabelle."

Captain Loyal eyed me like he didn't entirely trust me. Which was fair. "You'll confine yourself to doing that?" he asked me. "You'll stay clear of our business with the looters?"

"The looters is totally *your* job," I promised.

"We'll go to Harbor Town, then," the captain agreed.

CHAPTER TEN

Harbor Town turned out to be a nice little place. Nice for a seaport, anyhow. Being smallish and not real busy kept it from being as dirty and lawless as most ports. Along the waterfront were all the usual kinds of taverns and low taprooms all ports have, but not many of them. Such a small place didn't have drunks and loafers enough to fill many.

We found decent rooms where Dan could finally have a proper bed, and Izzy and me stayed with him there daytimes to see he didn't get lonely or bored. All Foresters are educated past all reason, and now that I was a "Forest Friend," Dan was determined I was going to get educated, too. When he wasn't nagging me to come to Evergreen Forest with him and join the school there—I naturally didn't tell him I'd already been offered a place in it and turned it down—he told me about things like electricity, and how radios worked—he knew everything about how radios worked—and what the Ancient Texts said the world had been like before the Ants pretty much destroyed it and humans had to start over.

"How could people not work?" I asked him, after one lecture. "Food doesn't just grow without people making it grow, and houses to live in don't build themselves, either."

"Machines did everything. Machines even built the machines that did the farming and building."

"Well, what did the *people* do all day, then? Watch the machines work?"

"I guess they did the same things we do now when we're not working. Read and write and draw and paint… Study. Fun things."

"Some fun," I muttered—although I like reading myself, in fact. "I'll bet most of them just got into trouble. Anyway, if machines did the work, what did the Ancients need Ants for? I thought Ants were invented to work."

"That's the funny thing. The Ancients invented all these machines, and then they found out humans did some things better and cheaper than a machine. It takes metal and fuel and so forth to make machines and to keep them running, while all it takes to make people is—people."

Before Dan could say any more, I suddenly knew what some of the jobs Ants did were. I got them from Izzy's mind. "Raising babies and taking care of the sick," I blurted.

"What?"

"That's what Ants did. Or some Ants, anyway. Because sick people and babies don't want machines to take care of them."

Dan stared at me for a minute. "Did Isabelle tell you that?"

I nodded.

Dan grunted. "All right. That fits. In fact, it's kind of appropriate, because the whole idea of making Ants started with making babies."

Then he went on to tell me the Ancients figured out ways to see that all their babies were born healthy, and went on from there to find ways to make babies "better."

"What 'better?'" I asked, kissing the top of Izzy's head. "All babies are perfect just the way they are."

"You know what I mean. They wanted babies who would grow up taller, or stronger, or prettier than they would have been without—whatever they Ancients did to make them taller or stronger or prettier. When they wanted workers, they used the same method—whatever it was, because, as I said, we don't know—to make better workers."

"What's 'better' about workers who kill people?"

"Exactly," Dan answered, grim. "My guess about that—my peoples' guess—

is that the Ants killed humans because humans didn't treat them very well. None of the Ancient Texts say that, but humans probably just wouldn't admit it in a book. Humans treated Ants badly, and the Ants rebelled."

"Instead of taller or prettier, the Ancients should have made babies that grew up *nicer*," I suggested, and Dan agreed.

The captain and Dr. Masterson asked some people they knew to watch around town for the looters, and once they'd done that, there was nothing for any of us to do but sit back and wait for news. When Dan had other people to keep him company, me and Izzy and Shy went out and explored the town. Shy had money and bought Izzy little treats, like sugar-sticks and beads to string. Izzy loved to string beads. In her mind, stringing beads was "work," and like all Ants, Isabelle loved to work. Shy and me also taught Izzy things, like to eat polite, and dress herself, and wash. She learned so well that nobody where we were staying took her for anything but a real human child, though one who didn't talk much. The Ancients had done a good job with her kind. More than one Harbor Town human told Shy—who they generally mistook for Izzy's mother—that she was the best-behaved child they'd ever seen.

Sometimes when Shy couldn't come with us, Izzy and me went walking alone, and one time, along our way, we stepped in a few places to ask if anybody there'd seen my dad. The places were taverns and such, but I figured it would be all right because Izzy didn't know a tavern wasn't respectable. That's what I planned to tell Shy if she found out, anyway. Nobody we talked to knew the name of "Dunn" until we got to the last place on the dirty end of town. There, the barkeep looked me up and down. "What was the name again?"

I repeated it.

"What's he to you?" the barkeep asked.

"What d'you care?" I asked back. "I got business with him."

He nodded toward Isabelle. "She yours?"

Keep in mind that I was about six when Izzy was born. "No, she ain't, thank you for asking," I snapped. "And she ain't Bill Dunn's, neither, if that's your next question."

The barkeep grunted and went back to what he'd been doing when I walked in, which was wiping down pint-pots with a rag so filthy it looked like it might've done earlier service in a toilet.

As I turned to leave, he added, "If I see Bill, I'll say someone's looking for him."

My heart jumped a little. "You know him, then?"

"I didn't say that. I didn't say one way or the other. I said if I saw him, I'd say someone was looking for him." He glared at me. "And that's *all* I'll say. I ain't your message-boy."

"Good enough. I'm obliged." I gave him a coin. He didn't deserve nothing, but it made me feel grand to do it.

It was as promising an answer as I'd gotten anywhere, and I was excited.

As we rounded the corner onto a bigger street, we got even more interesting news. A shopkeeper I knew a little, a man name of Rick, stepped right in front of me and Izzy, blocking our way, and then stared into the distance and pretended not to see us. It was too obvious a hint for me to miss. I stopped where I was and squatted down to fuss with Izzy's buttons like they needed attention.

Rick asked, quiet, "You one of the ones looking for—" I felt a jump at my heart, but Rick finished his sentence with "—strangers selling steel?"

I was disappointed—but only a little. Second best to finding my dad was finding strangers selling steel. "Yes. You see any?"

I figured I'd get whatever information Rick had and take it back to Wise.

"Got some fellows—strangers—at my place. They asked for a room to do a little business in. Not the usual business, if you get me."

I didn't get him, but lied and said I did.

"Anyway, they're upstairs now. There's four or five of them, and I've heard the word 'steel' said a dozen times. You might want to check them out."

"How?" I breathed.

Rick scratched his chin. "Well, they're upstairs at my place, as I said. Wait outside, and see them when they come out, I guess."

"But—there's a back door to your shop, too, right?" Rick's shop was a middle one in a row of shops all connected to each other. The door to the front was on one street, while the door to the back let out on the street behind.

"Yes." Rick added, a little nervous, "Notice, I'm not saying for *sure* they're the men you're looking for. They're strangers to me. Complete strangers."

"I understand."

"I'm a man who keeps his mouth shut. That's my reputation, and I value it. I put a very high value on it, in fact."

This time when I said I understood, I was being honest. It was clear to me that whoever the men in Rick's upstairs room were, Rick was afraid of them. I understood being afraid.

"I need to see them," I said. "But I'll have to come inside your place to do it. I can't wait outside unless you can tell me for sure which door they'll leave by, because if I'm by the wrong door, I'll miss them. Don't worry, though. I'll do it subtle, so the men don't know they're being looked at."

"They're at my place," Rick repeated.

"Right."

"*Upstairs.*"

"Upstairs at your place. Right."

Rick repeated that I'd have to wait for the men outside.

I'd already explained why I couldn't. I said again, "I can't. But I'll come see them subtle."

Rick stopped pretending he wasn't talking to me and stared at me frank and open.

I was just thinking maybe I was wrong about what "subtle" meant and had said the opposite of what I intended when Rick started away, shaking his head. "Damn stubborn female," he muttered as he went. "Glad she ain't mine."

I stood for a few minutes, thinking up a plan. What I came up with wasn't a great plan, but it seemed like it might work.

"I shouldn't involve you in this," I told Isabelle silently, eyeing her. "You're too little. But I have to. Come on."

I led her to a shop with toys for sale and bought Izzy a ball. The woman at the shop chucked Isabelle under her chin and told her to have a good time with it.

Isabelle answered with her favorite word, which was, "No." She wanted beads.

"She means 'yes,'" I told the woman as I hurried for the door. To Izzy I said, silent, "Learn your job with the ball first, and then I'll buy you beads. All right?"

At Rick's, I headed straight upstairs, ignoring the people who were downstairs drinking and talking. It didn't seem like a comfortable place to drink. There weren't enough chairs, and some of the women had to sit on laps.

The upstairs corridor was lined with doors on both sides, most of them closed, but men's voices were coming from an open one at the far end of the hall. I thought to myself that the end of a hall was a good place for somebody who didn't want to be seen. Nobody could stroll by it unintentional. Luckily for me, I didn't need to stroll by a room to see into it. I had a pair of eyes I could send to see for me. I grinned at Izzy, and asked, "Ready to learn your new job?"

Isabelle said she was.

I sent Izzy about halfway down the passage and told her—not aloud—"This job is called 'catch,' and this is how it works. You stand right there, and I'll throw this ball to you. Catch it and throw it back to me. All right?"

I could give Isabelle a good mental picture of how a game of "catch" should go, but I couldn't give her the skill to play it. I hit her in the head twice before I changed her "job" to just stopping the ball when I *rolled* it.

She couldn't always stop it in time, either, but that was all part of my plan. My third roll went all the way to the end of the corridor before Isabelle caught up to it, and that was perfect for what I had in mind. As she bent down to get it, I silently ordered her, "Look into the room, Isabelle."

Isabelle looked. She had a good, long look.

Then I said, "Bring me the ball," and she brought it.

I knew the men would eventually get annoyed with Izzy's little "visits," and they did—but not before Isabelle'd had five good looks. In five looks, she managed to see almost everything but the man who sat farthest from the door. She hardly got a glimpse of him.

The other four men in the room were sitting around a table, passing something between them and talking about it. The first four of Izzy's looks, I only tried to "see" the men. On her fifth look, I told her to look especially at what the men were holding.

She did, and I saw it with her. It was a metal bar—steel—greenish—rectangular; with a square notch in it running the bar's whole length. Exactly like the bar the man at our camp—the man with burned hands—had slung his bundle from, and that Captain Loyal'd bought from him for four squirrels, put under the floor of our wagon, and told us not to touch.

By now, the men'd yelled a couple times for us damn kids to get the hell out of here, but I wanted one more good look, so I rolled the ball again anyway, all the way to the end of the hall. The men had had enough of our racket. Just as Isabelle got to the ball, they shut the door to their room right in her face.

Isabelle didn't care if she was yelled at. To be honest, she didn't really see much difference between humans yelling and humans talking nice. But getting a door slammed in her face hurt her feelings. She turned to look at me, her lower lip stuck out and shaking.

Which made me mad. She was just a little kid. I'd get my "one more good look" anyway, I decided—a *real* good look—just to spite the bastards for making Izzy cry.

Just then, a woman stuck her head out of one of the rooms. She looked at Izzy and asked, "What's the matter, honey? My! You're young!" Looking over at me, she shook her head, disapproving.

"Come to get our dad," I said quick.

"Oh, is that it?" The woman laughed. "You'll have to wait until his time's up. Go down and sit in the bar, why don't you? It's more comfortable." Then she laughed again, and pulled her head back into her room, calling to us meanwhile not to drink anything anybody gave us.

As soon as she was gone, I told Izzy, "Wait here." Then I walked to the room where the men were and knocked.

One of the men opened it, but only a crack. I gave him my best smile.

"I'm here to apologize," I said. "My little sister and me didn't mean to disturb you. We didn't know anybody was here."

Which was a lie, of course—not that it matters.

Seeing I didn't look dangerous, the man opened the door a little wider. He said, "Fine, fine. Get out of here now."

I looked past him, into the room. "I'm sorry," I called, straining forward to see more. "I apologize to all of you. We didn't mean to be rude, see?"

The men muttered this and that back—mostly fairly friendly. I guessed when they weren't looting dangerous stuff and selling it to people who'd be burned and maybe die from it, they were probably nice enough. I studied all their faces, and once I'd done that much, figured I'd done all I could. After saying "Sorry!" a few more times—mostly to the back of a shut door—I took Izzy with me downstairs. On the way, we passed one of the women I'd seen downstairs earlier. The man whose lap she'd been in was with her, and in case they were looters too, I memorized their faces. Rick met me and Izzy and hustled us out.

At the inn, the captain and everybody were back, and the men were with Dan in his room. Shy met me as I came in, all happy and excited because Dan was sitting up by himself for the first time since he'd been hurt.

Then her face changed. "Oh, gods," she moaned. "Claire, what did you do?"

"Got some information," I told her, hurrying past her to get up to Dan's room. "Let me tell everybody what I found out, and then I need to go back out and buy Izzy some beads. I promised her I would and then I didn't, so she's a little bit mad at me right now."

So—I told them.

Everybody was their normal selves when I started, but for some reason got less and less cheerful as I talked. By the end of my story, Captain Loyal looked completely grim, in fact. Maybe I'd interrupted them at a bad time.

"You were *where*?" the captain asked.

"Rick's shop. On Water Street. You've probably seen it."

"Yes, I know the place," Captain Loyal said, stiff. "And you were upstairs there, you say?"

"Yeah. We were upstairs, and there were these men, see…"

"You were *upstairs* at Rick's."

I'd already said I was. "Well, that's where the men were," I pointed out. "Me'n Izzy went up there, like I said, with Izzy's ball…"

"Rick *permitted* this?"

"Well, yeah. I mean, what he said was to wait *outside*, but the problem was the shop's got two doors."

I looked at Dr. Masterson. He was staring funny at me, too.

"And I couldn't watch two doors at once," I explained.

"Rick's," the captain repeated.

"Yeah, Rick's. With two doors that I couldn't watch at once, and that's why we went upstairs." I shrugged. "Rick didn't seem to mind."

I think the Captain Loyal I saw then was probably the Captain Loyal sailors saw when they messed up *bad*. His voice cold as snow—and his face matching—he asked, "Did it occur to you that in the time it took you to buy a ball for Isabelle, you could have run back here and asked someone else to come watch the second door *for* you?"

It honestly hadn't. "Well, I didn't want to bother nobody in case I was wrong. Because I was afraid I *might* be wrong, and they were just doing business. Which they were."

"They were—! Did you *observe* this 'business' they were engaged in?"

"No. Well, yes. Or, not exactly. I think I observed what they were doing business *about*, though, which was metal."

The captain and the doctor and Mr. Wise all looked at each other, and got more interested.

"Metal?"

"Steel," I said. "A bar just like the one that's in the wagon. *Exactly* like it."

The Foresters—except Dan, of course, who couldn't—all stood up straighter. "Steel," the captain repeated.

"A bar of steel," I agreed. "They were passing it around the table they were at, and talking about it. One of the men said he wanted all he could get."

More looks went among the Foresters.

"What's your plan, Loyal?" Dr. Masterson said, very low.

He said it in Forester, but Shy was right there. I used her brain to understand what the doctor said.

The captain said, "Let me think," and then stepped into the hall outside and stared at the floor.

Evidently everybody else was used to the way the captain thought, because nobody seemed surprised or followed him. While Captain Loyal was outside, Dr. Masterson asked me, very soft, "Did you…um…see anything else at Rick's besides some men in a room, Claire?"

The captain, his forehead wrinkled, was now leaning with one hand against the wall, and drumming his fingers on it.

"I saw some other men," I said, watching the captain. "The place was pretty quiet on the whole. A lady spoke to us. She told us there was a room we could wait downstairs in, but of course Izzy and me couldn't do that. Also, somebody was kind of yelling for a while, but not like anything was wrong or anything. She sounded happy, if you want the truth. That's it, I think. Oh, and the lady who talked to us said not to drink anything."

The captain walked back in.

"Everything's fine," Dr. Masterson said. "Her innocence is her armor."

I had no idea what he was talking about (nobody wears armor anymore), but there wasn't time to ask. Captain Loyal sent Wise and the doctor off to keep watch at Rick's and told Shy to go with them to be a messenger between them and us. Then he asked me to tell the whole story again, which I did.

"What's the problem with this 'Rick's,' Uncle?" Dan asked when I was done. He'd been stuck in bed the whole time since we'd come to the harbor town and didn't know any place in it but one room in the inn.

"I'll tell you later," the captain said.

I don't know what he might've told Dan, but when Captain Loyal came to me later to talk again, he didn't say any more about Rick's. What he wanted to talk about was the men I'd seen *at* Rick's—though he asked me about them without, as I said, actually mentioning Rick's itself.

"Describe them again," he said.

"Are they still in that room?" I asked. "I mean, were they when the doctor and Wise got there?"

"You've put your finger right on the problem," Captain Loyal said. "We have no idea. The men we want could be any of the men we've seen come and go."

"Oh, that's bad," I said. "Well, let me think again." I brought a few pictures to my mind.

Isabelle was sitting near us while we talked. She was always near me if she could be. When I thought of the men at Rick's, she naturally thought of them too, which was handy. What I didn't remember, she did.

"All right. One's got real dark hair, see? As black as yours, only curly. His whiskers is real dark, too. I bet five minutes after he shaves, his jaw is already blue again."

I went on from there, telling everything about the man me and Izzy remembered. The captain listened close, and nodded occasionally.

I'd finished with the first man and started on the second, when Captain Loyal said, "Wait a minute. I'm getting confused. This man was wearing a striped shirt? Or the first man?"

"The first man." I thought for a minute. "Maybe you could write this down."

The captain said that was an excellent idea and got paper and a pen.

"Start again with the second man," he said, sitting down in one chair and using the seat of another for a desk. "No, wait. Look back at the first one." Growing up with telepaths, Captain Loyal knew my memories were like pictures I "looked" at. "What was the shape of his face?"

"Let me think… Sort of this-ish," I said, pulling my chin down and puffing out my cheeks. "And his eyes were set real deep."

Halfway through my description, the captain stopped writing words and sketched a picture. "Like this?" he asked me, showing it.

"*Just* like that. My! That's good! I wish I could draw like that! Did you take lessons?"

The captain didn't answer for a minute. Then he said, "I did, yes. From my father."

"He must have been a real good artist."

"Much better than I."

I looked some more at the picture. "I don't see how he could have been. I don't see how anybody could draw much better than that. Those are his eyes exactly. Only his eyebrows were kind of thinnish for a man's and more high-arched. Yeah, like that."

It took a few tries, but before the captain'd run out of space on the paper, he'd made a really good picture of the man I'd described.

I asked, "If you weren't a sea captain, would you like to be an artist instead?"

"I certainly find making art satisfying," the captain said. "There was a time in my life when I couldn't imagine anything better, in fact."

"Why didn't you do it, then?"

"Become an artist?"

"Yeah."

Captain Loyal wiped his pen. "The urge left me when my father died."

"Oh."

After a minute the captain added, "My present life is also a very good one, of course. I have no complaints." He spoke calm, but I noticed he didn't look at me. "Shall we do another picture?"

"You could still be an artist."

The captain shook his head. "Tell me about that third man."

One by one, we did all five of them, though the fifth man, the one Izzy and me hadn't been able to see much of, was just a few lines.

"It's funny," I said, looking at the fifth man's picture. "I feel like I'd know him from just that much. It's because you got the nose so good, I think. That's the thing about him you notice. That long nose."

"Where are you, Mr. Long-nose?" the captain asked the picture, joking.

"I guess you haven't found him yet, then."

"No, not yet. But with these pictures, I think we well may."

*

Dan was able to come downstairs for dinner that evening, instead of having it off a tray in bed, and we were all so happy to see him up that we stayed at the table late, laughing and talking. Izzy ate too much and had a nightmare. Her nightmare mixed into my dreams and woke both of us up.

It was the first nightmare Isabelle'd had since Shy had been able to "read" her, and I think Shy was more upset by it than either Izzy or me was. Shy'd never seen things like people being killed before or felt when a mind died sudden. She'd known minds that died, of course. Telepaths died on Annasland, same as everywhere. But all the ones she'd known went slow; fading out so peaceful it was hard, sometimes, to know when they were gone. What Shy saw—felt— happening on Izzy's island was minds being torn away, like if an arm or a leg was ripped off a body. I comforted Izzy by getting her out of her bed and into mine while Shy sat beside us and watched, very sad.

"She's seen too much for such a little girl," she said. "Poor little Isabelle! I wish I could take some of your memories away from you and store them in my own mind where you couldn't find them. Who's that man she's thinking of now? She's so afraid of him!"

I said it was the man who'd fired the actual shot that killed Isabelle's mother. "You'll see that part sometime," I told Shy. "Izzy'd like to forget him, but I bet she never will."

I didn't think any more about the man that night. Shy and me thought only nice things, so Isabelle could sleep. But the next morning I went—without Izzy—to talk to Captain Loyal about him.

I began, "Those pirates who kidnapped Izzy… You know them?"

"I know *of* them," the captain said. "I don't know who they are."

"That's what I thought. And if you don't know who they are or what they look like, that makes it pretty hard to catch them, right? Well, I know somebody who *does* know what they look like. She knows *perfect*."

Captain Loyal stared at me for a minute. "Isabelle, you mean," he finally said.

"Yep. Isabelle. Also me, because what Izzy knows, I know. Let's draw them. Just like we did the looters."

"We can't do that," the captain said. "Ask Isabelle to deliberately recall the most terrible day of her life? Definitely not."

"Izzy says she'd do it. She's saying it right now, in fact. She'll do it."

"If Isabelle said she'd light herself on fire, would you let her?"

Well, fair enough. I wouldn't.

I said, "Those are bad men. They're evil. But with pictures of them to go by, you might be able to find them and stop them hurting more people. That's worth something, right?"

I thought he was tempted. Then he repeated, "Absolutely not."

Captain Loyal could be even stubborner than me sometimes. We didn't make the pictures.

Later in the day, everybody but Dan and Izzy and me went out somewhere. I didn't know where they'd gone. I hadn't even felt Shy leave. But Dan was reading, which is the same as saying he was off in another world, and Izzy was playing with her beads, so I was bored. I tried to start on a new book myself but couldn't get interested in any of the ones I could find, and I wasn't tired enough to nap.

The inn we were staying in was four stories high, which made it the tallest building I'd ever been in, so I climbed up to the top floor and looked out a window, just for the fun of it and because I thought the view from there might be exciting. It wasn't, though. Four stories looked tall from the street, but I'd been up plenty of hills that were higher. The people I could see hurrying up and down the street looked like people, not ants; and I didn't notice anything new about the town's buildings from where I was except that the one of the shops' roofs could have done with a patch.

Just as I turned to go back down to our rooms again, though, I saw Rick go by, and the sight of him reminded me we were still looking for the looters. I decided I'd take a little walk over Rick's way—not all the way *to* his place, since I'd promised Captain Loyal I wouldn't, but just *near* it—in case a looter or two happened to be going in or out.

Izzy loved apples, so the first thing I did was buy one from a farmer's handcart. I put it in my pocket, and then headed over toward Rick's. I walked past the shop, but no one was around, so I went on walking down the waterfront almost to the end of town, looking at the ships in the harbor. A new one had come in overnight, a trader as dirty as the *Antelope* but bigger, so more dirt. A pretty dinghy was tied up at a pier. Besides neatly stowed oars, she had a biggish motor, and by her sleek shape, I judged she'd move fast and handle smooth. I wondered what ship she'd come from, since there was nothing to match her in the harbor, but just as I started to go closer to see what name was painted on her transom, it began to rain a little, so I turned back for another pass at Rick's instead. I kept close to the storefronts, where eaves and awnings kept me out of the wet.

Near a narrow passage between two buildings, a hand suddenly landed heavy on my shoulder.

"You the one asking for me?" a hoarse voice asked.

I pulled away, beyond reach of the hand, and ready to run if the man the hand belonged to took a step more in my direction. Once out of his range—I hoped I was out of his range—I looked him over.

The light was bad, and the man's face was half-covered by a hat pulled low and a coat-collar raised high. All the same, I recognized my father.

"Hey." I smiled.

In return for my smile, I got back a curled lip and a grunt. Dad's eyes raked me up and down a couple times—disrespectful, and as far as I could see, without knowing me.

"What you want, girlie?" he asked harshly. "You sure as hell ain't what I thought you was."

I stopped smiling. "What did you think I was?" I asked him back. "Who do you think I am?"

Dad said what he thought I was. The word he used didn't flatter me.

Getting red—I could feel it— I said, "Guess again. You used to know me pretty well."

"Don't play games."

"It's not a game. I thought you'd recognize me."

My dad turned away, back toward the narrow passage. "Never saw you before," he muttered.

I grabbed his arm, angry. "You know me," I insisted. "You've known me ever since I was born."

The word "born" finally got his attention. He pushed me—rough—out into the street where the light was better, and studied my face hard, and not like he was pleased to see it.

In a way, the last thing I would have wanted right then was for him to hug me. He smelled bad, and where a little rain had dripped onto his face through a hole in his hat, it had left a trail of clean. But in another way, I wished he *would* hug me, just because when we got to this place in my daydreams, he always did. I could wash up again later, I told myself.

He didn't hug me, though. Straightening up, he said, "You're...Clara, I reckon. That's right, ain't it? Clara. Something like that. What do you want?"

I told myself this was a reasonable mistake for a man to make. Men never care about things like names. "Claire," I corrected him. "It's Claire."

"What do you want, *Claire*, then. Not money." My dad looked me up and down again. "You're the one's got money."

"No, not money. I just want to see you."

"So—you seen me." With something like a laugh—but not a real laugh—Dad turned away again.

"And to talk to you." I started after him. "I need to talk to you."

He didn't look back, and only stopped when I grabbed his arm and held it. "Talk then," he growled. "Make it quick."

"It's about Mother. I need to talk to you about Mother. What happened to her?"

"Your mother?"

"Of course mine," I said impatiently. "Whose do you think?"

From somewhere not too nearby, I suddenly felt a mind make contact with mine.

Dad hesitated. Then he asked, uncertain, "She died or something, didn't she? Ain't that it? She died."

My anger was getting bigger. I said, "You told me she ran away. You said she wanted to be with another man."

He seemed relieved to be reminded.

"That's it," he agreed. "She run off. With...another man, like you said."

112

"Where'd they go?"

A minute before, he hadn't remembered anything. Now Dad started getting into the story. "I dunno where. I went after 'em, but they'd covered their tracks and I couldn't find 'em. Only then I finally did find 'em, and I threatened to blow his brains out, see?" Dad talked faster. "Yeah, and I'd a done it, only there was people around. But the bastard got his own back on me. He got his own back. He was a officer, and he told the story to all his officer friends, and after that, I never could get on no good ships. That's why I'm a poor man. I never got on no good ships because of him and his stories."

Without warning, the moment Rose had warned me would someday come was suddenly on me. She'd said one day I'd remember the whole night my mother died. Now I did. I saw it through my own eyes and hers. I looked through my mother's eyes at my father's face. His arm was around her neck, which he pressed with the dull side of his knife. It was a warning. It was a warning, but it filled my mother with fury. My mother's fury was my fury. My mother's cry of, *"If you so much as touch Claire, I'll tell!"* was my cry. *"I'll tell!"* she repeated. *"You know I will!"* and then both my mother and me felt it when Dad's arm stiffened around her, and the knife—the blade this time—raked across her throat. We felt a moment's panic and then an instant's pain as the blade penetrated. Then the rage, the panic, the pain, all faded into emptiness. I was alone in my own bed again, cowering under blankets still warm from my mother's body, and I was empty. I felt for my mother's mind and couldn't find it. For the first time in my life, she had gone beyond the reach of my silent cries.

In the present again, I was calm. Dead calm.

"You're the cheat," I said quietly. "You're a cheat, and a liar. She didn't run off. You killed her."

"You don't know nothing about it," Dad said, his eyes shifting to one side. "You was sleeping." He shoved me farther into the street, away from him, and for the third time, started toward the narrow passage. This time, he moved quickly.

"I know *everything* about it," I called after him. "You choked her and then you cut her throat. I saw you do it."

The mental "voice" I'd heard earlier was stronger and nearer. I wasn't alone, but Dad didn't know it. That made me bold. I repeated, hot as flame, *"I saw you!"*

Dad whirled and came at me, hands raised. I didn't have time to run. His dirty left hand closed on my shirt front, and his dirty right arm circled my neck, turning me around. He held on to me the same way he'd held on to my mother and then he dragged me one step, two steps, toward the dark passage.

At the third step, I started to struggle. His arm seemed strong and heavy as a band of steel, and I couldn't get it off my neck. I reached up my hand and scratched his cheek with my nails, and when Dad turned his head away to avoid my nails, I grabbed a handful of his greasy hair and pulled with all my strength. Some came out in my hand. I pulled harder. His arm tightened around my neck until I could hardly breathe, while his hand let go of my shirt and fumbled at his pocket. I guessed that was where he kept his knife, and I fought harder. I had a knife too, I remembered. I tried to reach it.

"Hang on, Claire! I'm coming!" the silent voice urged me. It was Shy's, of course.

At the same time, from somewhere closer by, a different voice shouted aloud. "Hey! You there! Stop!"

Still holding me, my mother's murderer kept moving toward the passage. I let myself go limp and made him drag me.

There were footsteps behind me. A man's voice—the one I'd heard shout— demanded, "What's going on?"

"Daughter," my dad said, short. "Takin' 'er home."

I stopped reaching for my knife. If the stranger saw knives, he might think his best choice was to leave quick. I tried to speak, instead.

"Murder!" I tried to say. "Murderer!" My voice came out a hoarse whisper.

Dad pulled me harder. The tip of his knife pricked the skin of my back. He was hiding his weapon between our bodies. He wasn't ready to kill me—not in front of a witness—but he wanted me to know he meant business.

Shy said again for me to hold on, only now her voice was close—almost beside me. She could see my dad now. She could see the stranger-man, who hadn't left but was afraid to come closer. Then she was in front of me, her own knife in her hand.

Dad half let me go to lunge at Shy. I gave him what I'd give the bandit on the trail—punches, kicks and head-butts. They weren't as strong as what I'd done to the bandit. I was weak from being choked so long. I couldn't see right, or keep steady on my feet. But I did the best—or rather, the worst—I could.

When Dad came after her, Shy jumped away nimble as a cat, then came right back for him again as soon as he moved toward me. It was like a dance, and they did the step twice or three times before my dad figured out that *my body* was his best protection from Shy. He pulled me against him and put his knife to my neck this time. He didn't care who saw it now. He pricked me, and blood ran down, and I froze—just like he wanted.

Shy dropped her knife—threw it down, is more like—and pulled out something else from her jacket pocket. She pointed the thing at my dad.

I'd never seen nothing like what Shy had in her hand. It was gun-shaped—but not a gun. It was metal—but not gun-metal. It had a gun-barrel—only not. At sight of it, my dad jerked me back so hard it felt like he would break my neck.

He started to say something, but before he could finish, the world went pure white.

Next thing I knew, I was on the ground. Shy was trying to pull me up, but my bones had turned to water. I felt sick, like I might spew.

"Come on! Come on!" Shy kept saying. "We've got to get out of here!"

Dazed, I looked around. My dad was lying behind me, sprawled out on his back like he was drunk or asleep, his eyes closed.

"What happened?" I asked. I sounded sleepy.

All Shy would say back was, "Come on!"

The stranger was still nearby, and now that my dad was down, he came forward to help. Between them, Shy and him got me on my feet.

"Thanks," I whispered. "Thanks."

With a snort like a hog, my dad came back to life. He rolled onto his side, his hands grabbing for me. He caught my ankle. Shy kicked him off. He grabbed again. Another kick. When he came at me the third time, Shy pointed the thing in her hand at him and the world went white again, only not as white as before, and I stayed conscious this time. Then there was black smoke and a smell like burning, and when I looked, my dad was sprawled out on his back again, and his face and neck were burned black to the bone.

The three of us—me, Shy and the stranger—stood where we were and just stared. There wasn't any question my dad was dead. Half his head was—gone. Just burned up and gone.

Then Shy said, "Come on!" again, and pulled me by my arm. I could walk now, though not steady. The two of us ran away, Shy snatching up her knife as we passed it, and left the stranger standing where he was, staring at the smoking meat of what used to be a man and muttering unintelligible to himself.

I paid no mind to where Shy was taking me until I realized she was helping me down into the trig little dinghy I'd seen earlier. There was a fellow in the dinghy already—a youngish man, dressed like a sailor. As Shy settled me on a thwart, he cast off and steered for the harbor's mouth. I turned to lay against Shy, my head buried in her jacket, and cried.

*

I didn't cry for long. There wasn't time for crying. The dinghy took us to the *River*, moored outside the harbor because she was too big to come in. Brand new, only barely commissioned, *River* was the prettiest ship I'd ever seen. Long, low, and sleek as an arrow, just riding at anchor she looked like she was making twenty knots.

I raised my head at sight of her, tears still pouring out of my eyes, and asked, "How?"

Shy told me the plan Captain Loyal had made at the inn, while he was standing in the hall looking fierce and drumming his fingers, had been to radio—somebody; Shy didn't know who—to send a ship to come and be ready to go after the looters if they escaped the harbor town shipboard themselves.

"The looters cast off this morning," Shy said. "The captain asked for the

Muriel or the *Anna* to come, but *River* was closer. She's his new command anyway, so it just made sense to send her."

"Ten thousand gods," I murmured—the first time in my life I'd ever said a thing like that in a religious way.

I asked about Izzy. Not aboard yet, Shy said, but on her way. "We need to get out of here as fast as we can," she said. "I'll take you to sick bay."

Sick bay was empty. Dr. Masterson wasn't aboard yet, either. Shy helped me to lie down on a sort of table there and covered me up with blankets. I was colder than I'd ever been in my life, I think, and my whole body hurt.

I lay with my eyes closed and let Shy mentally fuss about what she should do for me; whether she should help me sit up, or let me lie down; get me water—pillows—soup—anything—or let me just be. I didn't know myself what I wanted, so I couldn't help her decide.

Finally I asked, "What did you do to him?"

Shy's brain froze up for a few seconds. Then she said, "He was going to kill you, Claire. You didn't see him—the look in his eyes. I had to do—what I did. I had to. I'm sorry."

"Don't be. What was the white fire, though? That's what you shot him with, wasn't it? White fire."

Shy said it was energy. She'd shot my…mother's murderer—I wouldn't let myself think of him as my dad—with an energy weapon. "Valiant—the man in the boat—was showing it to me when I heard you call. I just grabbed it and ran, and sent Valiant for help."

"Is it Ancient?"

"Well, made from Ancient plans, anyway. It can be used just to stun someone. That's what I meant to do. Just stun him, like I did the first time. I never meant to kill him. I'm so sorry, Claire!"

Shy read in my mind that I wasn't sorry at all, but didn't seem shocked. She was getting used to me.

Dr. Masterson came in a minute later, kind and concerned as always. Dan and Isabelle were on their way, he told me. He'd hurried because he wanted to get to me first and make sure I was fit for how Izzy was going to act when she saw me, which was totally hysterical. She'd expected me back at the inn hours ago and was absolutely sure now that pirates had got me. Nothing Dan or the captain said could make her believe anything else. The doctor examined my neck very gentle and told me I'd have to stay in sick bay where he could keep an eye on me for at least a day or two.

"He must have been an animal," he muttered, turning my chin this way and that. "Only an animal would do something like this."

The doctor cleaned and bandaged the cut on my neck and then made me a sort of soft collar to wear that held my head still so's my neck didn't hurt so much. Then he fixed me up a bed and helped me into it, with pillows under other places that ached. Finally, he gave me something to drink that made me miss knowing when the *River* got underway an hour or two later. I was sorry not to have been on deck to see us turn for the open sea, but sleeping like I did made everything that had come before seem like a dream and easier to bear.

When I woke up, I found the apple I'd bought Isabelle in Harbor Town sitting on my chest. Izzy'd found it in my jacket pocket, but instead of eating it herself, she'd saved it for me to have. It was the whole apple, too, aside from just one or two little bites she hadn't been able to resist taking, and it gave me back my faith that there was still goodness in the world.

CHAPTER ELEVEN

I stayed in sick bay for our first two days at sea, but Dan and Izzy were there with me, so I wasn't lonely. The doctor made Izzy a collar like mine. She didn't need it, but Izzy always liked to have whatever I had. Shy visited as often as she could, but she was a sailor, and the *River* was short of crew, so she got put straight to work.

On one visit, she told me her normal ship was the *Anna*. "Or rather—*Phantom*, or whatever they might be calling her now," she added, smiling. "She's always the *Anna* to us, but she gets new paint and a new name every year or so. She was black and yellow when I left her. I wonder if she's another color now?"

"Why a new name? Are you trying to find a lucky one?" Sailors always want a lucky ship, luck being their best protection against storms and pirates.

But Shy said no and repeated that to Foresters, the ship was always *Anna*. "We change her appearance from time to time because she's a scout ship. It's better to scout anonymously."

"So you mean she's a spy ship."

Shy stuck with the word "scout."

Shy was proud and happy to be calling *River* "her" ship for now, but said she'd be just as happy to get back to her berth on the *Anna*. *Anna* was a former trader the Forests had bought and overhauled, but though she was solid, she wasn't at all flashy like the *River* was. An unflashy ship slipping in and out of ports unnoticed matched Shy's natural style.

Shy said right after Izzy and me saw them, the men in the room at Rick's had scattered like leaves. Luckily, before they could get entirely away, Captain Loyal'd showed people the pictures me and him'd drawn, and offered a reward for information. Money'll get you anything. Within a few days, he got news several of the men'd been seen in a smaller port. They were picked up, but Long-nose wasn't with them. Long-nose'd left Harbor Town in a different direction, horseback, and disappeared.

The day after the *River* sailed, Shy said a Forest "informant"—meaning spy—spotted him in Coast-town boarding a trader.

My heart jumped when she said the trader's name. It was the *Bee*.

"It's just a matter of time now," Dan said from where he was lying in a bed near me. "The *River's* faster than the *Bee* and better captained." *River's* captain was Dan's uncle, of course, so no wonder he thought that.

Next day, Dan was allowed to get up, and the day after, I was. Dan only got a berth in the crew quarters, but Izzy and me had our own cabin, like officers. I liked that.

I met Wise in a passage. He took my hands but didn't have time to say more to me than just that he was sorry about my dad before he had to hurry away again. He was Mr. Wise to me now, the *River's* first officer, and nobody's busier on a ship than the first officer. I was glad, really. I didn't want to talk about my dad anyway.

The second officer, a youngish Man named Mr. Toby, mistook me for one of his new recruits the first time he saw me, and barked at me for looking slack. He apologized to me for it later, but to be honest, I was kind of proud of the scolding. Nobody'd ever took me for a sailor before. After it, I tried to stand straighter, look livelier, and generally live up better to Forest Navy standards, so as to deserve the compliment.

Besides Shy, Izzy and me, there was only one other telepath on the *River*. His name was Seal, and he was Dan's age.

Dan was very grouchy about Seal—not because he didn't like Seal, but because he wanted to *be* Seal and couldn't. Dan wanted more than anything in the world to be a radio-operator on a ship. His mom wouldn't hear of it.

"I don't get it," he sighed. "Father's lived on Annasland all his life and never had any adventures, and he lets me do anything. By the time my mother was my age, she'd done all kinds of crazy things, but she wouldn't even have let me go to the continent if Uncle Loyal hadn't promised to have me safe in Evergreen in a week."

When I asked what his mom had got up to, Dan told me she'd been radio-operator on the first ship that made it from the continent to Annasland.

"They didn't even have a chart!" he said.

I'd sailed off once with nothing but a biscuit tin, but didn't mention it. "What else?"

"Well, they landed at just about every island they passed without knowing what was on them. At one place my uncle was almost killed by Ants."

"Your uncle was on the voyage, too?"

"Mother's uncle. My great uncle. Then their radio broke, and they kept going anyway."

"Her uncle looked after your mom though, right?"

Dan's gloomy scowl turned into a wicked grin. "About as much as mine looks after me. When I radioed Mother to tell her I wasn't in Evergreen, she said she'd tear Uncle Loyal in half the next time she saw him." He added, "She's really got only herself to blame. Everybody's always said her Uncle River and my Uncle Loyal are two of a kind."

The name "River" caught my ear, naturally. I asked, and it turned out Dan's Great Uncle River was the same River as Sarah's husband and Laura and Robin's dad. He was also—somehow—Captain Loyal's uncle. I couldn't see how, but that's what Dan said.

If that wasn't enough to tell me maybe the *River* was a bad place to hide from Sarah Farmer, five minutes later I turned a corner and there was Sarah's friend Timmy, the ugly sailor, coming down the passageway right toward me. He wasn't "Timmy" on the *River*, though. He was "Mr. Burns," and the chief engineer. I ducked away quick before he spotted me.

I'd been on the *River* almost a week before I saw Captain Loyal, but at sight of me he left what he was doing to hurry over with both his hands out. Looking at my neck, where the bruises were starting to turn green, he said, sincere, "Claire, I am so sorry."

As I said before, I didn't want to talk about it. "Is Shy in trouble?" I asked. "She thinks she is."

"Trouble?"

"About that weapon."

Captain Loyal made a face but said she wasn't. He said word about the weapon was bound to get out sooner or later anyway. Then he asked what I thought of the *River*. Looking proud, he said, "Her trials had to be cut short, but—"

He didn't have time to finish the sentence. At that moment, Mr. Toby stuck his head down a hatch and waved a spyglass at him. "Sir! A ship!" Mr. Toby said, breathless.

There was only one ship on the water could make Mr. Toby as excited as he was, and me and the captain both knew what ship it was. We asked together, "The *Bee*?"

"I think so."

I let out a whoop. The *Bee* was in sight, and the chase was on.

CHAPTER TWELVE

I'd believed before that the *River* was moving about as fast as any ship could move without flying to pieces. Now I saw she'd really been just loafing along. There wasn't nothing sneaky about our approach to the *Bee*. Captain Loyal made straight for her. We only slowed for a minute because we had to when the *River* switched from running on her batteries to her engines. Once her engines was engaged, she was faster than ever.

Even at her top speed, though, it was going to take some time to catch the *Bee*. *Bee* was fast, too. Also, *Bee* had the advantage that all she had to do was sail where she wanted until we engaged her, while *River* would have to keep maneuvering for position. Shooting at *Bee* from behind wouldn't allow the *River* to use any weapon but her bow cannon, and—barring a lucky hit, of course—bow cannon would never stop her. Battle stations was called, but my station was just my cabin, and anyway, I reckoned we still had an hour of straight chase before things got interesting.

To pass the time, I went back to teaching Izzy to sew, keeping one ear cocked meanwhile for signs we were getting close to a fight. Shy sent me mental reminders about the shortest route topside from my cabin and said if the *River* foundered, our longboat would be the aft one. A vision of waves—high ones—

and a sensation of pitching and tossing came along with the reminders. Shy was afraid.

The only thing *I* was afraid of was that I'd miss all the fun. There was going to be a sea-battle—a real one—and it looked like I was going to spend it teaching an Ant-child to sew. The gun deck was just above me. I could hear the guns being got ready. There were shouts from below, and someone passed my cabin door running. The ship's intercom asked—again—for status updates from all sections. Shy's thoughts, and Seal's when I could understand them (I still hadn't learned to read Seal real well), were mental checks and rechecks of duties and equipment mixed with hopes they'd be heroic, or at least not mess up too bad. I might have had some hero dreams myself if I could have imagined any way I could save the ship by teaching Izzy to sew.

More orders barked out, more running footsteps, more rumbling of guns being positioned... I paced the cabin. It was six steps one way and five the other and walking it didn't calm me much. Passing the porthole, I caught a glimpse of the *Bee* far ahead to starboard.

Eventually, Shy's mind told me to take Isabelle and shelter with her in the compartment across the passage. "You'll be safer nearer the center of the ship."

I didn't want to go. I wouldn't be able to see a thing from an inside compartment. But for Izzy's sake I did what Shy said. Izzy didn't mind the change. Once I'd sat her comfortable on a blanket, she went straight back to sewing, laying every stitch as exact as she could. Sewing was work, so naturally she loved doing it.

The ship got quiet. Everybody was ready for action.

But action was still a ways off. I tried pacing again. Still no help.

After a time, it came to me that while I'd been told to *go* to a central compartment, nobody'd ordered me to *stay* there. In fact, nobody could *order* me to do anything. I wasn't under orders. Dan was not far away in the aft crew quarters. I thought if I moved quick enough, I could pay him a short visit and get back before Izzy even knew I'd gone.

The passage outside was empty. Everybody else was at stations. There was a ladder to the bridge nearby. I decided I'd sneak up it and have a peek at what the captain was doing before I went aft to see Dan.

Though I tried not to think this plan clear enough to be read, Shy's mental voice slapped me down with a firm, "No."

"Nobody'll see me," I promised. "I'll be very sneaky."

"You'll get in trouble. You have no idea how much trouble you'll get in."

"Just one quick look. I swear."

Luckily for me, Shy was too busy to keep arguing.

The bridge might've been designed for sneaking into. The ladder to it came up through a narrow, dark well at the back. I crept up as high as the ladder's third step, where I could see most of what was going on but duck back down quick if anybody turned my way.

Captain Loyal was ten steps in front of me, leaning forward on a table but staring straight ahead at the *Bee*. His fingers was drumming. Mr. Wise was beside him, and Valiant and two other crew members was bustling about taking messages from other parts of the ship and monitoring dials and gauges and what-not. Everybody was calm, and nobody talked except just a word now and then in Forester. No one looked my direction.

I went one step higher on the ladder. I wanted to see what the captain saw. One step wasn't enough, so I went up another.

"Gun ports opening," Mr. Wise said, quiet.

He meant the *Bee's* gunports. Still no sound from the *River's*.

"What do you think, Captain?" Mr. Wise asked a minute later. "Port or starboard?"

The gesture he made told me he meant to be asking if the *River* should come up on the *Bee's* left or right sides.

The captain straightened and put a spyglass to his eye. "Port, I think. Not yet."

Then he said, "Damn. There she goes." Despite the swear, he was still perfectly calm.

The *Bee* had made her move. She was veering to starboard.

River moved to head her off. "Closer," the captain ordered. "Ignore her guns on the first pass. Clear her deck."

This order told me the *River* was going to try to take the *Bee* rather than sink her. A quiver of fear came again from Shy, who of course had "heard" the captain through me. I wasn't scared at all.

We were sailing through the *Bee's* smoke now. We were that close. But the *Bee* had some reserves the captain had evidently not reckoned on and was pulling away from us. It was just by a little, but even that much was bad. Where we were, we might hit her with a few shots from our bow guns—if the gunners was good enough—but we'd never catch or sink her.

The *River's* gunports were opening now, too.

Captain Loyal leaned on his hands again, and drummed his fingers faster.

When the ports were all open, he straightened up and said, short, "Flank speed."

Now, in case anybody don't already know it, "flank speed" is all the speed a ship's got in her, and it ain't ever ordered casual, being somewhat hard on the engines and other parts of a vessel. In fact, as the *River* surged forward, I was almost shook back down the ladder by vibrations from the engine. Ahead, the *Bee* turned stronger to starboard, putting more distance between herself and us. Not for long, though. The *River* started gaining on her again.

A few minutes more, and we were looking straight down the *Bee's* starboard side. I counted her gun ports. Two less than the *River's*. By now I could make out the men behind her aft swivel-guns, which were turning our way. I automatically braced myself.

Captain Loyal started to say something, but before the words could leave his mouth, the *River's* port engine let out first a bang, and then some other noises that weren't normal for it, and the whole ship shuddered.

Every ship's station called in at once.

Timmy—that is, Chief Engineer Burns—was the only member of the *River's* crew who talked like I did—ignorant—and always in Valley-speak. I picked out his voice from all the others.

"Got a problem here, Cap'n," he shouted over a lot of background noises. "We're shutting down."

Everybody on the bridge burst out with something, mostly curses, so loud nobody heard me yell, "Shutting down? What's he talking about? We can't shut down!"

That is, nobody heard but Shy, who told me again to get back to my cabin as fast as I could.

Captain Loyal, calm as before, ordered that the *River* not be turned an inch from her present course. "How fast are we losing way?" He leaned over the intercom, "What's our situation, Burns?"

"Can't we go to batteries?" I cried. I was all the way up the ladder now, one foot on the bridge. All right, both feet. "They're getting away!"

All heads except the captain's turned toward me, but nobody answered me because they were too busy listening to Timmy say, "Got a small fire here. Think we can have it under control pretty quick, though."

"Batteries!" I repeated. "Can't we go to batteries?" I pointed ahead, frantic, at where the *Bee* was leaving us behind. "Look! We're losing her! Dammit, we're losing the damn *Bee*!" I was mad enough to spit, but didn't.

Shy's friend Valiant said to me, very flat, "Did you somehow miss hearing that there's a fire in the engine room?"

"But just a small one!" I cried. "And Timmy said it was almost under control anyway."

No answer from Valiant—or from anyone.

Captain Loyal's back was still to me, but he wasn't drumming his fingers anymore. From the line of his back, I knew I should have taken Shy's advice to go back to my cabin.

After a silence that lasted about a week, the captain finally straightened up, turned to me, and said, very quiet, "Dunn, what the hell are you doing on my bridge?"

His voice was so cold it almost frosted the windows.

I didn't have anything smart to say. The bridge was his, no question. I mumbled, "Sorry, sir."

I was below the captain's dignity to deal with. He turned away from me like he would have from a maggoty corpse and left it to Mr. Wise to yell at me to "get out of here *right now,* dammit!" adding, "I'll have more to say to you later, Dunn!"

I was sure he would.

*

All the way back to my cabin, Shy scolded me. She said didn't know any reason I wouldn't be put ashore at the first port we came to.

"You aren't even supposed to be on this ship!" she lectured. "*River's* not a passenger ship! You're only aboard on sufferance! The least you could do is behave!"

I was suffering, all right. I'd been reprimanded—public—by the captain for invading the bridge, and cursed out by the first mate. I was suffering a *lot.*

Back in my cabin—me and Izzy's cabin—I stared for an hour out the porthole while Izzy went on turning her sewing into a bag for her beads. She was very proud of her work and confused about why I wasn't excited about it, too. That's the trouble with a telepath. No matter how much you try to make your mouth smile and say the right things, they know if you really don't care.

I was still watching out the porthole when the *Muriel* arrived, come to protect us. By staying on course and pretending we were still in the chase while we were really shutting down and stopping, Captain Loyal had fooled the *Bee* into sailing away, but there was no saying she wouldn't circle back to attack us again once she got wise to the trick. More hours went by, and Izzy and me sat alone; nobody but each other for company, and nothing but trips to the toilet for entertainment. I didn't hear from Shy, who was busy and also too mad at me to want to chat—which was mostly a relief.

At dinnertime, Seal brought us food.

He said the problem with the engine hadn't been too bad and was mostly fixed already, but Captain Loyal had ordered a going-over of all the ship's systems that hadn't been checked out thorough before the *River* sailed. The *Muriel* was leaving us, going after the *Bee* in *River's* place, but two smaller ships were on their way to watch over us for the night.

Near Izzy's bedtime, Dan came to visit. By then I'd talked myself into thinking that what I'd done by going onto the bridge wasn't as serious as Shy was making it out to be. I wasn't technically allowed to be on the bridge, sure; but since coming aboard I'd gone a few other places on the *River* I wasn't technically supposed to, and nobody'd appeared to mind much. As for the things I'd said, they were only meant as friendly advice. There was no harm in giving friendly advice even when it was ignorant and offered at a bad time, like mine'd been.

When I said as much to Dan, though, he just looked at me.

"You went on the bridge," he pointed out.

"Only for a minute!"

"During a battle."

"Well, how was I supposed to know I shouldn't?" I'd known perfectly well that I shouldn't. "All I did was look. Looking don't hurt. And anyway, the battle hadn't started yet."

"Claire—" Then, with a sigh that reminded me of his Uncle Loyal, Dan said, "It's not my place to lecture you, so I won't. Don't lie to yourself, though. You're in big trouble."

I looked at Dan's face careful, hoping to see some little sign he was joking. There wasn't any. "Will I get thrown off the ship? Shy thinks I might."

"Depends on whether Uncle feels like putting into a port to drop you off." Dan crossed his arms. "Look: I've got some advice for you. When you're called before Mr. Wise—it'll probably be him, though it might be Mr. Toby—don't make any excuses for what you did. In fact, don't say anything at all except 'yes, sir,' and 'no, sir.' And say them like you mean them. Otherwise, you might find out what it's like to be marooned."

*

I didn't sleep that night for worrying about being marooned, so I was wide awake to hear it when, near dawn, the *River's* engines started up again. They sounded like they had before the chase, smooth and powerful, and before long, we were moving. I got up, washed and dressed myself extra careful, and as soon as I knew she was awake, asked Shy if she couldn't please take Izzy to breakfast for me. I wasn't ready to face the *River's* crew in the galley.

Shy said, "No."

She said being embarrassed was only what I deserved, and she wasn't in any way minded to help me out of it. When I pleaded, she added, very fierce, that she wouldn't help me even for Isabelle's sake, and that I ought to be ashamed for even asking.

Then she gave in and came after all.

At the cabin door, just as she and Izzy were ready to go out, Shy turned back to hiss at me that if I *ever*—today, or at *any* time—tried to get out of trouble by crying, she'd never speak to me again. "I mean it," she scolded, her face all patchy red with pure rage. "When you're called before Mr. Wise, don't you dare let out one single tear! Whatever he says, you just stand up before him with your back straight and strong, and you *take* it! Take it like a— Take it like a *Forester*! You hear me?"

Then, before I could even start to answer, Shy stomped off, pulling Izzy after her. From the passage, her mental voice came back, "Oh, why do I even bother? She never listens to me anyway."

The door had hardly shut behind Shy and Isabelle before a sailor came to tell me I was wanted in Mr. Wise's cabin.

Mr. Wise spent the first whole minute of our meeting looking me up and down like I was something unappetizing that had washed up on the deck. I took it. I took it the way Shy'd told me to, standing in front of Mr. Wise's desk on the exact spot where the sailor had put me, my back straight and strong as Shy's principles. It wasn't easy, because what I really wanted to do was curl up and hide in a cupboard.

"So, Dunn," Mr. Wise finally said.

I answered, "Yes, sir," exactly the way Dan had told me to. I sounded miserable because I *was* miserable, but I did not cry.

The long breath Mr. Wise drew after that told me the lecture I was about to get would not be short.

He began, "Dunn, I was witness yesterday to a display of bad manners, indiscipline, and self-importance such as I have seldom witnessed before in all my years at sea. Do you know to what I'm referring? I believe you do."

"Yes, sir."

"I refer to your behavior, Dunn."

"Yes, sir."

Mr. Wise sat forward and folded his hands.

He asked me if it was possible I didn't know the bridge of a ship was off-limits at all times to crew unless summoned, and absolutely sacrosanct during action. Once Shy—who was listening in, of course—told me what "sacrosanct" meant, I answered him honestly, "Yes, sir."

From Mr. Wise's expression, I thought this might actually have been the wrong answer, so I changed it first to "No, sir," and then to "I knew I shouldn't be there, sir," which finally seemed to satisfy him.

"You knew you shouldn't be there, and yet—there you were!"

"Yes, sir."

"You wanted to be there, and you had not the self-discipline to stay away. Would you say that explanation answers the facts?"

"Yes, sir." My back had sagged a little. I straightened it quick.

Mr. Wise explained what he meant by self-discipline, and then asked, "Are you *capable* of self-discipline, Dunn? Are you capable of accepting any discipline at *all*?"

"Yes, sir."

"Are you?"

I'll be honest. I'd already answered the question, and I was annoyed to have to answer it again. A couple bad thoughts about Mr. Wise crossed my mind.

But to prove I had self-discipline, I didn't speak them out loud. Instead I said, humble, "Yes, sir."

A pretty long speech followed this—one I had the feeling Mr. Wise might have given parts of before. The speech had lots in it about Self-Discipline, Responsibility, Duty, and Honor, and also things about regular Discipline, which was apparently different from self-discipline though I couldn't see exactly how. Shy said she'd explain it to me later. I'd failed at Humility, too, it looked like. I wasn't exactly sure what "humility" was even after Shy told me. It was true that I generally thought pretty well of myself, but on the other hand, so does everybody. However, keeping Dan's advice in mind, I didn't argue the point but only went on listening careful to everything Mr. Wise said, putting in "yes, sirs," and "no, sirs" where I thought they belonged.

I won't deny I got tears in my eyes now and again. A few of Mr. Wise's remarks hit tender spots. But only one or tear—maybe two—made it as far as my cheek, and I managed not to sniffle at all.

Mr. Wise ended by asking me if I thought I'd learned my lesson.

"Yes, sir." I almost added that I'd learned a *whole lot* of lessons, but thought better of it, and only repeated, "Yes, sir."

Mr. Wise nodded, and looked down at his desk for a minute.

"I'm inclined to be—lenient this time, Dunn," he said then. "You've been through a lot lately, I know." When he looked up again, his voice was *way* kinder. "How are you doing, Claire? Your neck looks better. How are your spirits?"

Until now, I'd been staring straight ahead. It helped with keeping from crying. Now I looked direct at Mr. Wise. To my relief, he didn't seem angry anymore.

"I'm alright." Dammit, my voice broke a little. I didn't want Shy to never speak to me again, so I pulled myself together. "You don't need to worry about me. My dad was never worth nothing anyway."

I stopped myself from saying more about that. No point, really.

"Are you going to maroon me, sir?" I asked instead.

Mr. Wise cleared his throat. "Not this time." Then, unexpected, he smiled, and asked, "Still want to be a sailor, Claire?"

I started to say, "Oh, yeah!" but then changed it to, "Yes, sir. More than ever, sir."

"There's a great deal of discipline involved in being a sailor."

"Yes, sir. I know there is."

"A sailor has to obey orders. Without delay. Without question."

"Yes, sir."

When Mr. Wise seemed like he was waiting for me to say more, I added,

"I like orders, mostly. If I'm obeying orders, I know I'm doing right and don't have to be afraid."

Mr. Wise leaned back in his chair and cocked his head a little. "Afraid of being wrong?" he asked. "Or afraid of being punished?"

"Of being punished, I guess. Although being wrong is really the worst punishment."

Mr. Wise smiled broader. "That's a good attitude. Stay here for a moment, Claire. I'll be right back."

He was gone longer than he'd said he'd be—probably ten or fifteen minutes altogether—which I spent listening to the *River's* engines. She was running steady, but not fast. We'd definitely lost the *Bee* and given up the pursuit. That wasn't my fault, but I almost felt like it was, and I told myself that if I wasn't put off the *River*, I'd behave better aboard her from now on.

Finally, Mr. Wise put his head in the door and motioned me to follow him. We went down the passage to the captain's cabin.

Captain Loyal looked tired. That was the first thing I noticed. Shy, who seemed confused about what was going on, told me not to mention it, so I straightened my back, squared my shoulders, and kept my mouth shut.

The captain ignored me and looked at Mr. Wise.

"You're satisfied, Mr. Wise?" he asked, distant.

"I am, sir."

"Completely satisfied?"

"Completely satisfied, sir."

I wondered if they always talked so formal to each other shipboard. On the trail, they'd been all first names and friendly backslaps.

Captain Loyal drummed his fingers a minute, staring off—it looked like to me—at nothing. Then he said, "Claire, I cannot have rogue passengers on my ship."

I felt no call to disagree with him. "No, sir."

"I must be able to trust in the discipline and good order of everyone aboard."

Gods. When Wise'd smiled, back in his office, I'd thought maybe I was in the clear. Now it looked like I might be going to get put off the ship after all.

"Yes, sir," I said. "I know you do. And I—"

"Yes?"

"Nothing, sir."

"Nothing?" The captain eyed me. "I was hoping to be reassured that I could trust you."

"You can trust me, sir," I said quick. "I just thought maybe it was too late for me to say so."

"It's never too late," Captain Loyal answered. Getting up, he began, "Claire Dunn—" and then stopped, and asked, milder, "'Claire Dunn' *is* your legal name, isn't it? It's not another alias?"

"Oh, yes, sir," I said quick. I almost added that I wouldn't lie to him about something as important as my name when I remembered that I had and shut up again.

"Claire Dunn, you once told me you wanted to be a sailor. Do you still?"

"Me?"

A curt nod from the captain.

"Yes I do, sir. More than anything in the world."

"Good enough." Captain Loyal nodded. "Give me your hands," he ordered, and held out his own.

I wiped mine quick on my shirt and took the captain's hands like he wanted me to, though I didn't know why.

"Claire Dunn," the captain said again, very formal, "do you freely and with due forethought offer yourself for service in the navy of the United Forests?"

I was so surprised I just stared. Shy's brain said, reverent, "Ten thousand gods."

The captain stared back at me, waiting.

"He's attempting to enlist you into the Forest Navy," Mr. Wise explained. "Say 'no' if you want. Technically, he's not allowed to use coercion."

"I'm not coercioned!"

"Say, 'I do,' then. There's a six-months probationary period, and you can change your mind at the end of it. Or we can."

"Saying 'I do' will make me a sailor?"

"No," Captain Loyal said. "An affirmative answer will only give you a *chance* at being a sailor. You won't *be* a sailor until you've proved yourself disciplined and able enough to perform the duties of a sailor." In his more normal voice, he added, "You have many admirable qualities, Claire, but so far, you haven't demonstrated a great deal of discipline."

"I want to have discipline," I cried. "I really want to. Let me try!"

"Then you consent to enlist?"

I suddenly realized the captain and me were still holding hands, which meant what I said was serious, and official. "Yes!" I gasped. "I do! I do! Is this for real?"

"It's real if anything in life is real," Captain Loyal said, "which is uncertain." He let my hands go then, adding, "The only certainty in life is paperwork, and to prove that, here are documents for you to sign. Welcome to the Forest Navy, Apprentice Seaman Dunn."

The papers were in both Forester and Valleyspeak, and my name was already on them in several places, which meant the captain must have planned to enlist me before Mr. Wise and me had our little talk. Mr. Wise made me read the papers over very careful before he would let me have a pen, and my hand shook as I signed them.

"Now, Dunn," the captain said, finally smiling a little. "You are a sailor, and must therefore obey all legitimate orders from a superior. Agreed?"

So that was why he wanted to enlist me. So's he could give me orders.

Funnily enough, I was completely fine with that. "Yes, sir!"

"Good. Then you will stay off the bridge of this or any other ship unless authorized to appear there."

"Yes, sir!"

"You will hereafter also stay out of establishments known to be of a dubious character. *Rick's* is such an establishment."

Mr. Wise put in, "When did an order ever keep a sailor out of Rick's, Loyal?"

"I can't go to Rick's?"

"Not while you're under my command."

"What if there's men upstairs that—"

"You will summon help."

"But if I—" My eye caught Mr. Wise's expression. "I mean, yes, sir."

"Additionally, under no circumstances will you risk your safety or your life unnecessarily. Your body is Ship's Property now, and you must take care of it."

"Yes, sir. How will I know what's unnecessary, though?"

"You will ask guidance of someone older and more experienced."

I'd gotten myself into kind of a lot of trouble once or twice relying on my own judgment, so I said, "yes, sir," to this, too.

Captain Loyal let out his breath. "Glad to have you aboard, Sailor," he said. "Now get to work!"

Mr. Wise took me to the galley then, but not to eat. He said, "Seal will show you what to do," and left me with Seal, who was so excited to have me show up his brain was, like, buzzing. Until now, Seal'd been the youngest and least experienced sailor aboard the *River*, and the youngest and least experienced sailor, he informed me, got the job of washing dishes.

"I'll show you how." He led me to the sink. The crew had just finished their breakfasts, and there was a mountain—a *mountain*—of dirty dishes piled around it.

"I know how to wash dishes," I said, feeling sour.

"No you don't," Seal informed me. "You think you do, but washing dishes aboard ship is different from doing it on land. Everything aboard ship has to be done a certain way."

The "certain way" to wash dishes shipboard, Seal told me, was mostly by scraping instead of sloshing. We were literally surrounded on all sides by water, but we had to conserve it.

"Am I—? I mean, is this punishment duty?" I asked Seal, glad he was a telepath so I didn't have to ask out loud.

"It is if you're not the newest, youngest crew-member," Seal said. "For you, it's just your regular duty. This is where everybody starts."

This was good news and also bad news. "Fine," I sighed. "Show me."

Before we could start, though, Shy and Izzy showed up, both of them so happy they could almost not think right. Shy, who'd been mad at me for two days, now loved me so much she hugged me, so of course, Izzy hugged me, too. Izzy hugged me several times, in fact, and then showed me her bead bag. She'd finished it with Shy helping, and it was honestly done better than if I'd done it myself.

As Shy settled Izzy down at a galley table to play while I worked, she said, "I can't imagine what the captain was thinking to reward your bad behavior like this. Promise you'll behave from now on, all right? You're on probation for the first six months. If you get in trouble again, you'll be out."

"I can be good." I rolled up my sleeves. "You'll see."

Shy had work to do, so she left, and Izzy played with her beads while Seal and me washed dishes ship-style. The job wasn't as bad as I'd thought it would be, except for the pots, which was awful. Pots had to be scraped first and then rubbed clean with sand before they were done with water, and if you haven't tried it yourself, you can take it from me that the feel of greasy sand is disgusting. There was never going to be any fun in washing pots. I hoped the *River* would recruit a new sailor very soon.

I was almost done with the washing-up when Dr. Masterson strolled in. He congratulated me on my promotion from civilian to sailor—sailors in general pity and despise anyone who isn't also a sailor—and put out his hands to me. I thought we were going to do the Forester hand-hold, cheek-press thing, but instead the doctor turned my hands over and looked close at the palms.

"I'm not sure your hands are up to this." He nodded at all the dishes and pots I'd washed. "I can have you assigned elsewhere, if you want—for medical reasons."

I can't describe the noise Seal's brain made when the doctor said this.

"No, I'm fine." I shot Seal a little grin. "They don't hurt."

For once, I seemed to have said the right thing. Dr. Masterson smiled.

As the doctor was turning to say hello to Seal and Isabelle, Mr. Burns walked in.

I should have expected it, I guess. Everybody on the ship was bound to walk into the galley sooner or later. I remembered that Timmy—I mean Mr. Burns—didn't know my face, and hoped he'd forgot my name by now, too, but he hadn't. When the doctor introduced me, Mr. Burns gave a start.

"Did you say Dunn?" He looked at me close. "I know the name of Dunn. What was the first name, again?"

I decided it was better to just say the truth than make him figure it out. "Claire," I admitted. "Sarah Farmer might've mentioned me to you."

Mr. Burns stared at me awhile, then crossed his arms and tapped his foot, very pointed. "Well, by all the gods then, *Claire Dunn*, you need to get yourself on the radio to Mrs. Sarah and tell her you're all right! She's been half out of her mind with worry about you!"

Sarah Farmer was kin to about half the ship's company through Annasland's Forest master Peregrine and Infirmarian Helen, who were her nephew-in-law and niece, and—as two-thirds owner of D&R—two-thirds everybody's boss, too. Everyone wanted to know at once why somebody as important as Sarah Farmer would be worried about me.

Talking about Sarah made me think about Sarah, and my time with her all came rushing back into my mind where Seal and Shy, wherever Shy was right then, could see it. Before Mr. Burns could say more, Seal announced to everyone that me and Mrs. Farmer was *very close*. Then Mr. Burns added something Seal didn't know (because I didn't know it myself), which was that after I left, Sarah'd looked everywhere for me.

"She got word about a certain dinghy being found empty on a beach, and guessed you must be dead," he said.

Everybody had lots of questions. Shy and Seal's brains shot theirs direct into my mind, while everybody else asked theirs aloud all at once.

I told the non-telepaths the least I could get away with—that Sarah'n me'd met in Fortress; that she'd been very kind to me; that I'd been unkind back by running away to be a sailor—and mentally sighed to know I couldn't stop Shy and Seal from knowing all the rest.

Just as everybody was settling all this in their minds and calming down, Dan came roaring into the galley, his face red as liver.

He was furious, and he came right for me.

"You're—you're *crew* now?" he demanded. "*You*? I'm not, but *you* are?"

I said I was and apologized for it.

"Well, I call that an outrage." He looked around indignant at everybody. "I'm of full age, I'm a trained radio-operator, and I've been trying to enlist for two years. I have also *never* been on *any* part of the ship where I wasn't invited to go. And *she* gets enlisted instead? I don't call that fair at all!"

"Dan, meet your cousin," Dr. Masterson answered, very mild. "We've just discovered that Claire is a dear friend of Sarah's. I think that entitles her to be called 'cousin,' don't you?"

Foresters call just about everybody "cousin" who isn't an actual enemy.

"What Sarah? My *Aunt* Sarah?"

"It's not my fault!" I cried. "I didn't know she was your aunt when I moved in with her! I don't even get how she *can* be your aunt, in fact. And you don't have to call me cousin, either."

Over the noise of Dan's complaining, which continued, Dr. Masterson told me aside that Sarah and Dan's grandmother Anna were sisters. After thinking, he changed that to "stepsisters;" and then to "foster sisters;" and then added, "so to speak," which I guessed meant they weren't really sisters at all but were just spoke of that way.

"You know, Dan," the doctor said then, "the ship could really use another radio-operator. Maybe you should mention it to your uncle."

This was a hint, of course. Dan didn't get it. "He knows," Dan said, bitter. "I already told him I'd help out."

The doctor rolled his eyes at me.

"Well, go back and tell him you won't," I said. "Tell him you won't unless you're enlisted."

"I don't need to be enlisted to help. I'm family."

"Family's no reason to take advantage of you."

"Sure it is."

I rolled my eyes back at the doctor.

"The *River*'s shorthanded," Dr. Masterson nudged again.

Dan finally started catching on. "That's true," he agreed, thoughtful. "She is."

"Best interests of the ship..." the doctor hinted stronger.

As quick as he'd burst into the galley, Dan burst back out.

"Remember to call him *Captain*," I called after him.

I had help that night washing the dinner dishes. As the newest member of the crew, Apprentice Radio-operator Daniel of Annasland was obliged to do a spell of scrubbing pots.

CHAPTER THIRTEEN

The *Muriel'd* lost the *Bee* soon after she took over the chase. Nobody on the *River* was surprised to hear that. *Bee'd* had a good head start on *Muriel* from the first. Besides that, when the *Muriel* started getting close, the pirates sailed fast and confident into waters the *Muriel's* captain didn't know.

The waters were thick with little islands, Shy told me.

"All right," I said. "But the *River's* still going after her, right?"

Shy said no. "We don't know those islands any better than Captain Richard does. There's no chart of those waters."

Like not having a stupid chart made a difference.

Actually, it probably did make a difference, but in my opinion, it shouldn't have. Not where pirates were concerned. Shy said the *River* would stay on patrol duty, and be ready to give chase when the *Bee* was spotted again.

Dan moved from the galley to the radio room after just a couple of days. His radio skills were more valuable to the ship than clean dishes. I stayed where I was but didn't mind it. I didn't get to love scrubbing pots, but washing dishes and mopping the galley were fine, and taking meals to crew at their stations was even enjoyable. I went all over the ship with trays of meals—even the bridge. I was allowed on the bridge if I was bringing food. I saw everything and talked to everybody, and for the first time in my life, I was welcome wherever I went. Nobody knew me now as a thief who took stuff. I was a shipmate who brought people food when they were hungry. They brightened up at sight of me, and I liked it. When I wasn't working in the galley, I had lessons from Mr. Toby in mathematics and nautical things, which was like being back in school except this time I didn't mind it.

At one of my lessons, I asked Mr. Toby when we were going after the *Bee* again.

"Those are bad people on that ship," I said. Though Mr. Toby knew Izzy, of course, I didn't know whether he knew what had happened to her mother, so I told him. "We've got to get them, and soon."

"We're *this close*, Claire," Mr. Toby told me, measuring about an inch with his fingers. "We just need *this* much more intelligence."

"And then we'll go after her?"

Mr. Toby promised—almost promised—that we would.

A few days later, Dan was on duty in the radio-room when a call came in from the *Phantom* saying a small vessel believed to be a smuggler was heading into the same islands the *Bee* was hid in. The small vessel wasn't being chased. That meant she had to have some reason of her own to go among the islands. We all thought—hoped—the reason *might* have something to do with the *Bee*, and that if it did, the small vessel *might* have a chart of the islands to navigate by. Dan overheard the chief radio operator and Mr. Toby wondering together whether it would be possible for a Forest ship to take the little ship and seize her charts.

"Mr. Toby thinks the reason nobody ever catches the *Bee* with a cargo is that she sends whatever she's smuggling to the continent on other ships," Dan told me. "He thinks they pick up their loads somewhere in the islands."

"What's out in the islands to smuggle?"

"Nobody knows. Nobody except pirates have been out there since ancient times."

I remembered about the steel that Long-nose'd been selling. "Is there a Forbidden Site out there? With steel?"

Dan said the steel was most likely from the continent. "When the small ship comes out, I think either the *River* or the *Muriel* might try to take her and see what she's carrying."

*

Just as I was getting into my bunk that night, the *River*, which had been holding to a moderate speed and a course generally southeast, suddenly sped up and swung north. Something was evidently up. I was out of my bunk at first light and in the galley early, where Jerry the cook was getting out the trays used to carry meals to stations.

"Got a feeling we might need these later," he told me—*and smiled.*

Two things about Jerry were that he hated mornings, and he loved excitement. A smile from him before noon could only mean one thing.

"We're heading into action, aren't we?" I asked, smiling back.

The news was better even than I was hoping for. We weren't on our way to stop the little pirate ship, Jerry told me. Another ship'd do that when she came out of the islands. Instead, we were back in pursuit of the *Bee* herself. The *River's* batteries had finally been proved to Tim Burns' total satisfaction, and he reckoned them the surest means of pulling the *Bee's* stinger.

A long time ago, the *Muriel* had been the first ship to use electricity for everything. Her engine had turned turbines that charged batteries, and then the batteries turned her screw. Her batteries'd also lit her lights and powered her pumps and a radio-signal strong enough to be heard half an ocean away.

Now, a few refits later, the *Muriel* had two engines and batteries so good most of her systems could operate for hours—even days—with both engines shut down. But she still couldn't sail long that way. Her screws drained her batteries fast. *Muriel* could only keep moving if she ran her engine every couple of hours, for eight or ten hours at a time, to recharge them.

The *River's* batteries, on the other hand, were a new kind; bigger and better than any other batteries anywhere. They could keep her moving for five or six hours at a time—or even more at low speed. The *Bee* needed to be snuck up on, but no ship could sneak with its boiler fired, because even the best fuel smoked and stank. Being able to run long distances on her batteries meant the *River* could approach an enemy clean and quiet. I was almost prouder of her sneakiness than anything else about her.

At dusk that day we passed the first island in the chain, and from then on, we only fired up the *River's* boiler when it was full dark and her smoke couldn't be seen. We ran every night that way, charging up our batteries, but after dawn, when our smoke began to show against the sky, we shut down the boiler and ran on batteries. We didn't go fast, but was it better, Captain Loyal said, to sail far than fast anyway. Having no chart, we took a zigzag course, scouting the islands along the way. In the early afternoons, when our batteries got low, we found someplace to anchor and waited for dark again. Once we'd stopped for the day, the dinghy was sent out with a few sailors in it to scout some more.

I only went in the dinghy once, but Shy went lots of times. She was learning to be a navigator and scouting and drawing maps of what she'd scouted was good training for her.

"All I know to do is wash dishes," I complained to Mr. Toby. "What do I need to know to be a scout?"

"Trigonometry," he said. He'd been nagging me to get started on trigonometry for weeks.

So, I said fine, I'd learn trigonometry, then.

Wasn't as hard as I'd expected.

Since we were in uncharted waters where there might be enemies, just about everybody had to eat at their stations sometimes, which meant I had to carry a lot of meals. A *lot* of meals. I learned pretty quick not to ask Izzy to help me. If Izzy saw food, she couldn't resist helping herself to some, and if the plates were empty, she was apt to lick the crumbs. But by now, as long as Isabelle could hear me or Shy and had something to sort or clean or polish to keep her busy—and there's always lots to sort and clean and polish on a ship—even if I had to leave her, she was happy.

That's how I left her one day: Happy, sorting spoons into one box and forks into another.

I came back to find her different.

I could hear Izzy yelling long before I got to her, making the special high-pitched call Ants do when they're excited. I found her topside at the rail, being held back by Shy and some other sailors while she pointed and shrieked. Even Shy, who was getting better and better at reading Izzy, couldn't entirely understand her, but I thought she was saying she wanted to go home. As I ran, I called with both with my mind and out loud, but Isabelle didn't seem to hear me.

"She went crazy all of a sudden," one of the sailors told me as I ran up. "What does she want? For a minute I thought she was going to jump overboard!"

Izzy'd gone full Ant; wild like she was when I first met her. Her thoughts were a jumble.

"Let me listen." I put my hands on my forehead. "Let me just listen."

I closed my eyes and took a deep breath, letting my own mind go blank so Izzy's could fill it.

My calm made Isabelle calmer. After a minute, she started to make sense—a little. She was thinking about home. She was thinking about her mother. She was thinking about…

"Gods," I breathed, opening my eyes. "Izzy, are you *sure*?"

Izzy was very, very sure.

"Who's got the bridge?" I asked the other sailors—but didn't wait to be answered. Dragging Isabelle behind me, I ran up the ladder and burst onto the bridge without even calling out first.

Mr. Wise was there. I cried, "Sir, the guns! Roll out the guns and get ready to fight! They're there!" I pointed ahead. "There's an island just ahead and the pirates are on it!"

"Dunn…" Mr. Wise said, like a warning.

By now I was as crazy as Isabelle. Maybe more. I ran to the helm and grabbed the steersman's arm—probably a court-martial offense. "Turn," I begged him. "Turn your course! Go *there*!"

Mr. Wise dragged me back, but he did it gentle. He spoke gentle, too. Insane people have to be humored. "Dunn— Claire— What's going on?"

"There's an island," I panted, pointing again. "Just ahead. It's Isabelle's. She can hear her people. We have to go there because the pirates are on it, and we have to fight them! The pirates are on it *right now*."

Mr. Wise looked down at Isabelle, and then he looked back at me. He looked hard.

Then he looked ahead again.

"Wait… wait," he said, thoughtful. He pointed out a different island from the one I'd pointed to—a small one to our port. "Make for that," he told the helmsman. "Get behind it."

"Not *that* island," I cried. "The one we want is ahead! The pirates are there, and we can fight them!" I stopped a minute to listen to Isabelle. "They're taking people again. They're taking women to their ship!"

"You can hear Isabelle's people?" Mr. Wise asked me.

"No, but Izzy can, and I hear Izzy. She says we have to go fight those men and stop them taking her people!"

Mr. Wise said, very calm, "Dunn, we're not going to fight anyone until we've had a chance to scout."

Isabelle was trembling all over. Me too. As Mr. Wise reached for the ship's intercom with one hand, he put his other arm around my shoulders. He held me like that while he talked to Mr. Burns, asking everything about the engine— how she was running; how much time we had left on batteries; how much time it would take to fire the boiler. The touch helped both Izzy and me, and when Mr. Wise turned to ask us how near we had to be to Isabelle's island for her to hear her people, Izzy was calm enough to answer. She didn't know how to reckon distances, but she agreed with me that if she could "hear" her people, we were probably close enough for the pirates to see our smoke if the *River* fired her boiler. I told Mr. Wise this, and he nodded.

Anyway—we didn't fire the boiler. We didn't go after the pirates. Isabelle and me weren't told why. I wanted to fight. Izzy wanted to fight. I think Timmy wanted to fight. I *know* Shy wanted to fight. But in the end, the *River* sailed behind the little island Mr. Wise had pointed out to the helmsman, and scouts were sent across to it with spyglasses to climb up a high place and see if they could make out what was happening on Isabelle's island from there. While they did that, me and Shy took Izzy herself down to the engine room where the ship's steel hull blocked out her people's voices, and let her rock herself back and forth and cry weird, high, Ant-style cries until she wore herself out and fell asleep on Timmy's lap. When the scouts came back, the *River* quietly moved out far enough to give Izzy peace.

"Those men'll get away," I told Shy, angry.

Shy said the captain knew what he was doing. I wasn't so sure. I kind of thought he was wrong, in fact; and when I gave him his dinner-tray that night, I told him so. I was polite, of course.

"Why are we here?" I asked. I hadn't waited to be invited to talk like I was supposed to, but I made sure to sound respectful. "Why aren't we at Isabelle's island getting those pirates?" Losing my temper just a little—I admit it—I added, *"How can you just let bad people hurt good people and not do anything about it?"* I got hold of myself. "I mean, not that it's my place to tell you what to do."

Captain Loyal looked at his dinner. "Boiled peas and biscuit again," was all he said, very bland.

"That's all we've got." I snapped. "Anyway, what does food matter? *Pirates* is what matters!"

"I heard you speaking to Mr. Burns earlier... How's our fuel situation?"

I didn't bother to answer about the fuel. Fuel was somebody else's business; not mine. I took a breath and tried wheedling. I'd seen wheedling work for other girls. "Shy says the pirate ship's small. She says the *River* could take her, easy."

"Like swatting a fly," Captain Loyal agreed. "How do *you* feel about peas and biscuit, Claire?"

So much for wheedling. In about another minute, I'd explode. "Like I'm so sick of them I never want to see any ever again. *Why aren't we going after the pirates?*"

"Because the *River's* not a fly-swatter," the captain answered. "Get out of here, Dunn. I have work to do."

He flicked his fingers at me, and I left his cabin so mad it took me a minute to realize that Shy's brain'd suddenly got much happier.

147

"We're shorter on food and fuel than I realized," her mind said to mine. "But the *Anna* or some other ship must be ready to take the small ship. It's probably the *Anna*. The captain would never refer to *Muriel* as a fly-swatter!" Then she added to Isabelle, who was waiting for me in the galley, "Don't worry, sweetie. Your friends will be home again in just a few days."

Captain Loyal'd told me everything I wanted to know. I just hadn't understood him.

*

A week—more—went by with no sign of the *Bee*. I knew if we didn't find her soon, we'd have to give up the search. In uncharted waters with a big, fast, and hostile ship somewhere around, we couldn't risk letting ourselves get too low on fuel. Even with Mr. Burns reading the fuel gauges all kinds of artistic ways to make our situation seem better, I figured it wouldn't be much longer before the captain'd say we had no choice but to go back the way we'd come. To stretch out the time we could stay, we kept to our system of running on fuel at night and batteries during the day, but also added every power-saving dodge we could think of, including stumbling around instead of lighting the ship after dark, and cold food. We got used to living in the dark. It wasn't no worse, the older sailors said, than what all ships used to be like all the time. But after a week of cold food, I'd have given about anything to eat even plain boiled peas again, as long as they were hot.

The thing was, there wasn't *one single word* of complaint from anybody on the ship about any of this. The *Bee* was close now. We could feel her. And if getting her meant putting up with a lot of stubbed toes and bad meals first, that was just how it was.

One night, in place of the dinghy, the longboat was readied to go out, and the sailors to crew it were armed like they expected trouble. Naturally, I wanted to know about any trouble, so when I heard the longboat come back, I sneaked up on the deck and made myself invisible in a shadow to listen in to the chatter of the returning sailors. They had good news. They'd scouted out an island somebody was visiting regular to dump garbage on. A moored ship that didn't want to be found would be careful not to dump her garbage overboard, since a trail of garbage riding a current would be like a finger pointing back to where it came from. Sailors—possibly the *Bee's* sailors—were getting rid of their waste on a nearby island instead.

Captain Loyal answered the sailors with some Forester words, which, since Shy was sleeping, I didn't understand. But there was no missing the hopefulness of his tone.

While the sailors stowed their gear and the longboat, the captain, Mr. Wise, and the ship's navigator talked quiet together for a minute. Dan was there, too, which surprised me. I hardly saw Dan lately, it seemed like. He was always in the radio room. Just as I was thinking I'd go to the radio room myself in the morning and get him to tell me what they'd all said, the captain suddenly raised his voice and called out, "Bed, Claire. It's late."

Damn the man! He had eyes like a cat.

*

I didn't have to go find Dan next morning. Dan found me first. He was all excited.

"We found the *Bee*!" he announced. "*I* found her! Me!"

"Were you in the longboat?" I was surprised, because I hadn't seen him there.

Dan laughed. "No. I've been tracking her radio signals." He explained to me about how a ship's radio can be tracked by another radio—a different kind of radio—and the ship can be located that way.

"You remember that ship at Izzy's island?" Dan asked me. "The *Clover*?"

"I didn't know her name."

"It was *Clover*. The *Anna* captured her just after the scouts came back last night. Or rather, the *Phantom* captured her, if you want to be picky. That was Uncle's plan all along—that the *Anna* would pick her up as soon as she cleared the islands."

Shy'd guessed right about the captain's "fly-swatter."

"But the good part—the *great* part—" Dan continued, "is that as soon

149

as *Clover* was hailed, she sent a message to the *Bee!*"

"You found the *Bee* by that?"

"No, we found the *Bee* by the *Bee's* message back to the *Clover*. The *Bee's* captain has been careful until now, but this time he took a chance and radioed the *Clover* back, and we traced it! *I* traced it!" Dan was so happy and proud of himself, he did a little dance. "The dinghy's going to be sent out to scout the way to her, and by this time tomorrow, the *Bee* may be ours!"

I danced too—but just a few steps. I'm no dancer, as anyone who's seen me will say.

Then I noticed Isabelle wasn't dancing with us. Since she usually tried to do anything Dan and me did, I looked closer. Her face was as blank as new paper.

Dan noticed, too. "Izzy—what?" he asked, putting out his hand to touch her shoulder. "Is something wrong?"

Before Dan could reach her, Isabelle spun away from him and grabbed me hard around the waist. At the same time, thoughts started pouring out of her mind. They came faster than I could read them.

The thoughts were a thousand years old, but they were new to me. They were things Izzy'd learned from the brains of other Ants on her island, who'd remembered them, generation after generation, all the way from the time of the Cataclysm. Izzy'd never known what the ideas meant before, but she'd suddenly got the idea they had something to do with the *Bee*.

I tried to explain Isabelle's thoughts to Dan. "Izzy says this is all just like before. It's like—" I stopped.

"Like what?" Dan urged. He was standing right beside me, but somehow he sounded far away.

"At first, they were kind," I said, my voice coming out flat, and slow. "We were friends. Then we weren't friends anymore. Then they started taking some of us away. The ones they took away never came back. We never saw them again."

"Who? The pirates? Were the pirates friends of Izzy's people?"

He didn't understand, but the right words to explain were hard for me to find. "No," I said. "I mean the Creators. The Creators were our friends."

Isabelle's thoughts ran like a river through my brain—buildings, animals, people. Lots of people. Izzy liked people. Her mind kind of lingered on the people. Happy scenes; sad ones. Quiet days—and then war. War, and war, and war. War was everywhere. The pictures from Izzy's mind went by so fast I couldn't remember most of them afterward, but one scene stayed with me, and still does: Against a background of fire and…death, two friends—I don't know how I knew they were friends—reached for each other, grasped hands, and lifted each other up. Then they turned and ran in opposite directions. One of the friends was an Ant and the other was a human, but I thought I could feel that they'd once cared about each other. But something had killed the trust between, and without trust, they couldn't love each other anymore.

Sounding uncertain, Dan said, "The Creators were a long time ago, Claire."

"Yes," I agreed. "But now it's happening again. They're taking some of us away. They say it's to work, but we don't believe them. It's like before. The ones they take we never see again."

"The pirates are taking people, you mean."

"The Creators, the pirates… It's all the same."

From Izzy's brain, I picked out an image of the place in the *Bee's* hold where she'd been held captive.

"Oh, gods, Dan," I whispered. "That's the connection! Steel's being looted and Ants are being kidnapped, and everybody thinks those are two separate things, but they're not! The pirates kidnap Ants and show them steel from the Forbidden Sites. Then they take the Ants to the Sites and send them in to get more steel like the kind they were shown. No one knows the Ants. No one's looking for them. They get sent in and told to get steel, and they do what they're told until they die. There was steel on the *Bee*. There'll be steel on the *Clover*. Tell the *Anna's* captain to look for it. There's steel on the *Clover* to train the Ants what to look for."

I couldn't sleep that night. I couldn't even lie still in my bunk. I walked the *River's* decks until morning, and since word of what the pirates were doing with the women they captured had spread through the ship by now, nobody told me I wasn't allowed.

CHAPTER FOURTEEN

While I walked, the *River* sailed, quiet, to a small island near the island where the *Bee* was. The run over to it wasn't enough to fully charge our batteries, but we didn't dare keep our engines going longer. Our smoke couldn't be seen in the dark, but any sailor would know the smell. I heard Mr. Burns tell the captain he "thought" our batteries were charged enough now to run until the *River's* boilers was fully hot—but he wouldn't swear to it. Captain Loyal answered him with some words I didn't know, but which made Timmy laugh and call him "Jake." I didn't get the joke, but it seemed to tickle the captain.

We moored for the night behind the small island. At first light Mr. Wise called for a scouting party to go ashore, cross to the other side of the island, and take a look through spyglasses at the *Bee* herself and whatever else they could see. I finally had a skill worth more to my shipmates than my handy way with dishes, and it wasn't trigonometry. I got picked to go as one half of the scouts' "radio." Shy was the other half, of course, and between us we could talk as easy as we could have done with a real radio, only without any danger of our signals being tracked.

The island was small, as I said; long and thin, dry and brushy, and with a ridge like a spine down its middle. There weren't any trees but bent, stunted ones, and the only animals I saw were little, too. The animals weren't shy of us, which made me doubt they'd had dealings with humans before. The scouting party went straight up one side of the ridge and down the other, crawling on our bellies over its bald top so we wouldn't be seen. When we got to good cover, we stopped to have a look.

We'd named the island the *Bee* was moored off "Beehive Island," and now as I looked at it, I reckoned it was three or four times the size of the one the *River* was hid behind. I reported this to Shy, and also told her Beehive Island had a long sandy beach at its eastern end and gradually rose higher and higher over its whole length to where it ended in rugged cliffs and a sheer drop to the sea on its west. I thought the distance between the beach end and the cliffs might be several hours' walk, allowing for thick brush in places and a steep climb up the back of the western cliffs.

"The captain thanks you," Shy answered me.

We'd already figured the pirates must have some sort of permanent camp on the Beehive. The amount of garbage they'd dumped on what we now called Garbage Island suggested they'd been in the islands quite some time. Through the spyglass, I looked for it.

A minute later, I said to Shy, "I'm guessing the pirates' camp is straight inland from where the *Bee's* moored. It looks from here like there's a trail back that way." I also took a look through the spyglass at the *Bee* herself and said, "Damn! That's a nice ship!" because she was. Unlike any pirate ship I'd ever seen before, the *Bee* looked like she'd been built special for pirating. Trading in souls and death had apparently brought somebody lots of money.

Through Shy, I heard Captain Loyal ask, urgent, "Can she confirm the camp is where she thinks it is? Can she see it?"

"No, just the trail, but where else would it be?" I asked back. "That's where I'd put *my* camp."

Captain Loyal said he'd trust to my pirate instincts on the matter.

He wanted to know if the *Bee's* guns were still on the *Bee* or if some had been moved ashore.

As soon as he said it, I saw what he was worried about. Half the *Bee's* guns would be plenty to defend a land-based camp on all sides from raiders afoot, and if the other half were still in place on the *Bee* herself, the *Bee* would be a floating battery against sea-borne enemies.

I was sorry to report that none of the scouts could make out any guns at all. The *Bee's* gun ports were shut, and the island was brushy enough to hide cannon ashore.

"The captain says come in, then. We'll take the longboat out tonight."

*

I was mopping up before heading to bed that night—Izzy'd been asleep for an hour already—when I heard the captain and Mr. Wise arguing.

I wasn't snooping, mind you. I was just late finishing cleaning up the galley and happened to be around the corner when they got into it. The two argued in Forester, of course, but Shy was on watch, and although she was honestly trying not to listen, she heard the argument through me and I understood through her that Captain Loyal wanted to go out with the longboat, and Mr. Wise wouldn't let him do it. The captain's position was that he should have a look at the *Bee* himself before he asked anybody else to go to battle against her, while Mr. Wise thought if the longboat was spotted and the *River* had to rescue her, the captain of the *River* should be the one at her helm.

I thought the longboat was the only thing they were arguing about—I favored the captain's side—until I heard the captain ask, sarcastic, "Still worried about breaking your word to my uncle, aren't you, Wise?"

Mr. Wise said he didn't know what the captain was talking about.

"You promised him you'd hold me back," Captain Loyal said. "That you'd stop me from doing 'dangerous' things. I know you did. Don't bother to deny it."

Mr. Wise answered, "If I've ever made any promises of that nature, it's only been to myself. You're reckless, Loyal. It's your only fault. You do reckless things. But in this case, what I'm saying is just good sense. A captain stays with his ship as surely as a Master remains in his Forest. I'm sure you're intelligent enough to understand why."

I finished up my mopping as quiet as I could and tiptoed away.

Before the moon rose, the longboat was launched with Shy aboard and Mr. Wise commanding. I was in my usual shadow, watching, but the captain wasn't there to see me this time—the first time I'd known him to miss a scouts' launch. The raiders were dressed in dark clothes, and those who were light-skinned had smeared their faces and hands with soot from the boiler. Once the longboat was lowered, they became part of the night.

I went back to my cabin but got called up again five minutes later by Valiant, who came to tell me I was wanted on deck. He knocked at the door soft, so as not to wake Izzy. I pulled on my trousers over my nightshirt, went up, and found a place on the deck where I could sit. Captain Loyal and Mr. Toby came up a minute later and stood near me.

"Listen for Shy," Mr. Toby ordered as he came.

For half an hour, Shy's thoughts were just a low murmur about what she was hearing in the longboat, which wasn't much. The captain drummed his fingers on the rail and looked back at me over his shoulder every five minutes to ask, "What's happening?" but there was nothing interesting to tell him. The longboat had to risk going in close to see about the *Bee's* guns, and Mr. Wise was doing it slow and cautious. Aboard the *River*, the electric engine was humming and her gun ports were already open, just in case things went bad for the scouts.

The pirates' camp was exactly where I'd thought it was, Shy reported. "There's a watch on the ship, and a watcher in a tree on the shore," she said. "Other than that, we don't see any guards."

"What about the guns?" the captain asked urgently. "Afloat or ashore?"

Shy said they still didn't know and would go closer.

After another quarter hour, the scouts managed to get the longboat to where they could see the *Bee's* whole lee side. Shy raised her spyglass, and then her and me together said something like, "Whoa!"

"What?" the captain and Mr. Toby asked at once.

"Guns," I said. "Being brought aboard. They were ashore, but now they're being brought back. Looks like...two...are in place. No, three. Three in place and two more ready to be mounted. Another one on the beach. Lights are strung in the trees from the beach back toward the camp. Mr. Wise thinks they're bringing the guns from there."

Captain Loyal and Mr. Toby looked at each other. "They're leaving," the captain breathed.

The longboat backed off and found a dark place to sit while the scouts studied the situation. Everything they saw said the *Bee* was getting ready to sail. Besides remounting her guns, she appeared to be filling her water tanks.

"They're taking their time, Mr. Wise says," Shy told us. "They don't seem to be in any special hurry."

"The *Bee's* not leaving because she's seen us, then," Mr. Toby said, sounding relieved. "Claire, when does Wise think she'll be ready to sail?"

Tomorrow, was Mr. Wise's answer.

Captain Loyal turned to the mate. "We can't let them leave, Jim," he said. "We *must* take the *Bee* where she is."

Mr. Toby—I hadn't known his name was Jim before—seemed doubtful about this. "Wait and see which way she goes, and then cut her off," he suggested.

The two of them then had a longish discussion about this that probably would have been an argument if Mr. Toby'd had a higher rank. Mr. Toby wanted to do things cautious. I'd noticed before he was a cautious man. Captain Loyal said the situation required us to be bold. He said the *Bee's* captain knew the area better than we did, and the *Bee* was fast.

"We'll lose her in a long pursuit," he warned. He glanced up at the stars, judging the time. "Either way, attack or chase, we'll be doing it by daylight, and that's not to our advantage. Claire, what does Wise think?"

Mr. Wise, Shy told us, thought the pirates wouldn't go tonight. "They still have too much to do to leave tonight. She'll go tomorrow, under cover of darkness."

"Tell Wise to come in then," the captain ordered.

I did; then went down to check on Izzy. Since she was still sleeping peaceful, I went back up on deck after to see the longboat come in. I didn't hide, since the captain hadn't said I couldn't stay.

When the boat was in and being stowed, the scouts all gave their opinions about what we should do next.

I gave my opinion, too. Mine was that we should make a two-pronged attack on the *Bee*, with the *River* coming up from one side and the longboat—with a couple of cannon aboard her ready-primed—advancing from the other as a distraction.

I volunteered to be the one in the longboat.

Captain Loyal stared at me. "You're planning to fire the cannon?"

"Sure! That's the distraction part."

"From within a longboat?"

"Well, that's where the cannon'd be, so, yeah."

"Dunn," the captain said, flat, "you'd be killed. The recoil from one cannon, let alone two, would tear the longboat to pieces."

"Well, but I can swim," I pointed out. "So I might be all right. I just need to fire both the guns off right together and then dive for it quick. I figure it needs to be two shots. One might not be enough. But two shots from one side would be enough to distract the *Bee's* gunners so our gunners could hit her unexpected from the other side, and I bet I could do it!"

The captain turned on his heel and went below, groaning. Mr. Wise followed him. They seemed to be friends again, to my relief.

The rest of us went on talking until dawn. The *Muriel* was only a few days away from where we were, but a few days might as well be a year if the *Bee* left before she arrived. The *Anna* was closer, but slower and lightly armed. She also still had the pirates from the *Clover* penned up in her hold, too—not the best way to head into battle. Shy sketched charts on the deck with her finger, plotting this route or that to where the *River* or the *Muriel* or the *Anna* might be able to cut the *Bee* off, but not even Shy knew for sure if the charts she sketched were right. The *Anna* had captured the *Clover's* maps of the area, but we wouldn't have them until we met the *Anna*.

Only one other plan besides my cannon-in-the-longboat one sounded good to me, and that was Dan's. Dan thought a two-pronged attack would work perfect, only he wanted one prong to be a land attack on the pirates' camp.

"The land raiders would need to come up from the backside of the Beehive, though," Dan said. "They can't come from the same direction as the *River*. We need the pirates' attention to be divided."

Someone asked, "Anybody know what's on the backside of the Beehive?"

Nobody did, and we finally went to bed with nothing sure or settled.

When I got to the galley in late morning, the cook was going through his stores and bringing out things to make the evening's dinner. They were nice things, like dried meat and fruit, that he'd held back until now.

"I always make a good meal before a battle," he said when he saw me looking. "You never know who's last it might be."

I told him this was a gloomy thought. I didn't say it wasn't true.

"What do *you* think we should do?" I asked Cook. "Sail straight in, all guns firing, or sneak?"

"Whichever's fastest. Time's getting short." He shoved a couple of biscuits in front of Izzy and me. "Go finish your sleep if you want. I won't need you until later."

I decided to eat my biscuit first. I was tired, no question, but I was also hungry, and anyway I wanted a minute to think.

The *Bee's* company was about the same size as the *River's*. The *Bee's* guns were about the same, and her speed and the skill of her captain were both—I hated to admit it—about the same as the *River's*, too. But the *Bee* had some advantages over the *River*, like that *Bee* had lots of fuel, and knew the local waters.

It seemed to me, though, that her advantages could be cancelled out by attacking the *Bee* where she was moored. Fuel and an experienced pilot couldn't help her until she was moving. And an attack with even a *touch* of surprise in it would put the advantage square on the *River's* side.

A cannonade from a longboat would be surprising—but only if the *Bee* missed seeing the longboat coming. I couldn't entirely see how I'd manage that. Also, if Captain Loyal was right, I might get killed doing it.

Dan's idea, to make the diversion a land-attack instead of one from a longboat, was better, but how would we know where to send the landing party in unless we scouted first? And as Cook said, time was short.

I finished my biscuit without noticing. Cook asked me if I wanted another.

"No," I said. "Izzy does, though. Can she stay with you and eat one? I need to talk to somebody."

Cook said Izzy could stay as long as I needed her to.

I went to the captain's cabin and stood a minute in the passageway, getting up my nerve to knock.

CHAPTER FIFTEEN

I t turned out I needed all the nerve I could raise. The captain's voice when he called to me to enter was…uncheerful. To say the least. When I opened the door, I saw Mr. Wise was with him.

"What, Dunn?" asked Captain Loyal, impatient. "Make it quick."

Mr. Wise's mood seemed a little better, so I spoke mainly to him. "I kind of had an idea," I began. "Actually, it was Dan's idea. I didn't entirely think it would work Dan's way, but I've thought of another way that might."

Out of the corner of my eye, I saw the captain lean back and glare at me.

"I'll just take a minute," I promised, talking faster. "Dan's idea was a two-front attack. One side'd be from the *River* on the *Bee*, and the other side'd be raiders from the land side on the *Bee's* camp. I knew you'd want to scout first, and time for scouting's running out, but I've got a way around that problem."

Captain Loyal started to say something, but Mr. Wise cut him off. "What's the harm?" he asked the captain. He turned back to me. "Five minutes, Claire. As you might guess, we're busy."

"Right. Well, my version of Dan's idea is that I go scout—just me—and *while I'm scouting*, Shy and the raiders follow me in. See? It'll take longer than *just* scouting or *just* raiding, but not as long as doing them one after the other would." When neither Mr. Wise nor the captain said anything, I tried to make myself clearer. "What I mean is, if I scout first, and then I come back and we make a map and all that, it'll be night, and the *Bee*'ll leave before raiders can get to the camp. Or if raiders tried to go in *without* scouting, they could wander around for a long time trying to find their way and maybe get seen meanwhile, which would spoil the surprise."

Another silence stretched.

I was about to explain again when Captain Loyal finally spoke. "Thank you, Dunn. Your suggestion has been duly noted. Get out of here." He waved his hand in Mr. Wise's general direction, sighing, "Deal with this, would you?"

"Interesting idea," Mr. Wise said, thoughtful. "Claire, go through it again, will you? How much ahead of the raiders would you be?"

I don't think this kind of "dealing" was what the captain'd meant.

I went through the whole plan again, adding a few more things I thought of along the way, and ending with, "I honestly think it'd work. I'm just one person, and just one person'll be hard for any sentries to see—if the pirates even have sentries, which we don't know for sure they do. Also, I can move fast because I don't have to carry anything. I don't need weapons, because I can't fight a whole shipload of pirates by myself anyway; and I don't need a radio because I *am* one. I can do the fastest job of scouting that was ever done, and when I get to the camp, I can hide there and guide the raiders straight in."

Mr. Wise had been nodding right along while I talked. Now the captain nodded, too—though only a little. He also sat up straighter and cleared his throat.

"The plan's…not bad." He drew a breath. "It's similar to mine, in fact."

"The difference being that your plan's suicide," Mr. Wise muttered.

Captain Loyal ignored this.

I agreed, happy, "See? And I'm ready to go right away. All I need is the dinghy and some water to take along." After my trip in the *Antelope's* dinghy, I never wanted to go anywhere again without plenty of water. "It'll take a couple hours to get the raiders ready, but that's perfect. A couple of hours is just the head start I need."

Mr. Wise nodded again, but Captain Loyal said, "Not you, Claire."

"Of course me!" I answered. "It has to be me!"

"No," the captain said, firm. "There's…merit…in your plan. I'm not committing to it until I've had a chance to think it over, but it has merit. But it's also very dangerous, and you're the youngest sailor under my command. I can't authorize you for a mission of this kind."

I glared at him. "I'm *going*."

Mr. Wise started to say something. The captain paid no heed. "I'm not going to argue with you, Claire," he said.

My throat tightened up. It does that when I'm mad.

"Well, maybe *you're* not going to argue with *me*," I said. "But I'm definitely going to argue with *you*!" Spit flew out of my mouth as I said this. It was accidental, but spitting on an officer is a court-martial offense, and I don't know if it matters whether you meant to or not. "I know I'm not a trained sailor yet, but I don't *need* to be sailor. What I *need* to be is a sneak. Which I am. And if I get caught, I need to be a good liar, too—which I also am. I'm small, and I'm fast, and I'm not afraid."

"That's the problem," Captain Loyal put in. "You're not afraid."

"But the *main* reason I'm the one gets to go," I went on, glaring at him, "is that I've eaten more shit in my life than you Foresters probably ever even knew existed in the whole world, and getting those pirates is the one thing I can think of that'll wipe the taste of it out of my mouth! I am *going*!"

Gods. I hadn't meant to say *that*.

But Captain Loyal didn't yell back, nor Mr. Wise. And no word from Shy—who I knew was listening—about me using the word "shit," either. Shy usually went nuts over bad language.

Instead, Mr. Wise stood up, got a chair, and pushed it into the backs of my knees. "Sit down," he said, guiding me onto it.

Then he turned to the captain. "Our scout really *must* be either Shy, Claire, or Seal, mustn't it, Loyal? Those are our only choices. Any other scout would have to carry a radio. Dunn was lawfully enlisted, she's volunteering, and for the reasons she named herself, of the three possibilities, she seems the best qualified for the job."

All the time since I'd started shouting at him, Captain Loyal had been staring straight at me. Now he looked at Mr. Wise. "Wise, she's all of fifteen."

"You're talking to the wrong man," Mr. Wise laughed. "I knew you at fifteen. What were you trying to prove in those days, Loyal? I've always meant to ask."

"Irrelevant," the captain said, looking away.

"Is it? What about that thing on Johns Island, for instance? What the hell was *that* all about?"

"*That* was nothing more than a stunt," Captain Loyal said, tight. "And I was sixteen, not fifteen."

"Were you? Small for your age, I suppose. When's your birthday, Claire?"

Grinning, I told him.

"See? Coming right up." Mr. Wise got more serious. "As I understand it, Dunn's plan is to scout a safe path across the Beehive for the benefit of raiders who will form one prong of a surprise, two-pronged attack on the *Bee* and the *Bee's* company ashore. What've you got?"

The captain's fingers drummed up a storm.

"Or will we just let the *Bee* go?" Mr. Wise asked. "You've said it yourself, Loyal: We'll lose them in a chase. And if we run out of fuel and are left dead in the water, the *Bee* might think it was worth her while to come back this time and finish us off."

More finger-drumming, but slower. Nobody said anything for a minute.

Then, for some reason, Captain Loyal laughed. He just laughed. Like he was happy. "You're right. It's exactly the kind of thing I'd have wanted to do at Claire's age." He laughed again, seemingly to himself, and then opened the drawer of his desk.

"I can go?" I cried.

The captain didn't answer. Still smiling, he pulled out a sheet of paper, dipped his pen, and wrote a few sentences. Then he stood up, and after waving what he'd wrote in the air a few times to dry it, he handed the paper to Mr. Wise. "Here you are, Captain."

Mr. Wise looked at the paper, then looked again. "Loyal…no," he said.

"Refuse, and I'll resign from the navy entirely." The smile still on his face, the captain turned to me. "This is the *River's* new captain, Claire. What do you think?"

I wasn't getting what was happening. "Mr. Wise?" I frowned, confused. "I like him. Why?"

"*Captain* Wise," Captain—that is, Loyal—corrected me. "You 'like him,' you say?" To Captain Wise, he said, "See? You're popular already."

I finally figured out what was going on.

A captain's job is to look after his ship, and he never leaves it to go ashore except in a friendly port. The captain—Loyal, I mean—had resigned his captaincy to Mr. Wise so he could go ashore and scout the Beehive.

Suspicious, I narrowed my eyes. "You ain't thinking about going without me, are you?"

Loyal grinned like he was having the time of his life. "'*Aren't*' thinking," he corrected me. "Mind your grammar. No, as far as I'm concerned, this is your mission. But of course, that's the captain's decision."

It was interesting to see Mr. Wise take hold as a captain. He stared at me vague for a minute, his mind probably still on his sudden promotion, and then his look sharpened and he asked—demanded, more like—"Do you still have those clothes you were wearing when we first met you, Dunn? Go change into them. Don't wear or take anything ashore that could identify you as a member of this crew."

He didn't give any orders to his former captain, I noticed. Of course, Loyal didn't really need any. As I left, he was already pulling off his ship's jacket.

Saying goodbye to Izzy was hard.

Izzy'd heard everything, of course, through Shy. She didn't entirely understand. She knew I was going someplace she couldn't come, and she knew Shy was worried for me. I told her where I was going had something to do with getting her back to her island and her people because I thought it would cheer her up, but instead it made her cry. I changed my clothes, but I'd grown since the day I'd stole Wolf's suit, and the trousers were too short for me now. Tight, too. I didn't care, but Shy took one look and ran off to find some different ones. She came back with a bigger pair of Seal's that were baggy and too long but could be rolled up at the bottom.

I let Isabelle wear my ship's jacket like she'd always wanted to, and then, since she was still crying, I took the lanyard with my mother's broken ring on it from around my neck and put it on Izzy's neck instead.

"See? This means I'm coming back. I'd never leave my ring for good, would I?"

Izzy could see the sense in this and stopped crying.

Word was already getting around the ship about what was happening. Timmy heard and came straight up from the engine room to "volunteer" to pilot me and Loyal over to the Beehive in the dinghy. By "volunteer," I mean he told Captain Wise he was going to do it. I heard someone whisper that when Mr. Toby'd found out he was now the *River's* new acting first mate, he looked like he'd been told something terrible, but by the time I saw him he was ordering crew around as brisk as if he'd been first mate for years. He called for volunteers to be raiders, and every sailor on the *River* stepped forward including Jerry the cook.

Dan said goodbye to me with a hug and the news he'd been picked to be a raider and would see me later. "Stay safe," he whispered.

I said the same back to him. I hugged him back, too—long and hard. Why not? No harm in a hug that made us both feel better. The dinghy was ready, and five minutes later, we were underway.

CHAPTER SIXTEEN

"Whereabouts we goin'?" Timmy asked, leisurely.

Technically, Loyal still outranked me—he'd only bumped himself down to "seaman," whereas I was still "apprentice seaman"—so I let him answer.

"North side of the island," Loyal said, calm as always. "Put us down right opposite the camp, if you can."

End to end, the Beehive was much longer than Shelter Island, which was what we'd taken to calling the island *River* was hiding behind, but it was skinny—only maybe half again as wide as Shelter—and a lot ruggeder. The *Bee*, as I might've mentioned before, was moored on the Beehive's south side near a narrow strip of beach protected to the east and west by rocks and thick brush. The pirates' camp was straight inland of the beach. After discussing it, Loyal and me'd decided the best place for the raiders to come in would be from the exact opposite side of the island from where the *Bee* was, so they could attack the pirates' camp from the north at the same time the *River* attacked the *Bee* herself from the south. I think we both believed that if we couldn't find a way in for the raiders from the north, so that they had to come all the way up from the beach on the Beehive's east end instead, we might as well call off the raid altogether, but neither of us said this out loud. There was no way raiders or anybody could attack the pirates' camp from the west because of the cliffs on that end of the island.

Timmy said he'd put us down wherever we wanted.

We circled far out to sea, so no one watching from the *Bee* or the Beehive could see us, Tim and Loyal chatting away casual like old friends, which they were. Timmy told me he'd been the young sailor who showed Loyal around his very first ship, the *Muriel*, years and years before. He also mentioned—offhand—that Loyal'd almost sunk the *Muriel* once back in those days. I asked, but he wouldn't say how.

While Timmy was talking, I suddenly realized something Loyal and me hadn't considered before, which was that since the *River* was moored south of Shelter Island, and we were landing north of Beehive Island, we were going to start on our mission with two whole islands between my brain and Shy's. When the dinghy turned and headed behind the Beehive, the constant hum of other minds in my brain stopped like a switch had been thrown.

Timmy saw me start. "Want to go back?" he asked, concerned.

He thought I was scared.

I managed to laugh. "No."

I think Timmy didn't entirely believe this. Grinning, he said, "You can be the one takes the dinghy back, if you want. I've heard you're a dab hand with a dinghy. Loyal'n me can handle this." Kicking away a tarp concealing something stashed near the tiller, Tim showed me he'd brought a portable radio along.

I laughed again, meaning it this time. I said the dinghy I intended to go back to the *River* in was the *Bee's*. "I'm gonna capture it," I told him.

Tim laughed too, then, and nodded. "I believe you just might."

While the two men went back to talking, I enjoyed the first real silence I'd known since—when? Since the time I rowed off in the *Antelope's* dinghy, I guessed. I'd lived my whole life hearing telepathic brains around me, most of that time not knowing what the sound I heard was. Where we were now, there wasn't a single telepath in range, and the silence was both lonely and wonderful. It was a silence I could think whatever I wanted in, and provided I could get what I thought back out of my mind before Shy or any other telepaths came in range, it would be private.

After awhile of doing that—thinking private, I mean—I sat forward, and said, "I got a question for you, Mr. Burns, in case I don't get another chance to ask it. Sarah wanted you to find my dad, didn't she? Did you? Did you meet him?"

Tim didn't answer right away. "Saw him once," he said finally. "Never talked to him direct."

"But you talked to other people about him?"

"Yes."

What I'd been thinking about—private—was why my mother'd ever married my father. My mother'd been all goodness, whereas my dad—wasn't. "What did those people say?" I asked. "Did they know he was a bad man? Or did he hide it from everybody?"

Tim repeated that he'd never known my dad personal, adding, "But you can tell a lot about a man by his friends, and your dad's friends was low." He gestured toward the Beehive. "If you said the name of Bill Dunn in that camp, among them pirates, I bet there'd be some who'd know it."

I remembered what the *Antelope's* cook had said about me, and asked, "Do you think he might have been a good man once, and then something happened that turned him vicious?"

It was Loyal who answered this. "I think that's it, Claire," he said. "I think that's exactly what happened. Your father was born good, but bad friends and bad experiences embittered him."

Timmy looked for a second like he might disagree, but then nodded instead. "No doubt about it. That's what happened."

"So do you think when my mom married him, he might still've been good?"

"More'n likely," said Tim, and at the same time, Loyal answered, "Unquestionably."

I leaned back and smiled. Tim and Loyal were both very smart, and I trusted their judgment.

A minute later, Timmy pointed out a place on the Beehive's shore where the trees grew down to the water. "Good cover there. What do you think?"

Loyal said it looked fine, and we headed in.

As we got near, Timmy reached under the seat and brought out a long gun. He laid it in my lap. Loyal'd already pulled out another one from under his seat and was sighting on the shore.

"That works the same as a pistol," Tim told me.

I'd never fired a pistol.

"Keep it handy in case we need to shoot our way back out to sea. I don't see no signs of sentries, but we'll wait here a minute, and if there are any, they'll likely show theirselves soon. Watch careful, and if anything moves, let off a round or two while I back the boat."

We sat idling for ten minutes or so until Loyal said, "Take us in closer."

Tim cautiously moved the dinghy deeper among the overhanging trees until we touched bottom. "I'll pull her up," he said, starting toward the bow.

But Loyal said not to bother and jumped out. The water was no more than calf deep, so I followed. I left my long gun behind.

"I don't know how to shoot a gun," I admitted to Loyal.

Loyal looked a little sick when I said that, but all he answered was, "Fine. You can carry the rope instead." He slung a long coil of it over my shoulder.

I wished I'd kept my mouth shut. The rope weighed twice what the gun had.

Timmy looked at me. "Shy say the raiders are ready?"

I saw from Loyal's face he knew already I wasn't in touch with Shy anymore. Loyal knew about stuff like how far telepaths could hear each other.

Before I could answer Timmy's question—I admit I was planning to lie— Loyal answered for me. "They're ready."

"Back in a couple hours, then," Tim promised. "And tomorrow, when this is over, Claire and me'll race the dinghies. Eh, Claire? Me in the *River's* against you in the *Bee's*?"

"Mind you lose graceful, then," I said.

Timmy, his long gun sighted into the trees, softly wished us luck as Loyal and me started off. I still wasn't scared, but I was so excited I never heard the dinghy leave.

Where we'd landed, the shore was flat for a hundred yards inland, then rose steadily upward toward the island's central ridge. The hike to the ridge was steep, but the footing was firm and we made good time. We stayed alert and under cover, but there wasn't any sign of sentries. The same as on Shelter Island, the Beehive was generally brushy but the ridge bare as an elbow, and we crawled the last ten yards to it on hands and knees first, and then on our bellies.

When we got near the top, Loyal reached back and stopped me with a hand on my head.

"Let me," he said. "I'm sorry to be the one to break this to you, Claire, but you're not as adept at 'sneaking' as you imagine."

"I'm not what?"

While I was figuring out what "adept" meant, Loyal added, "You're not as good a liar as you think you are, either." Still holding me back, he eased his own head above the ridge in a place where there were a lot of head-sized rocks to disguise it.

It didn't immediately get shot off—which was good—but Loyal didn't seem to like what he saw. In fact, he said, "Damn," very heavy, and sighed.

Using the rocks to hide, like Loyal had, I took a look, too. The other side of the rise we'd just crawled up was a sheer drop, with stones—pointy ones—at the bottom of it.

"What now?" I asked Loyal.

We looked, and to the east, the situation seemed even worse. The ridge rose, which made the drop down from it longer.

To the west, though, things looked more promising. The ridge flattened to the west. Loyal and me crawled back down to where there was cover and walked a quarter mile or so west before crawling up to the ridge and looking again.

We did this twice. The second time, we sighted an easy path down from the top of the ridge to the wide, flat plain below.

Loyal pulled out a spyglass. "Let's have a look."

The *Bee's* captain might've been an evil man. I had a strong notion he was. But he wasn't a stupid one, and he knew how to site a camp. From the *River's* longboat, it'd looked to our scouts like the cliffs at the eastern end of the

Beehive rose up out of the flat land in the middle of the island, with the ridge separate. But from where we looked now, Loyal and me could see that the ridge down the center of the island and the cliffs at the far eastern end of it weren't separate at all. The ridge *became* the cliffs. East of where we were, the ridge kept on rising higher and higher until finally it bent like an arm around the end of the island. One side of the arm—the sea-side—was cliffs. The land side curled around and cradled the pirates' camp safe as a swaddled baby. No wonder we hadn't seen any sentries when we landed. There were only two possible ways into the camp, one from the southern beach, which the *Bee* was protecting, and the other by an easy but long walk from the west. Any sentries the pirates posted would be watching the west, where they'd see raiders coming for a mile.

I eased back down behind the ridge, sat up, and damned a lot of things and people.

Above me, meanwhile, Loyal scrambled higher and sat down comfortable on the ridge's peak. He reached down his hand to me. "Join me," he invited. "I regret to say we're in no danger of being seen. The only sentry"—he pointed— "is looking west."

"He knows nobody's coming over this ridge," I said, glum. "Nobody could."

"You're exactly right."

As I said before, eastward of where we were, the only way down from the ridge was by a long scary drop onto stones. Westward, where the ridge was low and there were no bad drops, the way to the pirate camp was by a long walk down a flat plain with poor cover that, as we saw now, was watched by at least one sentry.

"Well, how about there?" I asked, pointing east. I realized on second thought the place on the ridge I was pointing to looked like it had given way a few times before and was ready to give way again if any weight—mine, for instance—was put on it. I looked west. "Well, what about there, then?" I suggested. "We could go down there pretty easy."

"No," Loyal said. "The sentry would object."

"Take him out."

"Very risky. After dark, maybe."

Loyal was right, of course. Where the sentry'd stationed himself, there wasn't cover enough to hide a mouse in daylight. I said, "We can't wait for full dark. We have to go down soon. So—where, then?"

I pointed out a few more places. They were all bad.

I felt the first prickle from Shy's mind. "They're coming." I sat up a little.

"Time's running out," Loyal agreed. "We need to find a route across now, or we'll have to find one in the dark." He was still perfectly calm—or seemed like he was. I wondered what he felt like inside. "Suggest any possibilities that come to you, Claire. Don't be afraid to sound…unrealistic. Even a crazy idea may give rise to a better one."

I took his advice and said every way I could think up, including for the raiders to haul up the longboat with them to the top of the ridge, where we'd all pile in and ride it down to the plain below. "We'd get there so fast the sentry wouldn't have time to think, even."

Loyal thought this plan over—or pretended to. "Let's keep that idea for when we have time and resources to make a good, sturdy, purpose-built sledge, all right? I don't think a longboat would survive the trip."

On second thought, I didn't think it would either.

I said, "All right. How about this? How about if we wait until the raiders get real close, and then I go down the easy path and make sure the sentry sees me? While he's capturing me and taking me to the camp, you and the raiders can come down."

"But what if he doesn't take you back to the camp? What if he shoots you on the spot?"

"Well—what if he doesn't?"

Shy was closer now. I was beginning to understand what she was thinking.

"Dammit, we've got to do something!" I cried. "I am not going to just let those bastards get away! Let them shoot me if they want! Shooting me'd be as good a distraction as taking me prisoner!"

Loyal put his hand on my arm and held tight. "You're not going down,

Claire. Trust me when I tell you that, young and vital as you presently are, it is still perfectly possible for you to die. All right? You could die. And I don't want that."

I didn't believe for a minute it'd come to that, but when Loyal added, "Be quiet for a minute now, and let me think," I shut my mouth and stared across the valley.

When I looked at him again, Loyal was staring past me, toward the eastern part of the ridge. "There," he said, pointing. "See where the ridge curls?"

I'd already noticed the place he was pointing to. Just where the ridge started to curve around the end of the Beehive, there was a bit where a rockfall had left the ridge in a shape like the forward edge of a breaking wave.

"I thought of that before," I said, flat. "It's too far down from there, and it's all rocks at the bottom."

"Is it? Let's go see."

"It's all rocks," I repeated.

Despite me, Loyal started eastward, staying low until he was hidden behind the ridge again, and then trotting brisk.

I followed. Why not? I didn't have any better plan to suggest. "Shy wants to know where Mr. Burns should land them," I called as we ran.

"Are they here?"

"No. Getting close, though."

"Ask her to wait a minute. This won't take long."

The place Loyal led me to looked just as high and scary close up as it had from far off. Dropping to his hands and knees, Loyal immediately started toward the edge.

"Hold up, hold up!" I cried, pulling him back by his jacket. "Where the hell are you going?"

"I'm scouting," Loyal said back to me. "I'm going to look over the edge and see what's straight down. I think it's grass rather than rocks. That's my theory, anyway."

I was on my knees too by now. "*I'm* the one's going to look," I said, firm. "How do we know the cliff's strong enough to bear your weight? I'm not the only one could die, you know." Loyal was a slim man, but he weighed more than I did.

Loyal'd been perfectly easy with the idea of crawling straight to the edge himself, but he wouldn't let *me* do it until he'd tied the rope around my waist and braced himself to hold me if the cliff edge gave way.

"All right," he said then. "Take your look."

"Ready for us yet?" Shy's brain asked again.

For the second time, I answered her, "Wait."

I crawled to the edge, looked, then called back to Loyal, "Well, you're almost right. Down from here is past the worst of the rocks, anyway. The thing is, it don't matter how many rocks there is or isn't, because the rope's not long enough to reach the ground." Something caught my eye. "Also," I added, speaking softer, "somebody's moving around down there."

"Sentries?"

"It's so brushy, I can't see for sure. Probably." I crawled back. "Now what?"

"Now we go down," Loyal said. "Or rather, I go down."

"Down *here*?"

"Tell Shy to have Burns land the longboat half a mile east of where he landed us, and have the raiders come straight up from there. You go guide them in. Send them down from this exact spot if you can—but if it gives way when I go over it, anyplace nearby will probably work. Tell the raiders to bring all the rope they have."

He was serious. He was already looking around for the best place to secure our—too short—rope.

"If the ridge gives way when you go over," I informed him, "you're gonna be dead."

"In that case, suggest to the raiders that they try higher up." He'd found a rock he evidently liked. "What do you think?" he asked, putting the rope around it.

"Loyal, the rope ain't long enough!"

Loyal thought for a minute, then took off his coat. Holding it up by both sleeves, he said, "If we tie this to the end of the rope it makes another"—He cocked his head—"say, five feet."

Sighing, I stood and took off my own jacket. "Wish I had long arms like yours," I muttered. "Here. That's maybe three more feet or so—though if you want my opinion, it still won't be enough." I saw him eyeing my trousers. "No, don't bother. I've done it before. Trousers ain't sewn tight enough, and if you put weight on them, they come apart between the legs."

"Your experience is invaluable to us, Claire," Loyal told me. "All right, just the jackets, then. Once I'm down, pull up the rope, untie the jackets, and get it ready for more ropes to be attached when the raiders get here."

"The one who pulls the rope up'll be you," I said. "I'm smaller and lighter'n you, and I'm going down first."

Loyal stared me down, fists on hips, but I wouldn't give in. I wouldn't've give in if he'd still been my captain.

I knew I'd won when he reached under his outside shirt to tear a strip off his undershirt. "I'll go back and flag the trail," he said, sullen. "Tell Shy to follow the flags." He walked off.

Ten minutes later, he was back with a rag in his hand that was all that was left of his undershirt, but seemed cheerfuller. He even smiled. "Ready? I'll get as near the edge of the cliff as I can to let you down, and then be down after you as soon as I can retie the rope to the rock. Wait for me at the bottom."

"You mean you'll be down when the raiders get here with more rope," I corrected him. "Tying the rope to that rock would make an extra six or eight feet you'd have to drop. I don't need to wait for you. I'm fine."

"You won't be fine if you're spotted. You don't even have a weapon."

"I'm not going to be spotted! Wait for the damn raiders, Loyal!"

While we were arguing, I was crawling, holding the rope, very slow to the cliff's edge. Loyal offered one last time to go first, but when I said, "No," he moaned, gave up, took the rope's free end, and braced himself against my weight.

"Don't get killed," he muttered, digging in his heels. "That's an order, sailor."

Stones breaking from the ridge's edge pelted me all the way down, but the ones that hit me were all small ones, thank the gods. A couple big ones passed me by that could've stove in my head. When the rope was all played out—and the jackets, and the last piece of Loyal's undershirt, which he'd added—I was still a good fifteen feet off the ground, but the raiders were already coming up from the beach, so I told myself the worst that could happen was that I'd soon be with my mother, and let myself go.

I'd had the wind knocked out of me before, but this was the first time I'd ever doubted it would come back. For what seemed like hours, I tried to suck in and couldn't, but at last I got a little air, and then a little more, and finally a big noisy gasp filled up my lungs and I was all right again. I lay flat on my back for a while, panting.

When my heart'd slowed down a little, I moved my limbs one at a time, and when nothing seemed broke, I got up.

Once I was on my feet, I reported to Shy about the undershirt-flags marking the trail, and said the raiders could hurry all they wanted now. The path ahead would be scouted and ready.

Then I walked to the nearest big rock, climbed up on it, and had a look around.

The pirates' camp was farther off than I'd thought it would be, but a fire there lit up the sky and showed the way to it. I reckoned the fire was the sailors burning their trash to save dropping it at Garbage Island. The figures I'd seen from the ridge were silhouetted against the fire's glow, and they were nearer than I'd thought they'd be. There were two of them, but watching for a minute made me wonder if they were sentries after all. They never looked west, where they might have expected raiders to come from, nor back toward their camp. They seemed to be wandering around aimless.

A rustling in the brush nearby and some wet, snuffly breathing made my heart almost stop, and then the mystery of the two not-sentries was cleared up when a couple big pigs trotted by. The "sentries" were out hunting. They wanted fresh meat for the *Bee's* voyage.

One of the two hunters was working his way back in the direction of the camp. The other was coming toward where I was. I stood still, like I was part of the rock I was standing on, and he passed by.

The hunter was following the pigs, who now seemed to be sniffing around the place I'd landed. If Loyal came down, he'd land near where I had, and if the hunter saw Loyal, I was sure he'd be even happier to bag Loyal than a pig.

I didn't know what to do. If I yelled, the hunter would probably turn his back on the pigs and Loyal and look my way instead. But what if Loyal'd been right that any pirate who saw me would shoot me on sight? I decided the best thing for me to do was to distract the hunter by yelling—but from far enough away that if he shot at me, he'd stand a good chance of missing.

I jumped down from the side of the rock opposite the hunter and ran, bent over, as fast as I could in the general direction of the pirate camp. I ran until I heard a *thump* on the ground a ways behind me. Then I froze, and looked back. While I was looking, the second hunter, the one who'd been heading back toward the camp, saw me. He shouted and started my way.

Next second there were pig squeals, and a shot.

The shot was muffled but unmistakable. The second hunter came faster, his gun raised and pointed straight at me.

There are two parts to being a good liar: One is to tell *good* lies, if you can, but the second part is more important, which is to tell 'em *fast*. I hoped it was a pig or the hunter and not Loyal who'd been shot, but that was only partly because I liked Loyal. The other part was because I wanted Loyal to live to eat his words about me not being an "adept" liar. I wanted him to see I only needed time enough to draw a breath before I had a whole adept broadside of lies primed and ready.

In my best imitation of an excited, happy voice, I called out to the second hunter—ignoring his gun the while—"Hey, I think he got it! He did! He got that pig! The sow!" I turned and smiled in the hunter's face. "Pork tonight for you, I guess!"

Then, as the hunter was coming the rest of the way to me, moving slower and slower as he got near and lowering his long gun on the way, I babbled on about how sows was smaller than boars, of course, but fatter and sweeter.

My jabbering—and the happy tone of it—almost made me ashamed. At that moment, Loyal might be lying hurt or dead. What I said worked, though. The hunter looked past me, toward where his friend was.

"He got a pig, you say?" He raised his voice. "Hey, Bud! Did you get a pig?" Bud didn't answer.

That should've made Bud's friend suspicious, and it probably would've, if two pigs hadn't burst from cover just then and run past us, obviously scared.

"Ooooh! Get one! Get one!" I howled, jumping around in a way that made it certain the pigs would run even faster and the hunter would miss any shot he tried to take. "Two pigs would be even better than one! I love pig, don't you?"

The pigs ran off, and the hunter eyed me, sour.

"Who the hell are you?" he asked.

I didn't answer this right away. Instead, I said I guessed he'd better help Bud bring in the pig he'd shot. Naturally, this was really the last thing in the world I wanted him to do, so I added, confidential, "Only, if it was me, I'd wait an hour or so. While a pig's cooling off, fleas and lice and stuff jump off them and run all over. They'd as soon jump on a man as another pig."

This is true of pigs, or of any animal that's been killed. Just as I'd hoped he would, the hunter thought for a minute, then decided Bud wasn't such a good friend of his that he cared to get lice and fleas all over himself helping him bring in his kill. Leaving Bud to shift for himself, the pirate asked me again who the hell I was.

I thought of what Timmy had told me.

"I'm Clara Dunn," I said, prompt. "My dad's Bill. You know Bill Dunn, right? He's a sailor, like you, and I got word he's on your ship. Is your ship the *Bee*? I come up from the beach, there," I lied, pointing west. "I ain't seen your ship yet, but I heard it's the *Bee*, and I heard my dad was on the *Bee*, and I'm looking for him. Is he? Can you take me to my dad?"

The hunter looked at me like I was crazy—with good reason, because I'd just told him a crazy story.

"Girlie, I ain't never heard of no Bill—whatever—in my life."

"Dunn," I repeated. "Bill Dunn. He's my dad. I'm trying to find him. Somebody told me he'd be here."

"Well, somebody told you wrong, then. How the hell'd you even *get* here? Nobody knows these waters."

"Maybe he's using a different name. He does that sometimes." I described my dad then, feeling no call whatever to flatter either his looks or his charms. "Can you go ask at that camp over there if anybody's got a daughter named Clara? I know Dad would step right forward if you did that. We're real close."

The hunter gave one last look toward where Bud had gone. "Should be done by now," he muttered.

"Oh, he's no fool," I said, gay as a lunatic—which is what I felt like. "He's waiting for that pig to get cold, just like you or me would."

"First ones down the ridge," Shy's mind said.

"Look for the captain! Loyal, I mean. Look for Loyal!" my mind screamed back. "He's not with me! I'm afraid he's shot!"

While I was telling Shy this, I kept a smile on my face for the hunter to see. I had to.

The hunter took my arm, holding so hard it hurt. "You come with me, Girlie," he said, tugging me in the direction of the pirates' camp.

"Clara," I corrected him, coming along like I was willing. "What's your name? Are you an officer?"

Shy's mind was in a tumble. She was on top of the ridge, and since the raiders had to be silent, nobody could call any news up to her. She had to wait to find out about Loyal until she could go down and see for herself what had happened to him. I was halfway to the pirate camp, yammering away to the hunter about how I'd got to the Beehive by stealing the *Antelope's* dinghy and rowing (it's best to mix as much truth as possible into your lies), before Shy could finally tell me, "Loyal's all right. A little bruised in the fall, but all right. He shot someone—a sentry, it looks like. But he's all right."

My relief must have been obvious. The hunter—I'd got it out of him that his name was Bruce—glanced ahead at the camp and asked, "D'you see your dad?"

"Not yet! Not yet!" I cried. "Keep going!" To make things more realistic, I yelled, "Dad! Dad!" a few times even though we were still too far away from the camp for anybody there to hear me.

"Four to go, and then we'll all be down," Shy told me. "Claire, be careful!"

Once we finally got to the camp, I realized "careful" probably wasn't going to work. The pirates were closer to leaving than we'd thought they'd be. Aside from a pile of firewood and some rubbish here and there, the place was almost empty. Dark, too. The campfire was being allowed to go out, and some of the electric lights strung here and there had been taken down and packed up, while others were getting dim from having too little battery left. There were only a few sailors around. The rest, I guessed, must already be aboard the *Bee*.

I relayed this to Shy. The raiders were carrying a radio with them, of course, and I heard Shy order Dan to pass what I'd just said back to the *River* on it. There was a chance, and maybe a big chance, that the *Bee* would intercept the message, but we hoped it would take too long for the *Bee's* radio operator to locate where it was being received to cause the *River* any trouble.

I looked this way and that way around the camp, trying to send everything I saw to Shy. There were places where it would be better for the raiders to come in from, and places where it would be worse, and I wanted her to have a chance to look at them all.

In the middle of the camp, with its back to a big rock, was a chair. It was the only piece of actual furniture left, though I guessed from the way the grass and bushes were tramped down that there'd been tables and benches—even beds, maybe—around the camp earlier. The chair was a ridiculous piece of work. I don't have any better word for it than that, although "outlandish" might also suit. Carved, and curlicued, and touched here and there with gold that was only paint and not the real thing, it wouldn't have looked out of place in a palace, maybe, but in a rough camp, it was—ridiculous.

Sitting in the chair, not looking ridiculous but mean and brutal instead, was Long-nose. I knew him on sight. I hoped he didn't know me the same.

Bruce marched me up to Long-nose, with me pretending I was eager to meet him.

"Found a girl," announced Bruce—like Long-nose might've took me for anything else.

Then he repeated some of what I'd told him on the way to the camp, about the *Antelope* and her dinghy, and me rowing all the way to the island from—

Bruce got that far and then remembered I hadn't said exactly *where* I'd rowed from. He turned to ask me.

"Oh, a long way!" I answered. "A long, long way! So far, I ran out of water! I didn't like *that* much, I can tell you!"

Long-nose eyed me.

"Anybody know the *Antelope*?" he asked the other sailors, general.

One said he did.

I doubted the *Antelope* had sailed anywhere much in the last ten years except between the continent and Johns Island, but I repeated that it was her I'd come on, adding that she was a slack, dirty ship I was glad to get off of, whose captain was usually drunk.

The sailor who'd said he knew her snorted and agreed I'd described the *Antelope* to a hair.

Long-nose got up from his ridiculous chair and started toward me, walking slow and impressive. "And you rowed here all the way from— Where did you say?" His hand shot out and grabbed one of mine. Before I could react, he'd turned it over and was staring at my palm.

My hands is pretty scarred, as I've said before, and all day long I'd been chafing them crawling and climbing, too. From Long-nose's face I saw he believed now that at least the rowing part of my story was true.

He let my hand go. "What's your captain want?" he asked, thoughtful.

There was another shot from a ways off. Long-nose started, and looked up, sharp.

"Another pig!" I said, bright as a damn star. "My! You'll eat good tonight, I guess!"

"Bud's still out," Bruce explained to Long-nose.

Shy was meanwhile apologizing to me for the noise. "Another sentry," she reported.

"Get that fool back in!" Long-nose yelled to somebody. "How much pork does he think we can eat?"

"Another one coming," I told Shy, as a sailor headed out to bring in Bud. "Do it quiet this time, if you can."

Before Long-nose could forget his question to me, I launched into another series of lies.

"Well, what *I* heard was that what *he* heard was that there was something in these islands was *valuable*. Cap's minded to get in the smuggling line, see? And what somebody told him was that out there somewheres"—I waved my arm northerly—"is an island with buildings on it. And on the island with buildings, there's something worth coming into these islands for." I added, when Long-nose looked piercing at me, "He's a drunk old fool, though. I bet there ain't nothing like that."

The raiders had the camp in sight, Shy told me, and were fanning out to surround it.

A sailor trotted up, coming from the direction of the *Bee*. When Long-nose looked at him, he nodded.

"Time to go," Long-nose said. He stepped away from me, and looking at the half-dozen sailors scattered around the camp, asked, "What do you think? Should we take her with us?"

The sailors answered this with hoots and howls that meant "yes."

Bastards.

Long-nose seemed doubtful. "Maybe we should just shoot her here. I don't know she's worth taking, the way she blabs all the time."

Despite saying this, as he started toward the beach, Long-nose gestured to Bruce to bring me along. All the sailors were moving toward the beach by now. The raiders needed to make their move quick if they wanted to stop them, but I could feel they weren't ready.

I had to hold Long-nose and the sailors back, if I could.

I pulled away from Bruce. "Let me see my dad first, all right?" I begged. "I just want to see my dad and be sure he's with you."

Long-nose looked confused. In telling my story before, neither Bruce nor me'd mentioned my dad. Confusion made Long-nose hesitate, and I took advantage of it.

"My dad's Bill Dunn," I said, wiggling out of Bruce's hold.

Then I told Long-nose the same tale I'd told Bruce earlier, only with more details and a *lot* of tears. The tears come easy because I was starting to be scared. If the pirates got me as far as the *Bee*, the *River* might feel like she had to hold back for fear of hurting me.

"I want my dad!" I wailed. I looked around, like my dad might be hiding close by. "Dad! Where are you, Dad?"

Of course, I was really looking for raiders. I caught a glimpse of one and quick looked another direction.

Shy said, "Almost in place…"

Bruce reached for my arm again. I skittered away like a roach. "Where's my dad?" I shouted, and then commenced a fit of hysterics. The fit wasn't genuine, but it wasn't entirely put on, either.

Nobody knew what to do with me. The sailors looked at Long-nose, silently asking with moves of their eyebrows and shoulders if they should carry me away with them forcible, or leave me alone to shriek. From the tail of my eye, I saw some of the pirates who'd started off down the path to the beach earlier coming back again to investigate the commotion, and I screamed louder, hoping to bring more of them. Not much of what I said made any sense. I yelled that I wanted my dad, and then I yelled *at* my dad—who wasn't there, of course, being dead—telling him he'd got off too easy for what he'd done. I told him I wanted him to come back so I could watch him die again, only more horrible this time. "Why did you turn bad?" I wailed. "You didn't have to turn bad!"

I carried on until Long-nose'd had enough of me and decided to shoot me after all. He pulled out a pistol from his belt to do the job.

Over the sound of my own yelling and of Shy telling me, frantic, to *get down*, I heard Long-nose snarl, "Damn the dog, I'll give her something to scream about!"

When he leveled his pistol, it came to me sudden that he *might* not be bluffing.

At that moment, something in me changed—I think forever. For the first time in my life I believed what Loyal had told me. I believed I could die.

Long-nose looked me in my face and called me a dog again.

"Dog" was the last word he ever spoke.

The shot Long-nose intended for me went wild, while a puff of dust from the breast of his jacket told me someone else's aim had been true. I watched as Long-nose staggered backward toward his chair and then suddenly sat down hard at the foot of it. He stared at me the whole time meanwhile—stared me straight in the eye. I stared back and couldn't move.

Raiders were advancing from three sides of the camp now, shooting as they came. While Long-nose and me stared at each other, a cannon-shot sounded. It was from too close-by to be the *River's* guns, but the shot that answered it was the *River's* for sure. She was coming in on batteries, fast and quiet. Long-nose went on trying, feeble, to point his gun in my direction until someone behind me shot him again. Then his pistol-hand went slack, and his head fell back and rested for a minute on the seat of his throne. I watched as the light went out of his eyes, and then he slumped sideways and rolled onto his face in the dirt.

I never knew for sure who killed Long-nose. Foresters never brag on their own kills, or mention anybody else's. All I can say for sure is that it was Timmy who came up right after to kick the pistol away from Long-nose's hand and lead me away from the chair.

CHAPTER SEVENTEEN

The battle was over in an hour.

Twenty minutes after the raiders reached the camp, the pirates ashore who were still alive regrouped and made a run for the beach, but by the time they got there, the *Bee* was already surrendering. She'd been ready to run, but not to fight; and the *River* coming on her so sudden, guns roaring, made running look like a bad option, too. Her own gunners got off one or two shells, and then her captain shut down her engines and struck.

If he'd known the *River's* fuel situation, or what would happen to him next, he might have chanced it.

As the raiders rounded up the *Bee's* company, bound them, and marched them down into the *River's* hold where they'd have to fight their ways up three decks to get free, me and Izzy stood to one side and looked at every man as he passed us. Izzy's face was like chalk, but she stood firm, and I was proud of her. The two of us pointed out the ones we knew had dealt death on Izzy's island, and the killers were locked up separate from the pirates who were no worse than just sea-going thieves and cheats. The *Bee's* captain had a story he tried to tell everybody about how the *Bee's* dirty work was all done by Long-nose and his friends, but Isabelle and me knew him for the man who'd ordered her and the other women from her island thrown overboard to save himself and his cargo, and he was led apart even from the other guilty pirates. I never saw him again after that night. I don't believe he was ever taken aboard the *River*. When a party that included volunteers from the *Bee* went ashore next day noon to bury the dead, I believe the *Bee's* men probably found their old captain among the bodies. I never heard it mentioned that they did—but that's my belief.

Whoever killed him, it wasn't Loyal. Loyal was in a sickbay bed at the time, grousing and complaining about being forced to stay there to anybody who'd listen, which was nobody. He'd hurt his ankle coming down from the ridge, a hurt he told Shy was just a sprain when he insisted on coming along with the raiders to the pirates' camp, but which turned out to be a bad break when Dr. Masterson examined it. Dr. Masterson splinted and bandaged it and then threatened to break Loyal's other ankle, too, if he got out of bed before he was told he might. I think Loyal must've believed him, because he did stay in bed.

There were other injuries among the *River's* people, too. Dr. Masterson was kept busy for days tending to them. But no one on our side was killed, thank the gods, and the *River* herself had only minor damage. Once some of the *Bee's* fuel had been transferred to the *River's* tanks, she was back to normal, and lit up after dark, too, which was a relief.

I'd always imagined that after a battle the side that won would celebrate, but there was no celebration on the *River*. Mr. Toby shot a pig on the island, and we had a nice meal, but that was all. Mostly, everybody was just let down and quiet. We'd got the *Bee*, and maybe with the Foresters pushing for it, the pirates would even be punished for what they'd done. But the women they'd murdered stayed dead, and now that doctors on the continent knew to look for it, they were reporting dozens of cases of radiation sickness, which really meant there were hundreds of cases and might even be thousands before all the poison steel was found and buried. If it ever was. Which was doubtful.

My one spot of personal happiness was to be back with my friends and Izzy again, but it was a happiness that would end soon. In a few days, it would be time to take Isabelle back to her island. This was such a totally good thing for Isabelle that I was ashamed to be sad about it, but the fact was I'd miss her awful.

More partings would have to happen, too.

The Forest Navy claimed the *Bee* as a prize, which meant a prize crew had to be got up to take her to Making Happy Island for repairs and a refit. Dan was asked to be radio operator of the prize crew, and since it'd be his first chance to act as a real, full radio operator, he naturally said yes. His Uncle Loyal'd also be going with the prize crew—though only as cargo, more or less. The *Bee* would be the first of the Forest ships into a port where there were doctors, and Dr. Masterson said Loyal's ankle needed to be looked at by somebody who could do more for it than he could.

And there was going to be another big goodbye. This one took almost everybody by surprise.

The Forest Navy was glad to get the *Bee*, of course, since she was fast and new, but it turned out the Forests didn't really need any more ships. They had all the ships they could crew already. Because of that, when the *Bee* was ready to sail and Dan came to say goodbye to me, he had news that made us both miserable.

The *Muriel* was going to be sold.

"I can't believe they'd do this," he moaned, his arms around my neck and his face buried in my hair. "The *Muriel's* the Forest's founding ship! There *was* no Forest Navy before they bought her."

I couldn't believe it, either.

"What're they going to do with the *Muriel*?" I asked, also in a moan. "They won't let her go to just anybody, will they?"

"Well, not to pirates, at least." Dan let go of me and ran his fingers through his front hair. "Some trader will take her, probably. Gods, I hope I never see the *Muriel* as a trader. The sight of her loaded with cow-dung and turnips would kill me."

I tried to laugh. "Nobody'll waste her on turnips. She's a fine ship."

"No turnips yet, maybe—but once she's a trader, she'll come to turnips eventually."

Then he added that he'd always intended to serve on the *Muriel*, which I knew was true.

I also knew it was true that, in time, the *Muriel* might come down to shipping manure and vegetables, while newer, bigger ships took the cream of the trade. That's the way of things with ships. I pretended not to agree with Dan about that, though, so as not to make him feel worse.

Later I watched as Dan and Loyal—Loyal hobbling on crutches—and a few other friends rowed away from the *River* and boarded the *Bee* instead.

Mr. Burns watched with me.

"Never got our dinghy race, did we, Claire?"

"And we won't never, now." I tried not to sound as low and bitter as I felt. "Why didn't Loyal get made captain of the *Bee*? What does any captain have to do that can't be done with a broke ankle?"

Mr. Burns looked hard at me before he answered, quiet, "This is private, so don't noise it around, see? Loyal wasn't made *Bee's* captain because he quit the navy. Wrote the letter yesterday. He's going home."

I don't remember it, but my mouth probably dropped open. "Home?"

"Annasland."

Dan'd told me once he reckoned that since Loyal'd left Annasland twenty years ago, he hadn't spent two years there all together, in bits of a week or a month at a time.

"That ain't his home," I scoffed. "Not his natural home. His natural home's a ship!"

Mr. Burns agreed, but said Loyal'd made his mind up and that was that. "I don't know the Forest Navy was ever really Loyal's style, what with all the regulations and such," Timmy added, thoughtful. "He takes after his Uncle River. Likes to make up his own rules."

I got up the next morning knowing the day's breakfast was the last one I'd ever share with Izzy. *River's* boiler was already heating to take her home.

Shy ate with us, and both of us spent the whole meal reminding Izzy about how to eat, and wash, and dress herself, and use tools and make things, and…well, everything. Everything we'd ever taught her, including how to say words. Izzy knew a few dozen words now, and knew that if she spoke them to silent-brains, they'd understand her and answer her back. That was an important lesson for Isabelle. Her people—all of them, everywhere in the world—had almost totally forgotten how to talk with silent-brains. At breakfast, Shy and me reminded her again and again that if she taught the people on her island about talking, it might be a big help to them if Men ever came there again.

Most of all, we reminded Izzy that we loved her and always would. She said she loved us, too. Before we'd finished eating—not that Shy and me could eat—the *River* got underway.

Long before I could hear her people, I knew Isabelle could. It was almost like she left us right then. She stopped thinking intelligible and went back to thinking the way she did when Shy and me first knew her. Pure Ant. One long thread about everything at once. If I was guessing right—and I was just guessing—the thought Izzy was thinking was one that had started when the first Ant was made, and would go on until the last Ant died. Shy and me joined in with it as well as we could. We thought we saw the Creators in it. They looked like anybody, and were probably nice people. I thought I got another look at the Cataclysm, too—confusion and killing, with bits of normal life mixed in. In the middle of death, humans—Ants are humans—go on living as close as they can to the way they always lived. Everything Izzy thought went by very fast, and I couldn't keep up.

The closer we got to her home, the more excited Isabelle got, and when she could finally see her island, she ran for the rail like she had the first time we'd passed it, like she was going to jump overboard. Mr. Burns caught her and stuck her straight into the longboat, and stuck me and Shy in too, to hold her there. Once he'd put her sea chest beside her, Izzy calmed down. I took her long string of strung…things…out of her hand. There were not only beads on the string now, but also seashells, a toy boat Timmy'd made her, small metal ship parts she'd found around and a piece of a bent spoon. I hung it around her neck like a necklace so she wouldn't have to carry it. Izzy gave me back by own necklace in exchange for it, and for a minute her mind came back to me, and she was my Isabelle again. She chuckled, and patted me, and bragged silent about being pretty.

Next minute, Izzy's mind was on the island again. I thought Shy might just cry.

The sailors in the longboat all had pistols under their coats. I didn't know that until later. It made sense, I guess. Izzy's people were Ants, and their experiences with Men had been bad. Nobody'd have blamed them if they'd wanted a little vengeance. But when we brought the boat in, nobody rushed it. Timmy carried Izzy ashore so she wouldn't get her feet wet, and Shy and me came behind, lugging Izzy's sea chest between us. It was almost too heavy even for two of us to carry. Izzy'd been popular on the *River*, and everybody'd put things in her box they wanted her to have.

I'd put in the knife Shy'd given me back on the trail.

This was a big secret nobody could know, including Isabelle until she unpacked her box and found it herself, because the law against giving an Ant any kind of weapon was just about the only Man-law that was generally enforced. I excused myself for breaking it by telling myself I wasn't giving the knife to Izzy to use as a weapon. In fact, I was pretty sure the people on her island would think a knife was much too valuable to be wasted on sticking in a person. I was giving it to her because Izzy's people hadn't had a real knife since ancient times. All they had were wood and stone tools, and since there wasn't any glassy-type stone on their island, none of the tools they made were much good for cutting. A knife would be more useful to the islanders than almost anything else in the world, and I was willing to risk getting into trouble to give them one.

Shy must have felt the same. She knew what I'd done but didn't say anything.

The islanders were afraid to come out of the brush to greet Izzy, though Shy and me could feel they wanted to. They were afraid of the sailors. I kissed Izzy, and Shy kissed Izzy, and then, while we felt like we could still bear to, we turned around and started away, both of us crying, and trying not to. Isabelle followed us for a few steps, tearing her mind away from the Ant-thought for a minute to beg us one last time—she'd asked before—to stay with her.

Just like we had all the other times, we said we couldn't.

"I love you, Isabelle," I said out loud. "And I'll never forget you."

Shy said the same, silent, and took my hand.

"Never forget you" is just a boring, literal truth to an Ant, and Izzy didn't bother to say it back to us. Instead, she ran away into the brush, where right afterwards I could sense her people hugging and petting her, and feel their joy at seeing her again. They were looking at Isabelle mostly—but they were looking back through the trees at me and Shy and Mr. Burns and the sailors in the longboat, too. They were reading Izzy's mind about us and feeling surprised.

At the boat, Mr. Burns comforted me and Shy, saying, "Izzy'll be all right. They seem like nice folks."

In spite of being unhappy and lonely for Isabelle already, I laughed a little when he said that. It was the exact same thing Izzy was saying to her people about us.

CHAPTER EIGHTEEN

I spent my sixteenth birthday sitting beside a cot, holding a sick Ant-woman's hand and trying to help her die.

An hour after Shy and me'd said goodbye to Isabelle, Captain Wise had called us into his cabin and broke the news to us that the Foresters had found the Forbidden Site where the Ant captives had been taken to loot. Foresters, including telepathic Foresters, had gone to each known site, stopping at a safe distance from each one for the telepaths to "listen." At one, they heard Ants inside—sick, starving, and confused.

The Foresters knew the danger of the sites, and had already concluded not to go any nearer any of them than was necessary to leave food and other supplies for anybody inside, but when the telepaths heard minds, they threw away caution and rushed straight in, calling. When I heard Rose was one of the telepaths, I wasn't a bit surprised. She had that kind of heart.

When a dozen sick Ant-women came out from where they were hiding, every one of the Foresters, both telepaths and silent-brains, helped carry them to a deserted place, where the Foresters set up tents and beds and made fires for warming and cooking. In the Forbidden Sites, the Ants had lived by eating bugs and critters they caught, but by the time they were rescued, they were too sick to care about food. The Foresters fed them what they could manage to get down, holding up their heads to help them even though nobody was sure they wouldn't get sick themselves from touching somebody else who had radiation sickness. They washed the Ants, and helped them to put on warm clothes, and made them as comfortable as they could. Now, Captain Wise said, they were just waiting for them to die. It was all they could do. Nobody knew any medicine that would help.

The captain told me and Shy as much of all this as he thought we could bear to hear and that he could bear to talk about, and when we both said we wanted to be released from our other duties to go help, the captain answered it was no more than he'd expected from us. Radio-calls went out, and a dozen ships offered us transport, including a smuggler who bragged that he could get us anywhere in half the time a regulation ship would take. We took him up on it, and he was right. Only days later, Shy and me were at the Foresters' camp. I took one look at Rose and told Robin he should take his wife—not to Evergreen, like he planned—but back to Annasland.

"Evergreen doesn't have enough telepaths," I told him. "Rose needs a thousand brains to help her bear the load of what she saw here." I knew now about things like how telepaths shared mental loads.

He took my advice.

No one knew for sure how dangerous being with radiation-sick people might be for the rest of us, and no one wanted people as young as me and Shy to take chances, but we wouldn't leave. The other telepaths couldn't understand the Ant women; and worse still, the Ant women couldn't understand the other telepaths, though at least they sensed enough to know they meant well. But I could link minds with them as well as I had with Izzy, which meant that Shy could link minds with them a little, too. Ants feel lost and alone without other minds. Once the Ant women knew somebody'd heard and understood what had happened to them—somebody who cared—they felt peaceful. They called Shy and me by the name of Creators, Men they hadn't hated and feared, and when they slipped away, one by one, they went easy.

It was all over in a couple of weeks. The Foresters buried the dead and everything the dead had touched, and then planted trees in their memories.

Sarah came for the tree-planting and to take me "home" to her house in Fortress.

My first childhood ended when my mom died. At Sarah's, I had another. I ate too much, and was lazy, and spent all my wages from the *River* on trinkets and clothes. Wolf and Anne came home from Evergreen School, and we were like kids together, playing, and laughing, and talking, and, in the case of me and Wolf, even flirting a little. It came to me while I was with Wolf that I was a nearly a woman now, not a girl anymore. The idea was strange, but enjoyable. Wolf seemed to enjoy it, too.

Then one day we three looked at each other and knew childhood—second childhood—was over. Wolf went to work at D&R, like he'd always planned to, and Anne went back to school.

"What about you, Claire?" Anne asked as she was leaving.

I told her Sarah had invited me to stay and work at D&R too. "Thought I'd give it a try. Wolf likes it."

D&R was a good place to work. Sarah's son-in-law Tom was my boss, and I couldn't have found a better, more patient one anywhere. But I knew by the second week that a day-in, day-out, always-the-same-job wasn't for me. It seemed like I couldn't breathe right indoors. I needed to be someplace where the wind blew on my face.

Still, I stayed on at D&R for a little while, saving my wages until I had more than I thought Aunt Jane would be able to resist. Then I went to her—alone—and offered it to her in return for telling me where Dad had put my mother. I described exactly what he'd done to her, and since Auntie had no idea how I'd found out, she imagined I knew more. She imagined I knew whatever part she'd had in the business. I didn't, but I let her think I did, and guilt and money together made her confess that, while she'd scrubbed the floor, Dad had gone off in the direction of a nearby field carrying my mother's body wrapped in a blanket.

Sarah had the field dug up and brought a piece of the blanket the diggers found there to me to identify. I recognized it right away. As a child, I'd slept wrapped in that same blanket. Sarah wouldn't let me see any more than just the blanket, and for a minute I was furious. Then I realized she was right. I didn't want to see more. I didn't want a picture of what was left of my mother now to take the place of the one I'd always carried in my mind of her whole and smiling. Sarah saw to it my mom's ring got fixed good as new, and the day I put it on my finger again she took me to plant a tree in the Broadleaf Memorial Grove. We put my mother's ashes under it, and I think Mom's at peace there.

A week later, I went back to the *River* to be a sailor again.

The *River*'d changed a good bit. Captain Wise was a different kind of commander from Loyal. More comfortable with lots of rules, mainly. Chief Engineer Burns was gone from the engine room. He and his Mary were finally going to have the baby they'd been wanting for ten years or more, and Timmy took a job at D&R so he could stay home. I didn't have to wash pots anymore. I was "officer material," Captain Wise said, and made me Jim Toby's aide. As First Officer's Aide, I did just about every job on the ship, I think. On my seventeenth birthday I took a cold dunk overside, inspecting the *River*'s rudder.

The *River*'s job was catching pirates, mostly—some of them over and over again. I told one young one privately that the next time I caught her on a pirate ship, I'd shoot her. Word got back to Mr. Toby about it, because telepaths like me can never really be private, and I was on punishment duties for a week after.

"Oh, Claire, when will you learn?" Shy moaned at me for it—but I never saw the girl again so maybe it was worth it.

Six months or so after that, the *River* visited Ant Island.

This made Shy very happy. Ant Island was a place she'd been trying to get to for years, because it was the main site of the Ant Reintegration Project. Shy, as I may have mentioned before, was heart and soul in favor of Reintegration.

A few years before I was born, a lot of Hybrids had settled on Ant Island, making themselves a village with nice little houses and gardens and workshops separate from the Ant villages on the island. The Hybrid's idea was that the pure Ants would visit them to see what they had—Ants are very interested in what people have—and stay to get to know the Hybrids themselves.

The plan hadn't entirely worked. That is, the Ants had come and seen how the Hybrids lived, and liked it, and wanted to live the same, just as the Hybrids had hoped they would. And the Ants imitated how the Hybrids made nice things for themselves, just the way the Hybrids had hoped they would imitate them. The three Ant villages on the island were just as nice as the Hybrid one now. What the Ants *hadn't* done was stayed and made friends. In the whole twenty years the Hybrids had lived on the island, nothing had occurred between the two groups that could be called "reintegration." The Hybrids couldn't link with the pure Ants' minds, and the pure Ants didn't show any signs of wanting to link with the Hybrids'.

As we landed, Shy asked me if I wanted to come ashore with her. "It might be your only chance," she said sadly. "Some people want to discontinue the Project."

I hadn't heard this and felt bad for Shy's sake. I went ashore with her mainly to cheer her up if I could. We walked around the island, looked at a few things, waved to a few Ants (who didn't wave back), and afterwards went to the Hall in the Hybrid village to have dinner.

The dinner was nice. It wasn't the Hybrids' fault reintegration hadn't worked. They were as good people as you'd ever meet and serious about their work. While we ate, they told us everything they'd done on Ant Island, which initially was just to try to keep the full Ants from killing them. The Hybrids'd had to live offshore on a ship for the first whole year. It wasn't safe for them to be on the island overnight. The Ants had been brought to Ant Island in ancient times to farm it for silent-brained masters, which had been such a bad experience they'd never gotten over it. I remembered the things that had come from Isabelle's brain into mine about the kind of bosses some Men had been to Ants, and wasn't entirely surprised to hear this. Now the Ant Island Ants tolerated Hybrids, and even tolerated Men, when Men visited. But bare toleration was the best anybody other than real, full Ants ever got.

"The women who were thrown from the ship that kidnapped them from their island were brought here, and they were accepted by the Ants immediately," one of the Hybrid women told us as we ate. "We haven't been able to make it clear to them that it would be safe for them to go back to their home island now, but I'm not sure they'd want to go if they did know. They like it here."

Talking about the captive women reminded me and Shy of Izzy, of course, and we smiled across the table at each other—a little sadly, because we still missed Isabelle a lot. Then the conversation moved on.

But later, when I wasn't even thinking about Izzy anymore, I started getting a kind of strange tickle in my brain. A little later, Shy told me mentally that she felt it, too; and a half-hour after that, a few of the Hybrids reported they were also feeling something in their minds they couldn't quite describe—though it didn't seem to be as strong as what Shy and I felt.

The next minute, it came to me all of a sudden what was happening. A former captive woman, one of Izzy's friends, had seen Isabelle in my thoughts. From her, the memory of Izzy had spread to the other former captives who'd known her. Now it was spreading to all the full Ants of Ant Island.

The fact that every Ant on the island was now "remembering" a little girl only a few of them had ever actually known wasn't surprising to me or to Shy. That's the way it is when Ant minds link. What *was* surprising—or astounding; or something beyond astounding—was that for the first time, some of the Ant Island Hybrids' minds were caught in the wave of memory, too. The Hybrids and the full Ants of Ant Island were *sharing minds*.

Right along with Shy and me, the full Ants and the Hybrids "remembered" Isabelle wild and scared, orphaned and half-drowned. Then they "remembered" us feeding Izzy and caring for her, so that she got to be happy and feel safe again. After that, they saw all of us—not just me, Shy, and Izzy this time, but every sailor on the *River*—learning to be friends and to talk to each other. In our minds—Shy's and mine—the Ants and the Hybrids saw the fight on the Beehive, where the Men who'd captured Izzy's people were killed or captured themselves. They saw when we took Isabelle back to her own people, joyful and whole again. When they saw Isabelle go home, the women from her island realized they could go back to their homes, too. Evil Men had hurt them, but good Men had made their island safe again.

The Ant Island Ants and the Ant Island Hybrids saw all this together, and because of that, they could reach Consensus about it.

The two groups had never reached Consensus about anything before. The

Ants had never even understood that Consensus was possible with these not-quite-silent-brained-but-not-Ants-either "Hybrid" creatures. But once they'd reached Consensus about one thing—that not all Men were the same; that there were good Men and bad ones—the Ants wanted to come to Consensus with the Hybrids about everything. Still hesitant—Shy and I could feel their fear—they gradually opened their minds to let the Hybrid minds in so Consensus could happen.

For a long, exhausting week, Shy and I worked to help this Consensus along. The Ants and Hybrids could only link through us at first. But the more the two groups mentally joined, and the more they learned from—and about—each other, the easier the process got. Before long, all the island children, who were less afraid than the grown-ups, were "talking" with each other directly.

Shy sent in her letter of resignation to the Forest Navy.

"This is my work," she wrote. "This is Ant Reintegration as it was imagined from the first, where Ants and other humans rediscover their commonalities and learn to accept their differences. It's what I was born to be a part of."

Shy said at first that I should resign from the navy and be a part of Ant Reintegration, too.

I kind of wanted to do it. I still loved most of naval life. I loved my shipmates, and the sea, and the salt air, and the constant chance for adventure. But adventures didn't come along every day, and I was getting to know the ship's routine—and it was a routine—just a little too well. Being a sailor in the Forest navy was starting to become a...job. I was certainly good at communicating with full Ants. As far as I knew, I was better at it than anybody else in the world. The problem with me staying was that I wasn't sure I entirely believed in what all my communicating was supposed to take us *toward*. I believed now that Ants and Hybrids could "reintegrate." I'd seen it happening. But I had some doubts as to whether full Ants could ever reintegrate with full Men.

As I told Shy, "I'm not sure non-telepaths can ever understand how hurting one telepath can really, truly feel to other telepaths like they're *all* being hurt, and I'm not sure Ants can ever understand that Men's brains are so separate that some can have good thoughts while others have evil ones."

"They can learn to trust," Shy said firmly. "We can teach them."

Then suddenly, she seemed to change her mind. "No, Claire," she said, looking me earnestly in the face. "You're right. You should go. You would be stifled here."

It was nice of her to put it that way—that I should leave Ant Island for my own good. But of course, I knew Shy's unspoken thought. She thought if I stayed, I might do the Reintegration Project more harm than good.

Ants don't just *love* Consensus, they *need* Consensus, and since the Ant Cataclysm, Ant Consensus had always been perfect because Ants only had to take their own natures and interests—which are mostly identical—into account. They hadn't had to consider Men's points of view at all. By now, they didn't even remember Men *had* points of view. They'd never been able to read Men's thoughts and they'd forgotten Men's languages.

Shy didn't expect Consensus to always be perfect because though she was half Ant, she'd lived her whole life among Men, and Men can never all reach Consensus about anything. But even when Consensus wasn't perfect, Shy still loved it. She loved it as much as any Ant did.

I thought Consensus was fine for people who liked that kind of thing, but I wasn't that kind of person. Consensus was calm and steady—like Shy. I loved excitement and change.

Sometimes your friends know you better than you know yourself. The Ants couldn't learn the hard lessons they had ahead of them from any teacher but one who respected their point of view. And that wasn't me.

I rested my head on Shy's shoulder. "You're right: I can't stay," I told her, sad. "But you are, and always will be, my best friend."

We stood like that for a minute: heads together, hands clasped.

Then I sensed surprise, and Shy straightened up and looked past me.

"The captain!" she said.

Captain Wise's expression told us he was bringing bad news.

"It's Anna," he said as he reached us. "She wants to see you." I didn't know why that would be bad news until he added, "She wants to say goodbye."

Though he spoke to both of us, I'm pretty sure he didn't really mean me.

Anna'd known Shy since she was born, but the captain was aware that I'd only spoken to Anna a few times by radio. I'd liked talking to her. She was a nice lady, and very smart. But since we'd never had a chance to share our thoughts, we couldn't, as telepaths, be described as "close." I figured I'd stay with the ship and Shy would go to Annasland.

Only—Shy said she couldn't go. She wanted to see Anna, but she didn't feel she could leave Ant Island right now. Her work was at a critical point.

Turning to me, she begged, "You go, Claire. You go for me. I'll send all my thoughts and good wishes with you."

Telepaths can do that.

I couldn't say no to her. Shy had tears in her eyes. All I could do was beg her to come to Annasland as quick as she could.

The *River* couldn't go, either, it turned out. She was on patrol. Captain Wise promised to put out a call to all ships in the area. Ant Island was remote, and there was luckily a respectable trader nearby that was captained by a friend of his. Shy poured out her thoughts—her heart—to Seal and me to give Anna, and before long, we were on our way. I think Captain Wise's friend might have owed him a favor or two, because we made the passage to Annasland in record time.

CHAPTER NINETEEN

E ven a record-setting passage was too slow to get Seal and me to Annasland in time to speak to Anna. She died the night before we arrived. The telepaths on the island got the news to us as we landed, and a welcome party met us on the dock. The welcomers took Seal home to be with his family, and me to the island Guest House, where they brought me food I couldn't eat and afterwards led me to a bed where I lay down but couldn't sleep.

Next day I walked in slow procession with the whole island population to the Memorial Grove, and watched as Anna's children and grandchildren planted a pear tree there in her memory. Somebody told me at the time there was a special significance to Anna's being memorialized with a fruit tree, but afterwards I couldn't remember who'd said so or what the significance of it was, and I honestly didn't care anyway. Until I saw the earth packed down and smoothed around the tree that symbolized Anna's ongoing presence on the island, I couldn't believe she could possibly really be gone. And when I did believe it, I wished I didn't.

Dan had barely managed to get home in time to say goodbye to his grandmother, but Sarah Farmer had been on the island for a month already. Dan told me that on a radio call, Sarah'd heard something in Anna's voice she didn't like the sound of, and had taken passage on the next D&R ship heading out. I only saw Dan for a few minutes—just long enough for him to tell me that much—because he and Sarah were staying with Dan's parents and I didn't want to intrude on their family grief. I saw Rose and Robin at a distance, but didn't like to intrude on their family grief, either, and I didn't speak to Loyal for the same reason.

Fact was, I felt like a trespasser on the island. Everybody on it was grieving except me. I cried sometimes, but my tears embarrassed me—and not just because I'd never learned how to cry pretty, like some women can. I felt like my situation didn't entitle me to cry. The Annaslanders were mourning their best friend and most important citizen, and I was only disappointed because now I'd never know her. I spent a good part of every day walking all over the island, looking for places to hide my tears where not too many minds could reach mine and nobody could see me at all.

Unearned tears weren't my only problem, either. I hadn't been on Annasland a week before I felt like if I didn't leave there soon, I'd lose my mind. When telepaths linked with my brain, they shared their own thoughts and memories while meanwhile picking through mine. I wasn't used to so much "sharing." I didn't like it. "Sharing" felt to me like being stripped naked and made to live among a bunch of other naked people. The *River* might not come to pick me up for as much as a month, since with Anna already gone, there was no need for her to hurry, and I didn't think I could survive a month of mental nakedness on Annasland. My present life was respectable, but the telepaths would soon know all about my old life, too. They'd know every bad thing I'd ever done and every bad thought I'd ever thought.

Maybe they already did. I tried not to know for sure.

On one of my walks I found a high, narrow sea cliff where I was out of telepathic range of anybody, and sat down on it with relief to think about ways I could escape.

I'd had so much experience escaping before you'd think an escape plan would have been easy for me to come up with. As a kid, I was always escaping. Running away was always better than a beating from Aunt Jane. If my aunt's mood was bad, I kept ready to escape on short notice by sleeping in my clothes, and if she had a man in the house, I kept my shoes on, too.

Annasland being an island complicated things. Sleeping in my clothes wasn't going to help me get off Annasland.

I'd escaped from school. I ran away when other school kids mocked me for being dirty and ignorant and then one day I ran away and never went back. Of course, I could have washed anytime at a pump and not been dirty anymore, and I could have paid attention in class so I got less ignorant, too, but I didn't think of those things back then. Too busy escaping to think, I guess.

I'd escaped from about a thousand shopkeepers, constables, and do-good people. All that kind of escape took was good legs and a million lies.

I'd escaped from Rose.

I turned my mind quick away from Rose. I knew her better since meeting her again when we were tending the radiation-sick Ants together. I knew now she was all goodness and had only wanted to help.

I'd escaped from the *Antelope*.

I perked up when I remembered the *Antelope*. A ship at sea was a kind of island. Something I learned getting off the *Antelope* might help me get off Annasland, too. I'd left the *Antelope* in a dinghy. Annasland had a small fishing fleet. Could I steal a fishing boat, maybe?

No. I definitely could not.

I'd never felt the least bit of shame over stealing the *Antelope's* dinghy. In fact, I'd privately vowed I'd steal any ship's dinghy—even its longboat—if I was ever in the same circumstances again. But Annasland was no *Antelope*, and the islanders had been nothing but kind to me. I'd never be able to face myself afterward if I stole from them.

I was just thinking that what I probably needed was somebody like the *Antelope's* cook to help me when I felt someone coming up the trail. I hadn't entirely got the hang of the way Island Forest Hybrids thought yet, but the visitor seemed to be saying her name was Iris and that Sarah had sent her to ask me to come.

I said I would, of course. It wasn't as if I could really hide from anybody.

Iris was the chatty type, so the two of us "talked" on the way to Dan's family's house. Iris did most of the talking—mostly about Anna, and mostly about what the Island Forest had been like in the days when Anna was Forest master. I listened, but didn't have anything to add. Just as we got near where we were going, it came to me that the Annaslanders might not think my usual way of talking was respectful enough for Sarah, who was an even more important person on Annasland than she was on the continent. I asked Iris what Consensus suggested would be a proper greeting to her, figuring if what Consensus recommended had any words in it that sounded like they might have capital letters on the fronts of them, I'd be extra careful about my grammar.

Luckily, Iris told me any version of "happy to see you, Sarah" would be just fine. Nodding very serious, she said, "No ceremony is required. Sarah is both unpretentious and kind."

As if on purpose to prove Iris was right, a nearby door opened right then and Sarah called to me. She was smiling unpretentiously, and her arms were already kindly open. I ran the last few steps straight into them.

"Oh, Claire, darling," Sarah sighed, laughing and crying and hugging me all at once as she pulled me inside. "I wish the circumstances were happier, of course, but I am so, so glad to see you again!" Then she told me everybody else was at dinner in the Hall and started to help me off with my jacket.

But before I could get even one arm out, instead of saying I was happy to see her like Consensus had told me to, I found myself blurting, "Oh, gods, Sarah, I am so sorry!" and starting to cry.

It happened so unexpected even the telepaths were surprised.

Looking confused—I was too, honestly—Sarah asked me what on earth I had to be sorry *for*. "Has something happened?" she asked. Knowing me like she did, she probably thought I'd done murder at least.

I sobbed away without answering until she repeated the question, and then, my nose dripping and probably already red, I told her.

"I stole from you," I bawled. "And I stole your husband's stuff that was in his room I sneaked into at the library." (And slept in the actual bed he'd died in. I didn't mention that part.) "And instead of calling the authorities to have me punished—and the gods only know what they'd have done to me, you being a Farmer and all—all you did was treat me nice! You took me home and washed me and fed me and dressed me decent…" And loved me. I wasn't brave enough to say that part out loud.

Sarah tried to answer, but I couldn't shut myself up long enough to let her get in a word. "When I was in the dinghy and thought I was going to die (you know: that dinghy I got away from the *Antelope* in), the only thing I could think about besides my mother was that I wanted to write you a letter to thank you and tell you how grateful I was to you. Only I didn't have anything to write with then, and later when I did, my hands were all messed up." I cried harder. "But I could have written when my hands were better, and I *still* didn't. If it hadn't been for Timmy making me, I probably wouldn't have ever even told you I was still alive! Please believe me that I *was* grateful to you, even if I didn't say so at the time. I'm *still* grateful. I promise I am!"

Dammit, my sniffles were very juicy by now, and some of the drips were getting on the front of Sarah's shirt. She pretended not to notice. "Claire, you were young and very frightened," was all she said, patting me.

"Well, I shouldn't have been frightened," I answered. "What was there to be frightened of? All you were was kind and good to me! And that's not the only time I've run away from goodness, either. I've run away from a *lot* of goodness. I don't know why. I know why I run away from badness. It's because it's bad and I don't like it. But I don't know why I run away from goodness, and you taking me in like you did was totally good!" Something else suddenly occurred to me. "I never thanked that cook, either," I muttered. My nose was running too fast for my handkerchief to keep up. "I never even tried to find him."

I got just that far, and noticed Dan wasn't in the Hall with his parents at all. He was right in the room with me and Sarah. He hadn't said a word, and his eyes were big as moons.

Sarah, one arm still around me, said, "Oh, Claire, of course I forgive you—or would, if you'd done anything that required forgiveness." Then she saw where I was looking, and added, "Danny, dear, go to the kitchen and get us some dinner, will you?"

Dan was gone like a shot.

Sarah led me to a bench then, and she and I sat on it talking until Dan came back. Since Dan didn't hurry—at all—we had time to discuss a lot of things. I didn't know the cook from the *Antelope's* name. I'd never asked it. Sarah promised she'd find it out if she could so she could thank him, too. She said Rose already understood about me running away, and Robin was so grateful to me for my good advice about bringing his wife back to Annasland that he wasn't likely to be holding a little thing like one long-ago sudden departure against me.

"And Laura and Tom *certainly* understand," she said, laughing. "Especially the part about running away from good things. Anybody who knew Laura's father knows a lot about *that*."

The only thing I knew for sure about River Wolfson myself was that Dan wanted to be exactly like him. "Did Mr. Wolfson run away from good things?"

Sarah laughed harder. "For years and years," she said. "River ran away from good things because he didn't think he deserved them. Eventually he learned not to try to calculate how much happiness he was entitled to, and just accept what came along. That was only when he was much older than you are, though. You should be proud of yourself for catching on so young." Sarah smiled and brushed back some hair from my face. "River had a restless soul," she told me. "Just like you."

It was nice to hear somebody say I had any soul at all. Aunt Jane, for one, had doubted it.

A little bit later, as Sarah was telling me for the fortieth time that everything was fine and nobody was mad at me, Dan stuck his head in the door to check if the coast was clear. Sarah waved him in, and we all sat down together to eat the food he'd brought.

While we ate, we talked of course, and just like with Iris, our talk was mostly about Anna at first. She'd gone very easy, Sarah said. She said she thought the telepaths would probably make a point of reassuring me about that. She told a few Anna stories; Dan told a few Anna stories; I told an Anna story—my only one—and we all cried a little.

Then we moved on to more cheerful subjects.

Dan had been promoted to full radio operator, so we talked about that for a while. Spending eight or ten hours a day breathing stale air in a radio room sounded awful to me, but Dan seemed to love it. Sarah asked me about how things were going on the *River*—but only to be polite, I think. Sarah knew more about things on the *River* than I did.

"She keeps up with all the ships," Dan told me, looking proud. "At heart, Aunt Sarah's more of a sailor than I am."

Naturally, I didn't miss the opportunity to tell Dan I thought just about *anybody* was more of a sailor than he was. He was only a radio operator who just happened to work on a ship. Like I guessed he would, Dan took this as a compliment.

Then he asked Sarah, "How about if I tell Claire what we've been talking about, Auntie? I think she'll be interested."

The look on Dan's face as he said this would have made anyone get interested. I sat up straighter in my chair.

But Sarah shook her head. "No, leave it, Danny. Let me think the whole thing through first."

Of course, Dan didn't leave it—whatever "it" was. And I admit I didn't help Sarah any with getting him to leave it, either. Instead of agreeing with her that Dan should shut up and let her think, I just folded my hands, sat back, and listened to them argue. It was interesting. Where I came from, arguments generally involved yelling and sometimes weapons, but for fifteen minutes straight, Dan kept up wheedling and Sarah kept up telling him to wait but they were both perfectly mannerly.

As I've said before, wheedling works for some people. Eventually, Sarah gave in.

"Dan's taken it into his head that I should buy the *Muriel*," she explained. "To save her from being sold to a trader."

As soon as I heard it, I liked the idea myself. "For D&R, you mean?"

Sarah shook her head. She said D&R only went into the shipping business in the first place because years ago, there wasn't any other reliable way for the company to move its goods. "At this point, running a fleet is just a distraction from our manufacturing. Nowadays there are plenty of other shippers. No, Danny's plan is that *I* should own *Muriel*. Me *personally*."

"It'll be handy for you," Dan insisted. "Once D&R doesn't have ships anymore, it'll be more convenient for you to come visit Mother if you have your own."

Sarah pointed out—dry—that she didn't need a ship the size of the *Muriel* just to visit Annasland.

Dan acted like he hadn't even heard her. "If we had the *Muriel*," he said, with a gesture that included me as part of the "we" (which I didn't mind, by the way), "I could visit Ant Island. The *Anna* never goes out that way, and I haven't seen Shy for a long time."

I couldn't stop myself from putting in, "And maybe I could visit Izzy on Isabelle Island sometimes, too."

The Foresters had established what they were calling a "protectorate" around Isabelle Island. No ships, not even their own, were allowed near enough for the islanders to detect. Sarah being who she was, I figured if she was the one who asked them, the Foresters might bend the rule to let *Muriel* moor near enough to the island that I could pilot an unthreatening little dinghy the rest of the way in.

Sarah reached across the table to pat my hand. "You don't need the *Muriel* for that, darling," she said. "I'll speak to Wise."

Since she obviously meant she'd ask Captain Wise to go near enough to Isabelle Island for me to get there in the *River's* dinghy, and since Dan knew as well as I did that Captain Wise would do anything Sarah asked him to, Dan immediately started coming up with more reasons than just to visit Izzy that Sarah should buy her own ship.

He said, "You know, if the *Muriel* might be going by Isabelle Island anyway, we should explore a few of the other islands out that way. I think Uncle River might have seen some of them on the *Muriel's* first voyage. We might be the first ones to set foot on them since he did!"

Any mention of her husband always brightened Sarah right up. She immediately started looking more interested in maybe being a ship-owner. "Explore? We'd explore?"

"Could I come exploring too?" I begged. "If I can get leave from the *River*, I mean."

"Of course," Dan said, like Sarah'd already agreed to the plan. "We need you to, in fact. We're probably going to find Ants out there, and we'll need you to deal with them. I'll handle the radio, of course. Also, Kitty Alcock will absolutely want to come. Did I tell you she made Second Officer, Aunt Sarah? On the *Heron*."

Kitty Alcock was the daughter of the *Muriel's* first captain, and the *Heron* was the new name of the *Bee*.

The mention of Ants seemed to give Sarah second thoughts. "Danny, full Ants are dangerous! Even for Claire!"

I agreed with this—though not out loud. On the other hand, a lot of the best things in my life had come to me because I could talk to Ants, so I said, "No, I'll do it. I want to."

Dan was already moving on, as easy in his mind as if he was planning a picnic. "We'll need some other crew, of course. And a cook. Who were you planning to get to do the refit, Auntie? Tell them we want a battery array like the one on the *River*, not the one on the *Heron*. *Heron's* been back in the yard with battery trouble twice since we got her."

Sarah rubbed her forehead. "Danny, think about what you're saying! I don't know that a refit would be enough, honey. The *Muriel's* old!"

Dan ignored this the same as he'd ignored all Sarah's other protests. He said, "Uncle River's tree's got some little saplings around it this year. What if we put them in pots and take them with us? We could plant one in every new place we explore."

Years before, Dr. Masterson'd called me "cynical." I knew by now what the word meant but I wasn't sure whether to apply it to Dan or not. His suggestion to plant trees in his uncle's memory *might* have been perfectly innocent.

Whether it was innocent or conniving, Sarah liked it. She said it was beautiful, in fact.

Later, minds around me let me know when Helen and Forest master Peregrine left the Hall to come home. In fact, telepaths had been slipping little thoughts in—and out—of my brain the whole time the three of us had been talking. It didn't seem to bother me so much now. I saw Helen take one quick look around a corner at us, but she and the Master went to bed without interrupting our conversation. Dan, Sarah, and I stayed up talking all night, planning a voyage of exploration that I thought might only be a dream right up to the point where Sarah said quietly, "I spent some of the best years of my life aboard the *Muriel*. I'll bring River's bed from the library back aboard. The *Muriel* is where it belongs."

When she said that, I knew our plan was real. Sarah'd already told me she planned to die in the same bed her husband had. It would take some time for the refit first, but the voyage was going to happen, and Sarah was going to be on it.

As the first sliver of sun showed on the eastern horizon, Dan asked, "Where shall we go first?"

Speaking to Dan, but with my eyes on Sarah's face, I answered, "To see Izzy and Shy, and then to Farlands. *If* the Farlanders are still alive."

Dan had been trying for months to convince me—and everybody—that the Farlanders were still broadcasting, though only at low power and frequency. He was so sure he'd intercepted a few of their transmissions that he'd gotten the Farlands dictionary manuscript from Sarah to try to teach himself their language.

"They're still alive," he said, firm. "Their last good radio broke, that's all."

I didn't really care where we went, to be honest, so I said, "Farlands, then. We'll take them some more radios. And after that—Fartherlands."

Dan laughed. "There's no place called 'Fartherlands' that I've ever heard of."

"Well, it's out there," I said. "There's a whole world of 'Fartherlands' out there, in fact, and I mean to visit as many of them as I can." Then I suggested what nobody else'd dared to yet: "Let's get Loyal for captain."

I think Sarah almost said no to this, but then she changed her mind and said, "yes," instead. "I think he's dealt with his unfinished business here now."

I didn't know what she meant by "unfinished business." Maybe something to do with Loyal's dad. Whatever it was, a whole bunch of brains immediately agreed with her. Consensus said Loyal was ready to command a ship again.

I smiled to myself. Thanks to the Annasland rule about "sharing," as soon as the island was awake the entire population would start heading over to the art studio to "share" with Loyal that they thought he should captain the *Muriel*.

He wouldn't stand a chance against us.

I think Dan would have gone on talking longer, but Sarah—yawning—ordered us both off to bed. "You have years left to talk," she said. Then she smiled us and added, "You have years left to explore, too. I won't pretend I don't envy you that."

She offered me a bed in the infirmary so I wouldn't have to walk all the way back to the Guest House to sleep, adding that she and Helen had already started fixing me up a permanent room in the house, only it wasn't done yet. Funny how just a few hours, a shared meal, and a little talk can change things sometimes. At sunset I'd been an outsider on Annasland. Sunrise found me right at home there.

From the minute Sarah'd said the word "bed," I'd been ready to fall into one. Now, judging by the way Dan staggered off mumbling, "'Night, Claire," he was finally sleepy, too.

Sarah tucked me into bed and kissed my cheek. "Sleep well, Claire," she murmured.

I did. And dreamed of Farlands.

BY THE SAME AUTHOR

The *Antlands* series:
Book 1: Antlands
Book 2: Annasland
Book 3: Farlands

Other writing:
The Complete Raffles (Annotated & Illustrated)

Available now via your local Amazon store

ABOUT THE AUTHOR

Genevieve Morrissey is a passionate student of British and American social history, but through one of those strange little quirks of fate she spends most of her days talking with scientists.

In her *Antlands* series, she explores a future history of societies coping with the loss of civilization—and attempting to rebuild it.

Genevieve also enjoys reading obscure books, travel, good cooking, and solitude.

Stay up to date with Geneveieve and her writing via her website:

antlands.com